PRAISE FOR

Dog Days

"If this sparkly, witty, and occasionally vicious little novel is any indication of Wonkette's talent, then Cox ought to log out of cyberspace and start calling herself Novelette."

—Christopher Buckley, *The New York Times Book Review*

"A must-read for the Beltway crowd . . . fun for outsiders as well. . . . Cox is an irresistible observer of the Washington scene." —*People*

"Written with intelligence and shrewdness . . . chock-full of Cox's trademark snark. The story is clever, and Cox provides plenty of interesting twists and unexpected laughs right up to the very end. *Dog Days* also paints a sharp picture of the D.C. rat race, with everyone slurping down lattes, dueling in witty riposte, and dashing around the District while constantly suckling at the electronic teats of their BlackBerries. [It] will be a raging success for Ana Marie Cox. She's funny and quick and has a wonderful sense of comic timing."

—*Lincoln (NE) Journal-Star*

"*Dog Days* is funny, moving, and very smart; a fresh-eyed inside look at Washington from the keen mind of Ana Marie Cox."

—George Pelecanos, author of *Drama City* and *Hard Revolution*

continued . . .

"An acid political satire . . . at times *Dog Days* sounds like it was written by a more sartorially inclined Raymond Chandler."

—*The Village Voice*

"[A] jaunty political farce . . . This is [Cox's] first novel, and it's good enough that we should wish for many more."   —*Forbes*

"*Dog Days* is fun, a quick read rife with pop culture references and great wordplay. Cox has known success as the writer behind Wonkette, the political blog that covers the ins and outs of Washington, D.C. Can someone with the ability to write short, snappy quips . . . maintain that energy throughout a novel? In Cox's case, the answer is a resounding 'yes.'"   —*Ottawa Citizen*

"She's fast and she's funny [but] Cox is capable of real writing, as opposed to the quick bursts of sarcasm that blogging tends to bring out. What readers will probably take away, though, are her funny toss-offs. As a Beltway euphemism for sex, 'bringing each other to closure' is both original and perfect."

—*The Atlanta Journal-Constitution*

"I am impressed by Cox's wit. She genuinely can write . . . [she has] managed to take the real-life absurdity of Washington campaigns, including the sex and vulgarity, and make a novel that in the end offers some decent entertainment and a lesson."   —*The Press-Enterprise*

Dog Days

ANA MARIE COX

RIVERHEAD BOOKS
New York

THE BERKLEY PUBLISHING GROUP
Published by the Penguin Group
Penguin Group (USA) Inc.
375 Hudson Street, New York, New York 10014, USA
Penguin Group (Canada), 90 Eglinton Avenue East, Suite 700, Toronto, Ontario M4P 2Y3, Canada
(a division of Pearson Penguin Canada Inc.)
Penguin Books Ltd., 80 Strand, London WC2R 0RL, England
Penguin Group Ireland, 25 St. Stephen's Green, Dublin 2, Ireland (a division of Penguin Books Ltd.)
Penguin Group (Australia), 250 Camberwell Road, Camberwell, Victoria 3124, Australia
(a division of Pearson Australia Group Pty. Ltd.)
Penguin Books India Pvt. Ltd., 11 Community Centre, Panchsheel Park, New Delhi—110 017, India
Penguin Group (NZ), Cnr. Airborne and Rosedale Roads, Albany, Auckland 1310, New Zealand
(a division of Pearson New Zealand Ltd.)
Penguin Books (South Africa) (Pty.) Ltd., 24 Sturdee Avenue, Rosebank, Johannesburg 2196,
South Africa

Penguin Books Ltd., Registered Offices: 80 Strand, London WC2R 0RL, England

This is a work of fiction. Names, characters, places, and incidents either are the product of the author's imagination or are used fictitiously, and any resemblance to actual persons, living or dead, business establishments, events, or locales is entirely coincidental.

While the author has made every effort to provide accurate telephone numbers and Internet addresses at the time of publication, neither the publisher nor the author assumes any responsibility for errors, or for changes that occur after publication. Further, publisher does not have any control over and does not assume any responsibility for author or third-party websites or their content.

First Riverhead hardcover edition: January 2006
First Riverhead trade paperback edition: February 2007
Riverhead trade paperback ISBN: 978-1-59448-232-8

The Library of Congress has catalogued the Riverhead hardcover edition as follows:

Cox, Ana Marie.
Dog days / Ana Marie Cox.
p.   cm.
ISBN 1-59448-901-7
1. Political campaigns—Fiction.   2. Washington (D.C.)—Fiction.   3. Political fiction.   I. Title.
PS3603.08895D64   2006   2005054652
813'.6—dc22

PRINTED IN THE UNITED STATES OF AMERICA

10   9   8   7   6   5   4   3   2   1

For Chris, who was waiting on the other side of August

Acknowledgments

From the beginning, my mother, Shirley, made me feel that writing fiction was possible, and my father, Sam, never doubted I could do anything. I thank them for their support throughout my career's peregrinations as I looked for the job that would allow me to watch both C-SPAN and *The Simpsons* as homework. Nick Denton, of course, gave me that job. My agent, Gary Morris, saw a good book in me years before I did, though he had the sense to keep me from writing all the bad ones I thought of first. Sonya Geis laughed at my jokes and sent me good vibes from the other side of the continent. Megan Lynch, my patient and precocious editor, supplied ideas and solutions that bridged the gaps of my authorial inexperience. My verisimilitude advisers—Mike Feldman and Dick Keil—made sure there were no details too far off or too specific. John Dickerson rounded up the fan club when I needed encouragement and salted in criticism when I could take it. Tracy Sefl was—and continues to be—a source of witty banter, third bottles of wine, expensive accessories, and friendship. A posthumous shout-out to Billy Lee Brammer for *The Gay Place*, my inspiration and the best book ever written about Washington that isn't set there. Thanks to the joke jury and to all the Wonkette operatives and informants (especially A.B., C.S., M.M., and G.B.) who made my day job easier. And finally, I'd like to thank the staff of the Kerry–Edwards campaign. Thank you for all the forwarded pool reports and interoffice memos, thank you for letting me crash your parties and mock your progress. But most of all, thanks for working so hard for so little when so much was at stake. Campaigns can be foolish; what you're fighting for isn't.

Dog Days

1

Thursday, July 29

To: [undisclosed list]

From: Julie.Wrigley@clevelandparkgroup.com

Subject: Flash mob

Where: Four Seasons bar

When: As soon as the last balloon drops

THE CHAMPAGNE WAS COLD and expensive. The room was crowded
and hot. And you couldn't swing a Democratic Convention creden-
tial without braining a network reporter, a campaign staffer, or a
hit-or-miss celebrity who had come to Boston to lend his support to
the cause. If someone had set off a bomb in the bar of the Four
Seasons, political chat shows would only be able to book Republicans and the conventional wisdom packagers from *USA Today*. Not
that anyone would even joke about setting off a bomb. Democrats
were now tough on terrorism. They didn't joke about that kind of
stuff; it was in the memo.

Some people think that the convention climaxes with the nomi-
nee's acceptance speech, but for the scrum of journalists, staffers,
and consultants who had bullied and sweet-talked each other

through the last four days, these final hours at the bigwigs' hotel bar marked the event's true ending. Speeches had been given. Deadlines had been met—or closely approximated—sound bites had been dispensed, and unless you were unlucky enough to be booked on a news network's desperate attempt to milk the convention for just one more hour of airtime at midnight, your work here was done.

Melanie Thorton kicked off her shoes underneath the table, at a banquette she had slyly reserved earlier under the name of the junior senator from Wisconsin. ("Normally we don't take reservations for booths in the main bar area, Senator, but seeing as how you're expecting a large group . . .") Melanie was junior varsity in the John Hillman for President communications team; often, the most significant perk of the job was just getting to tag along. Tonight was a chance to cash in on little favors and her knowledge of the obscure staff members of obscure legislators.

She had worn flip-flops with her suit for most of the convention, sacrificing style for some degree of comfort during the twenty-two-hour days of constant shuttling between the war room, the convention hall, and the hotel.

For this last night, however, she had attempted to dress up. In theory, this would have meant her least wrinkled Ann Taylor skirt and a shirt with a small, unidentifiable stain under the right collar that she could hide if she left it unbuttoned far enough.

In the end, she wore jeans and dared the shirt, adding some really expensive shoes she had just bought—a pair of strappy Charles David sandals with a heel that was thin and wide, like an upright graham cracker. She had seen them in the *Lucky* magazine she allowed herself on the shuttle up to Boston and had become fixated on them. She would buy them if she made it through the week, she promised herself, dividing their $350 price tag by all the times she imagined wearing them. That afternoon, after Hillman's final convention hall walk-through, she had snuck out to Newbury Street and laid down her plastic. Now she realized that her carefully rationalized prorating had only justified the shoes' expense, not the searing pain they were causing. She reached underneath the table to feel if the blister on her left heel had grown from the size of a dime to a silver dollar.

Melanie's friend Julie Wrigley, sitting beside her, noticed. "Serves you right," Julie said with mock scorn. "Helping the economy like that. Didn't you get the talking points? The economy sucks, the president's tax cuts are a historic failure, job growth is down, and consumers are worried about paying their bills—not buying shoes that cost enough to pay for junior's flu shots for the next five years—that is, if flu shots are still available under the failed policies of President Jim Golden."

"Sorry if I fell off my talking points. I am 'working harder and earning less,' if that means anything," Melanie said. She wriggled her toes back into the shoes and eased the heel strap over the blister, wincing.

Melanie sat up and pushed her shoulder-length dirty-blond hair—*really dirty-blond,* she knew—out of her face. Her roots were showing. They had been for a few weeks now. In fact, they weren't roots so much anymore as saplings. Melanie tried to convince herself that this was her look.

She had an open face with wide-set green eyes and a smile that created a single dimple on her left cheek. She had learned early in life that it was a face people tended to think was honest—store managers waved her through blaring shoplifting detectors, and restaurant managers gave her free meals if she even hinted the steak she ordered medium-rare had come out well-done. This genetic accident, this appearance of trustworthiness, mostly reflected her inner stuff. She was a Girl Scout, she didn't cheat at solitaire, and she only took one newspaper out of the vending machine. But appearing so honest also made it much easier to do her job on Hillman's communications staff, which involved a lot of lying.

Well, not lying. Never exactly *lying*. She told stories with happy endings and uplifting messages. She cajoled. She sweet-talked and buttered up and occasionally, very occasionally, tweaked a fact so that it slid a little more easily into place. She had discovered this talent early on as well, easing B-pluses to A's and creating completely plausible reasons why she couldn't possibly do windsprints that day. And in spite of all the hours spent earnestly memorizing the reasons for the Whiskey Rebellion and Saturday nights in the library researching the Works Progress Administration, *this* would be the skill that got her a job in politics.

When Melanie was honest with herself—which was about as often as she was with others—she knew that changing the world was only what first attracted her to the game. There were pictures of her dressed up in a little corduroy suit, getting ready to play Michael Dukakis in her school's mock debate, to prove that she didn't start out on the side of spin. She had logged hours in protest lines and call banks all through school as well, just one of the warm bodies campaigns were always short on. But would she be here now if she didn't also love the dirty part? The trick of maneuvering a story into print, the knack of using whatever idea was in the air as leverage for a talking point.

Melanie loved knowing that she watched the news with an ear toward what got placed and who would benefit; she loved hearing her ideas spill out of other people's mouths. Working for the Illinois Civil Liberties Union in Chicago the year before, she had done the opposition research for a campaign to defeat a state measure requiring schools to observe "a moment of silence." The proposal was so bland few had bothered to even try to organize against it. But the movement had come apart at the seams after Melanie managed to get the *Tribune* interested in some of the less reliably unobjectionable proposals that the measure's sponsors also advocated—jail for adultery, mandatory instruction in creationism, the banning of homosexuality.

She suspected it was this come-from-behind culture war victory that put her on the campaign's radar. She had some friends from an Iowa senate campaign who were doing advance work for Hillman early in the primaries as well. One thing was for sure: There had been no résumé, no interview, just a phone call to Chicago the last week of April and a request that she be there by May. The campaign ate communications staff. In fact, one of her first tasks had been to come up with a spin on the high turnover. "We're just trying to accommodate the dozens and dozens of young people who want to put John Hillman in the White House," she had told the *Washington Times*.

Melanie was levelheaded enough to realize that not all manipulation was bad—she had learned that much in the library as well as in the trenches. Look at Lyndon Johnson, horse-trading and bullying for the sake of the Civil Rights Act. So if she spun in the service of access to birth control or tickled some junior AP stringer under the chin to get him to see things her way, well, the fate of the free world was at stake. Wasn't it?

Julie had put the champagne they were drinking on her boss's room service tab—"He'll just bill it to the client, anyway," she had reasoned. "That is the beauty of being a consultant: clients." She elbowed the guy next to her—a scruffy former speechwriter who seemed to be taking credit for something (all speechwriters do)— and obtained just enough space to reach for more champagne. Julie's elbowing arm was trim and forceful and sheathed in a perfectly pressed Prada pantsuit of summer-weight wool, under which she wore a shirt of such crisp whiteness it glowed against her summer-gold skin and sleek, dark hair in the bar's dim lighting. Years after starting out as a Senate aide, she was enjoying all of the benefits—they were chiefly financial—of being in the private sector. *Now* that *is the beauty of being a consultant,* thought Melanie, uncomfortably aware of how her clothes were always striver brands rather than arrived brands, somehow collecting grime each time they were folded in and out of her airline-regulation-sized carry-on with its smashed zipper and squeaking wheel. Her clothes didn't seem to fit as well as they used to, either. She had always been curvy—though she preferred "voluptuous"—but a diet of Subway veggie sandwiches (she tried), whatever was left in the office vending machine (she didn't try *that* hard), and alcohol (sometimes she didn't try at all) had made her jeans tighter than they had been even two months ago.

She wanted a cigarette. The bar was supposed to be nonsmoking and Lord knows the Democratic Party itself was supposed to be, but a thin haze hung at the top of the room anyway and she wanted in. The scruffy speechwriter was smoking now, so Melanie wondered aloud if she could get a cigarette from him. "Oh, sorry," he said. "I got this from her"—Melanie couldn't really follow his gesture, and suspected his vagueness was just a way of protecting his supply. He took a drag. "I *never* smoke." He smiled at her through a careful smoke ring.

He's full of it, Melanie thought. *Everything's about withholding information with these people.*

She surveyed the throng. The Four Seasons was one of those new downtown hotels that tried to look old, but in the bar they had given up and just gone with "generic expensive." Marble floors, scattered indoor palm trees, gold gilt anywhere your eye might rest, and furniture so anonymous that it seemed to disappear under the people who sat on it.

And who were they? They were people who, a year ago, Melanie would have admitted she was impressed by—the editor of *The New Republic,* White House correspondents who had earned nicknames from the president, campaign professionals with bit roles in history-making moments (Howard Dean's web-master, the leader of the Draft Clark movement, the Gore guy who got the first message that Florida was too close to call in 2000).

Today, she was still sort of impressed, but knew better than to admit it. In general, she felt it was only okay to be impressed by the really big names who normal people—her mom, maybe—would recognize: network news anchors like NBC's Brian Williams or movie stars like Ben Affleck—who seemed drawn to the campaign in exact disproportion to crowds being drawn to his movies—and, of course, John Hillman . . . who wasn't there.

Julie followed Melanie's gaze and read her mind: "It's like the fucking *Star Wars* cantina in here."

"Right," Melanie said, mindfully unimpressed. "Full of freaks."

"Freaks," Julie said, and switched to bland newsreader tones: "Who, come January, could be setting the agenda for a new administration—and a new era." She dropped back into normal register: "I bet Chuck Reed is already picking out his West Wing office."

"Oh, dear God." Melanie took a sip of champagne. "Is that confidence or arrogance?"

"I have to say, a win seems more likely after tonight's speech than it did yesterday." Julie's dark, slightly slanted eyes scanned the party, her full lips thinned into a smirk. Who here would be covering the next administration? Who would be working in it? The challenger's team always looked too young and too disheveled to make it, but the election could provide that magic upgrade. George Stephanopoulos had gone from wide-eyed wharf rat to the White House to ABC News.

Hillman's acceptance speech had been good. Or at least much better than everyone had expected. And his just barely surpassing expectations gave all the bored campaign writers the excuse they needed to make it a real race again. Melanie had watched the speech from the campaign's temporary war room in a grubby hotel across from the convention hall. Even the candidate's more-profuse-than-usual perspiration had been greeted with optimistic spin: "He looks human!" someone had exclaimed. *Kind of a low bar,* Melanie had thought, even as she made a mental note to mention the flop sweat to the next reporter who asked her if the candidate was "too stiff" to "connect" to real people.

Melanie found herself caught up in the wave of good feeling as well. After a hard slog through the early primaries, and then losing their precarious momentum to a series of small but painful gaffes, the campaign was picking up steam. They were ahead in the polls—not by much, but just above the margin of error, which was great, considering the high approval ratings Golden had been getting. They might actually win. People allowed their hopes to be raised. Bill Taft, the Buddha of the campaign, had even reportedly greeted Hillman as "Mr. President" when he stepped off the platform that night.

Just like they do every cycle, Mel thought. The bubble of hope broke. But across the room there was also a peal of drunken laughter. An almost foreign sound at a real D.C. party, where no one ever got drunk. Too drunk. And where only Republicans drank champagne.

"The problem with most Washington parties is that it never feels like anyone's going to get laid," Melanie said. "Even when people are naked and climbing into bed together, it doesn't feel like they're going to get laid."

"Hmm." Julie cast a sideways glance at her friend. "I have a pretty good sense of who's getting laid, actually. But really, the problem with most Washington parties is that there's not anyone there you'd want to be laid by. But this isn't really a Washington party, is it?"

Julie and Melanie picked out faces and murmured to each other the names of the famous-for-D.C. who were present and doled out shorthand evaluations: "dull as sand," "grabby," "looks like an alien's idea of a female human," "will never rise above cable." Julie had a perfect and highly compensated talent for summing up entire baskets of complicated personalities in a word or two. *It's like birdwatching,* Melanie thought. *More vicious, but not as pretty.*

Then Melanie saw a chance to flush out some excitement by poking at one of Julie's grudges: "I saw Karl Taylor come in earlier," she said, gesturing toward a tall, dark-haired man in a shiny suit. He was the political director for NBN and the editor of *The Point,* the most read of Washington's daily political tipsheets.

Julie narrowed her eyes. "Maybe you should go let him stare at your chest. I mean, say hi."

Melanie grimaced. "For the sake of the campaign, I probably should."

"His precious *Point,*" said Julie. "It started as an internal memo, and now getting a mention in it gives you the Good Housekeeping seal of approval."

"Well, anyone who can make political journalism sexy . . ." Melanie began, goading her.

Julie interrupted, "Well, he has given reporters something to jerk off to, if that's what you mean. Now, more champagne. Do you see our waiter? You'd think a ninety-dollar bottle of champagne would get you better service than this."

"Not when half the bar is ordering the hundred-and-eighty-dollar bottles."

"And Al Franken's probably ordering the eight-hundred-dollar bottle." She drained her glass. "Fuck. All right, scoot out and I'll get more provisions."

Melanie obliged and Julie set off toward the bar. As she disappeared into the crowd, Melanie spotted Hank Lensky and smiled. *Okay, it doesn't matter where we are, it's really a D.C. party now,* she thought. Everywhere she looked there was someone new who had to be maneuvered around or acknowledged—and with Lensky, she'd need to do both. He had to be acknowledged because he was a softly fading newsmagazine superstar at *Current* with the off-duty demeanor of an excitable junior faculty member in a ruthlessly competitive English department. He gestured wildly, he wanted to talk about the last time you insulted him by accident, and he wanted to gossip about who was doing the next cover package. He had to be maneuvered around because he hit on any girl who might be a little impressed by him—or recognized him at all, for that matter.

She reached for her BlackBerry, thinking she'd tap out a quick digital warning that Julie should be careful what route she took on her return. Lensky had roped Julie into one too many lengthy conversations, usually ending in a hopeful invitation to adjourn to another party. Mysteriously, the only other guests at these parties were other forty-something bachelors. "I feel like I'm just lucky they've never actually asked me to jump out of a cake," Julie had reported after a night watching dog racing.

Warning Julie was suddenly less important when Melanie saw fifty new messages waiting in her inbox, and the convention gavel had only dropped an hour ago. Most were just offering congratulations on the candidate's speech, which Melanie did take a certain amount of pride in. She didn't have much influence in the campaign, but she had been there for the speech brainstorming session and felt that at least some of her ideas had been incorporated. Ideas such as "the," "and," and "when." She sighed inwardly. *Just to be invited into the room should be enough,* she thought to herself, *it's a long way from running for student government back in Davenport.* But Melanie wanted to go further than the speechwriting room. *It will be different if we win in November. Put in my time now, as a glorified assistant to the communications director. Next stop: the White House.*

Where I will be a glorified assistant to the communications director. She was revived by a message on her BlackBerry screen:

To: ThortonM@hillman.com

From: Rick.Stossel@thinkmag.com

Subject: Polling

Congrats on a great convention . . . I think Hillman will get a huge bounce . . . How about you? Is there a huge bounce in your future?

It wasn't poetry. But Berrys didn't lend themselves to poetry. It was the message she'd been waiting for all night. Melanie looked around; Julie had yet to return. Twisting in her seat to shield the screen from her banquette-mates, Melanie thumbed a rushed reply:

To: Rick.Stossel@thinkmag.com

From: ThortonM@hillman.com

Subject: Re: Polling

I hear the beds at the 4 seasons are awfully springy. Where are u?

She spun the reassuringly mechanical wheel on the side of the thing, found "send" on the menu, and clicked.

"I DECIDED TO BEAT the rush and order a double," Julie announced, arriving with two waiters, accompanying buckets of iced bubbly . . . and Hank Lensky. Julie grimaced just slightly and flicked her head in his direction before regaining practiced brightness: "And you'll never guess who I found!"

Lensky grinned and swayed slightly. His hair was a gray-and-black wiry mass, thick and stiff enough to support a dinner plate without losing its shape. His tie was loosened at the neck of a chambray button-down. "Quite a night for you, Mel. Let me buy you a drink." Melanie raised an eyebrow at Julie as the waiters prepared to open their newly purchased bottles. Julie rolled her eyes and shrugged, mouthing, "Let him."

"Save your money for election day," she said, pointing to the bottles already on deck.

Lensky mimed tragic disappointment, then fluttered his eyelashes behind his thick glasses. *It's so third-grade, it's almost cute,* thought Melanie. She had noticed that Washington was full of these born-again bachelors, men whose success in the sober field of politics or political journalism somehow freed them to behave like the high-school lotharios they couldn't be at eighteen, when they were too busy getting their lunch money stolen and passing student council resolutions against depantsing. Their awkward flirting was a fun party game to observe, but it was never much fun to play. Lensky pouted: "You're not rejecting me, are you?"

"Rejection is such a harsh word. I'm tabling you for later consideration."

Julie had refilled their glasses and was scanning the room again, a skill she practiced with such efficiency that Melanie always half-expected her friend to emit sonar-like pings at the approach of any person of interest. Instead, Julie gave Melanie an elbow in the ribs, just before putting her arm around Hank: "Don't look now, but there's your good friend Rick Stossel," she said, brushing her arm up against his. "I heard he mentioned your piece on Hillman on Imus this morning, Hank. Very complimentary. Hey, you used to be on Imus a lot yourself, right? Why did you stop? Too early in the morning for you?"

Lensky looked around. "Yeah, something like that."

Julie couldn't help but twist the knife a little more: "Gosh, I swear you used to be on it all the time. And you were on Rick's show, too, a lot, I thought. . . ." Lensky's eyes narrowed at Julie, who kept hers wide, with a blankish, innocent smile on her face. "They revamped the whole thing about three months ago," he told her. "They wanted to get a wider range of guests."

Julie knitted her brows and nodded as though Lensky were explaining a calculus problem to her. "So that's why Ron Brownstein is on only every other week now instead of every show?" Julie could pull the wings off flies like this now—it was one of the benefits of being in the private sector. On the Hill and on campaigns, staffers needed reporters more than reporters needed them. After years of currying favor on Capitol Hill, Julie took pleasure in pulling rank.

Melanie inclined her head toward her friend and mouthed "Stop." Julie winked back then ignored Lensky: "Mr. Stossel is looking good, isn't he? I hear the ratings for *Capitol Insider* are getting better ever since he started doing that 'reading list' segment. His star has really risen lately. I guess there's no better shortcut to success in Washington than creating an insiders' club with arbitrary rules for membership."

"Yeah, everybody tracks that," Lensky added, looking wistful for the days when he used to not only appear on Stossel's show but also have his articles highlighted by the host.

Melanie spoke up: "I think it's kind of brilliant, really. He's made himself a tastemaker just by declaring himself one."

Lensky smiled. "All the more reason I should go over and pay my respects. You girls want to come over with me? I know he's a big fan of yours, too, Melanie." Lensky's slightly tipsy cadences sharpened up at that and he shot Melanie a more-sober-than-she-had-thought-possible look.

"Well," said Melanie, considering her options. "That's only because I'm fucking him." She smiled sweetly at Lensky as he choked on his drink.

Julie laughed—and then lost a little of her high-priced subtlety: "Ha-ha! Oh, that's a good one, Mel!"

Lensky pounded on his chest, gasping. Julie glared over the diminutive investigative reporter's hunched shoulders and tried to will Melanie into shutting up. Through gritted teeth, she hissed, "What are you doing?"

Melanie continued to smile and stood to thump Lensky's back helpfully. She leaned over and whispered in Julie's ear: "Hiding in plain sight, sweetie."

Lensky sputtered back to normal, slightly flushed. "You got me there, Mel. Whew." He took a restorative swig of beer. "Sorry to have implied anything. Of course you wouldn't be screwing Stossel. He's way too visible. And it's too juicy. And hey," Lensky chuckled, "he'd probably have to cover it himself!"

Julie looked at Melanie square in the eye. "And then there's the fact that he's *married*."

"Oh, right. Hmm." The recently divorced Lensky looked at his shoes. "That, too."

Not like that matters in this town, Melanie thought to herself, observing Lensky's discomfort. She drew herself up. "Right," said Melanie. "Right."

Julie took Lensky's arm. "Let's go say hi, eh?" She spun him around and started off. Turning her head over her shoulder, "Wanna come, Mel?"

Melanie waved: "No, thanks—we're fucking later!" she said brightly.

Julie looked upward with exasperation. Lensky looked back over his shoulder quizzically. Julie jerked him forward.

Melanie could see Rick for herself now, surrounded by his own small gaggle of admirers. He still had traces of pancake along his jaw from doing television earlier. He was wearing a black suit, as usual, and his dark hair kept swinging in front of his eyes. He had the kind of body common in Washington, his skinny past evident in thin wrists and a gawky neck. He carried his moderate gut well, despite a slouch expertly calculated to show everyone how unimpressed he was. In his early forties, he was older than Melanie would have usually aimed for. But he was the national correspondent for *Think* magazine, the kind of omnipresent journalist who drove town car drivers crazy with a schedule that on any given day might include a hit on *Good Morning America*, a call-in to Imus, lunch with a senator, and a shouting match with Chris Matthews. He also had his own Sunday afternoon show on the upstart news network America Now. And he wrote his share of cover stories, too.

Their courtship—or what passed for it—had begun with maddeningly terse e-mails from the high-flying power broker that managed to fuse flirtation with trace amounts of condescension. "Nice work on the plane today," he had written her after she spent a rare day out of the war room traveling with the campaign and listening to the daily briefing, "but you shouldn't wear pleated pants."

Melanie didn't think that she was the kind of girl who only responded to men who tried to woo her by putting her down. But the attention he gave her—both positive and negative—was addictive. Then there was the public flattery—not in his pieces, but in the thirdhand compliments that found their way back to her. The gaming of that backchannel network probably impressed her more than the compliments themselves—and maybe just as much as who he was. He was someone her mom would recognize . . . though maybe not right away.

At first the attention had been embarrassing, especially when every other journalist in town had been writing stories about "the communications meltdown in the Hillman campaign." But when his public flattery had been combined with sly invitations to drinks and a locked-eyes series of compliments that started with "the smartest woman in politics" and continued through "the way those boots show off your legs," she found herself wondering what it would be like to have the romantic attention of someone so in demand. At any given moment, half of D.C. was trying to get him to buy their line, mention their story, or get booked on his show. From dinner with the *New York Times*'s senior Washington correspondent he would Berry her e-mails asking her what underwear she was wearing or call her between cable TV appearances. "It's not that power is an aphrodisiac," she had told Julie later. "It's having someone powerful desire you."

As she looked at him from across the bar, he winked at her over Julie and Lensky, who hadn't quite made their way over to him yet. She grinned back and pulled out her Berry again.

To: ThortonM@hillman.com
From: Rick.Stossel@thinkmag.com
Subject: Re: Polling

I am somehow stuck in a conversation with Tom Edsall about campaign finance and he's given me 15 minutes already on independent expenditures and I could be on for an hour more. Set off a bomb, break a window. Do something. Let's leave.

To: Rick.Stossel@thinkmag.com
From: ThortonM@hillman.com
Subject: Re: Polling

I can see how that could get you excited. 5 minutes? In front of the bar?

She looked up just in time to see Rick look down to his belt to check for her messages. Melanie smiled to herself.

"You still working?" a voice at Melanie's elbow inquired. Melanie shoved her Berry back in her purse. Paul Lead, the *Washington Post*'s shortish gossip columnist, looked at her over the world's largest reporter's notebook. She felt a prickle of tension between her shoulder blades. She had some secrets to hide—she had just BlackBerried one of them—and although Lead's nose for dirt had been thrown off by a temporary posting to the paper's Baghdad bureau, he made her nervous.

"Oh, you know"—Melanie shrugged—"the spinning never stops."

Lead nodded, lowering his notebook and holstering his pen in its spiral. "It's true. What I wouldn't give for a good, honest war zone," he said wistfully. By unfortunate accident, the *Washington Post*'s e-mail protocol conflated his first initial and last name. Everyone called him "Plead." As a handle, it was Dickensian but apt.

"Riiiight," said Melanie, steeling herself for the inevitable.

"All these parties. 'Are you on the list, are you off the list . . .' " Lead grumbled.

It's coming, she thought, *in the next sentence he will mention Baghdad.*

"I wish I were back in Baghdad. . . ." He sighed.

"Who doesn't?" Melanie replied.

He's like a walking drinking game. In fact, Julie and Melanie had tried to work one out once: If he mentions Baghdad take a shot. Bosnia a double. If you throw up before he puts his head on your shoulder you win.

"Feh. I guess I like not getting shot at."

"As opposed to all the free food and booze?" she asked.

"It's so fattening!"

"How could I have overlooked that. . . . They're real slave drivers at the *Post*, aren't they?" She didn't hate him particularly. He was just the worst possible combination of possible Washington traits—tiresome and a potential threat. He was boring and dangerous.

"Oh, now you're making fun of me."

Melanie sighed and attempted to look for the flashing notification light on her Berry without appearing to look for it. She was unsuccessful—she had probably drunk too much champagne to pull off subtlety. Lead scowled: "And now you've clearly got something more important to do."

The light was flashing, and even though she knew it was going to piss Lead off, she reached back into her purse and with one hand, fished the Berry out. "Sorry, Paul," she said. "Work, you know, work."

"Uh-huh."

To: ThortonM@hillman.com

From: Rick.Stossel@thinkmag.com

Subject: Re: Polling

    I'm waiting for you now.

Melanie jerked her head up and looked around. Rick was just outside the bar's exit, leaning against a pillar in the lobby, nonchalantly checking the insta-polls.

"Oh, crap," Melanie said as she put the pager back. "Really, sorry. But this is sort of important."

"Right." Lead looked toward the lobby. He looked like he might be pulling his pen out again.

"Uh, the dial groups just wrapped up," Melanie said, walking backward, still holding her champagne glass. "And they're through the roof!"

"Hmm. Can I call the campaign about that?"

"Yeah, sure!" Melanie said, wondering if, in fact, there was a dial group wrapping up. *Sure there was!* She turned around and began to trot toward the exit, the room spinning in front of her. *Hey, I'm kind of hammered,* she realized. *Fuck, where's Julie?* Melanie looked around quickly. *She'll understand. Right? Right.* She reached for her Berry with one hand. "Fuck," she muttered to herself. "Fuck!" she yelled, sprawling headfirst onto the floor. She caught herself hard on one hand and two knees. The champagne glass shattered. One of her pricey high graham cracker heels snapped. "Fuck."

Glancing up she saw Rick look toward her, through the bar's entrance, horrified. Hillary Clinton's chief of staff was standing next to him, and seemed frozen in mid-sentence. The entire bar was frozen in mid-sentence, really.

Melanie sighed, rolled over on her backside—into a small but still quite damp puddle of champagne. If she said "fuck" again in front of all these reporters, the FCC might get involved. She restrained herself and started to stand, shaking on her uneven heels. Julie hurried over as a busboy started sweeping up shards of glass. "That's her heel," Julie pointed out as she arrived. "Don't take that—it's worth more than the champagne."

"I fell off my shoes," said Melanie, as though the scene needed an explanation.

People had started back to their conversations. Julie waved at the remaining gawkers. "She'll be doing another show at midnight, folks! Be here all week!" She handed Melanie her heel and said, more quietly, "Where's your boyfriend when you really need him?"

"Ha-ha." Melanie glanced out and saw Rick start toward the elevators. "I gotta run."

"I don't think you're gonna get anywhere very fast."

"Yeah, yeah," said Melanie, lopsidedly loping out of the bar. "Hold the elevator! Going up! Hold the elevator!"

From inside the elevator, Rick's hand shot out. Melanie grabbed it and limped in.

It was just the two of them. He let the door close.

"Well," he said. "That was smooth."

2

Friday, July 30

Good morning from the staff of the Four Seasons! The temper-
ature today is 91 degrees.
Quote of the day: "Politics are such a torment that I would advise
every one I love not to mix with them."—Thomas Jefferson

MELANIE WOKE TO FEEL Rick's arm lying across her naked chest.
Across the room, sunlight blurred the edges of the thick hotel
drapes. She blinked and the dry scrape of her eyelids reminded her:
I slept in my contacts again. She reached up to rub her eyes and felt
the slightly sticky crumbs of mascara flake off her lashes: *I didn't
wash my face, either . . . again.*

Lately evenings had a way of shattering; in the mornings she
always had memories of a good time but couldn't reconstruct a
clear path from one event to another. It was partially how the campaign ate up her days and ate into her nights. It was partially the
constant influx of information, from cell phones and Berrys and
bourbon-soaked admissions. Conversations that started at one bar
with one person got carried over to text messages and cell phone
calls over dinner, and it became difficult to remember if you had

read something or heard it or maybe just thought about saying it yourself. The drinking, she supposed, didn't help her any. But then again, maybe it did; sometimes it was the only way she knew to get away from the daily swirl. Her head felt cloudy and polluted—like the sky over New Jersey—but as hangover weather went, it was mild. It was less than she deserved. She closed her eyes and felt around in her head for the jagged pieces of the evening before, handling their sharp edges as gingerly as her headache would allow. The problem with these evenings is that there was always one question stealing the fun from her memory: Had she done something really stupid? If so, had anyone noticed?

She wouldn't have to search hard for the previous night's divot. There had been that unpleasant incident at the bar, falling off her new shoes in front of almost the entire Washington press corps and most of the Hillman campaign. Her ankle felt tight and sore. That was the thing about being falling-down drunk: You fell down. Melanie sighed. Before that, there had been drinking with Julie. After that, there had been drinking with Rick in his hotel room. This hotel room. Raiding the minibar. Rick ordering up ice for her ankle, "but not for the scotch!"—she had yelped in the background as he called the front desk. . . . Oh, and he had gotten serious for a second there, and scowled darkly at her for blowing their cover. "Right, yes, so important for the concierge not to know you have a guest! In your room! Who is not your wife!" She had giggled helplessly. *"Quel scandale! Quel fromage!"* Still giggling, she hobbled across the room to the bed.

"Mr. Stossel, if you are that concerned about your reputation, you really shouldn't let young, single women into your hotel room at all."

"Yes, well, they seem to follow me everywhere." His scowl was cracking.

She half-stumbled, half-pushed Rick onto the bed. "It's the scent you give off. Smells like . . . someone who can get me early exit poll results!"

"And here I thought you were just after my body."

"Well"—Melanie had smiled—"as long as I'm here . . ." And the buttons on his shirt fumbled loose and his hands sought her heavy breasts. Their bodies were both campaign-white and campaign-soft; they canceled each other out. During an election year D.C.'s standards of attractiveness—already graded on a generous curve—tracked to availability and not physical beauty. *It's like the Special Olympics of sex,* Melanie thought. *Everyone's a winner!*

The sex last night had been pretty good, she was mostly sure. What she could remember of it wasn't a progression of events—first base, second base, third base—but a series of still pictures, like a pornographic flip-book. His hands on her, their chests pressed together, the view of him kneeling over her, his hair hanging into his face. Then oblivion.

It was not like it had been the first few times, where they had stolen time in supply closets and restaurant bathrooms and once, memorably, at three A.M., on the squeaky secondhand sofa in her boss's office. The minute the staff had left they had dropped their pizza, abandoned the beer, and even left a cigarette smoldering. The couch made enough noise for a third person.

The rattling buzz of a BlackBerry brought her back from wincing as she thought about any couch stains. Rick started awake in response: "Whahuh? Gimme."

"I'm not sure it's yours. Hold on." Melanie started to grab the agitating gadget off the bedside table when his hand brushed hers aside.

"I'm sure it is. . . ." He picked it up, glanced at the screen, and smiled crookedly at her: "Unless it's not." He chuckled at the message and handed Melanie the Berry.

It must kill him that I knew it was mine, Melanie thought. He was a congenital early adopter. His phone, his Berry, and his earpiece were the highest-end versions available to mortals. His techno-lust benefited other passions as well. Rick instructed Melanie in the geekery required to communicate and cover their tracks. He preferred, for instance, to bypass her desktop e-mail and message her Berry directly, and had asked her to do the same. "No traces that way," he had explained. Melanie, on the other hand, had a just-barely cordial relationship with technology—she loved her Berry, but it sort of mystified her. She had used it as her cell phone for a while, and had walked around D.C. looking like she was talking into a toaster pastry until someone explained to her that the outlet on the side of the Berry could be used to attach an earpiece. Then she had to decide which was worse: the Berry's ungainliness or having to wear an earpiece. Melanie had spent her high-school summers back in Iowa working at McDonald's; headsets and earpieces would always remind her of hairnets and the smell of industrial cleaner and grease. She wound up just getting a real cell phone. Now she turned to the e-mail that had started the commotion, and read it aloud.

To: ThortonM@hillman.com

From: Julie.Wrigley@clevelandparkgroup.com

Subject: Belt?

Why am I wearing your belt?

Rick laughed: "I guess it's better than wearing your underwear."

"Don't think that hasn't happened, pal."

Rick leered at her: "Do you have a webcam set up for that kind of thing? I could arrange it if you don't. . ."

Melanie threw a pillow at him. He batted it away and picked up the hotel phone. ("Hello, to whom am I speaking? Carlos? Carlos, this is Rick Stossel in room four ninety-seven. Could you send up a pot of coffee—a large pot of coffee—and, Carlos, what is your *greasiest* breakfast? Right, I'm on Atkins. . . .")

She thumbed a reply:

To: Julie.Wrigley@clevelandparkgroup.com

From: ThortonM@hillman.com

Subject: Belt?

   Oh, you don't remember? Last night really meant something to me, darling.

To: ThortonM@hillman.com

From: Julie.Wrigley@clevelandparkgroup.com

Subject: Belt?

   Ha ha. I'm sure it did. Can you talk? I think I know where to reach you. . . .

To: Julie.Wrigley@clevelandparkgroup.com

From: ThortonM@hillman.com

Subject: Belt?

   You can reach me on my cell. I don't know what else you could be talking about.

"Hey, babe," Rick called to her, "I'm jumping in the shower. If room service comes, just sign my name." Melanie nodded, wondering how closely Rick's boss tracked room service tabs and whose role she'd play in the expense report. Was she a colleague? Was she a rival reporter or a political consultant? A source? *A source of something.* He winked at her and shut the door to the bathroom behind him.

Melanie sat up in bed and debated whether to turn on the news. She knew what to expect from it: rehashes of Hillman's acceptance speech, along with judgments of the convention's "success." The campaign's B-team would be out in full force on the morning shows because in an hour the A-team would be on a charter back home to D.C. Melanie was on the A-minus team and had, with much cajoling, convinced her boss to both let her out of morning-show duty and allow her to fly down on her own. The precious few hours of R&R were a good way to ease into the down period between conventions, and an even better way to avoid getting on a chartered plane that had begun to smell of stale beer and tomato juice and sweat by this point in the campaign. It was also the best way to enjoy a $100 room service breakfast and a lingering good-bye.

Her phone played a snippet of "Champagne Supernova," which meant Julie was calling. Rick had downloaded and installed a whole set of tunes and with a mysterious wave of his hands she had aural caller ID. He'd given himself Ravel's "Bolero." Melanie pawed through the tangle of underwear next to the bed—*What am I going to wear out of here?* she wondered—to answer the call.

"No, seriously, why am I wearing your belt?" Julie never bothered with "hello."

"What, doesn't it match your shoes?"

Julie sighed. "Of course it doesn't. Where did you get it, anyway? It's like, made of . . . plastic or something."

"I prefer to call it 'pleather.'"

"I'm going to buy you a real belt, just so you can see what they're like."

"Feel free." *Maybe I should loan her my crappy accessories more often,* Melanie thought.

"But first, why am I wearing this? I must have been drunk."

"Without it, your pants would fall down."

"Cute. I thought that was why firemen wore suspenders."

"I'm serious. We were at the bar at the Four Seasons, and your pants were falling down."

"Hmmm. It's sort of coming back to me. Was this before or after Lensky invited me to find 'cold tea' at a Chinese restaurant with him?"

"So that's what they're calling it these days."

"Apparently, that's code for wine if you want to get served after hours."

"How handy. I think this must have been before that."

"Right. Well, thanks for the loan," Julie's voice became sly: "I imagine that your pants stayed on fine without the belt?"

"Ahem."

"My God, girl. You know that appalling runt from the *Post* saw you guys leaving together. Of course, Lead wouldn't know gossip if it were fucking him, so you might be fine. On the other hand, *everyone* saw you leave together. They don't need to read it in Lead's column to know that it's true."

"I know, I know . . ."

"I don't want to play bad cop here."

"So don't, Sarge. How did your night end, anyway?"

"Oh, you know, the same ten people as usual. We crawled around looking for this mythological 'cold tea' for an hour or so and then things kind of petered out. We ended up in a convenience store eating cheese and crackers with those little plastic red spreaders. I don't even have a hangover."

"That's so not fair."

Rick walked out of the bathroom, hair wet, the too-short sleeves of the Four Seasons robe exposing his pale forearms. "Who's that?" he mouthed.

"Julie," she mouthed back, not even bothering to cover the phone. Melanie was suddenly conscious of the thin, sticky layer of sweat on her body. *The sheets of the Four Seasons don't deserve to be this dirty,* she thought, and gathered them up around her.

On the other end of the cell phone, Julie trilled: "La-la-la-la-la . . . You're not as quiet as you think. Are we still pretending that no one knows that you two are bringing each other to closure?"

"Yes, yes we are."

"We'll talk about this later. What shuttle are you taking?"

"Three-thirty something. Delta."

"Cool, me too. I'll see you there. Along with the other ten people."

Melanie flipped her phone shut and watched Rick sort through the piles of newspapers that had been delivered to the door. He was naked underneath the robe and his toothbrush stuck out of its pocket. He tossed the entertainment sections, the sports sections, and the business sections on the floor and sat on the bed, laying out the three front pages (*Washington Post, New York Times, USA Today*) side by side in front of him. He looked at them like a captain preparing for a voyage would look at maps. He not only looked for news, but how it was told and who was telling it. At the end of the week on his show, during the "Reading List" segment, he would anoint a few lucky journalists by reading from their stories. "Smart take," he would say, ensuring that whomever he had tapped would get a pleasant herogram from his boss—and that Rick would have a new friend.

He turned his head toward Melanie suddenly: "Why aren't we watching television?"

Rick always wanted to see who was on if he wasn't. He needed to see if they were talking about his story or someone else's—and he needed to see if he was being quoted.

Melanie felt for the remote and flicked on the screen; the bouncy LodgeNet theme was quickly replaced by the somewhat nasal sneer of a Fox News commentator.

"Hey . . ." Rick started.

"Let's see what the competition's up to, okay?"

". . . sure, it was a success, if by 'success' you mean nothing went wrong," said the squeaky thin blonde who served as one of their pundits-on-call. "But John Hillman's one task for this convention was to convince the American people that he's not some pointy-headed, bleeding heart liberal and I'm just not sure showing footage of him leading civil rights protests at Harvard accomplished that. . . ."

Melanie exhaled. She had been unaware that she had been holding her breath. Rick put his arm around her, punched her playfully with his other hand. "Way to go, kiddo." He shook her slightly. "Breakfast is on me!"

Melanie managed a smile.

Their relationship wasn't exactly Tracy and Hepburn, though it was true that Melanie hadn't been certain she liked Rick at first. He was cocky and brusque, so sure that what he had to say was worth hearing that he tended to steamroll over anyone who didn't talk fast enough. Early on in the campaign, he had sent her a note pointing out some spelling and grammatical errors in a press release:

To: ThortonM@hillman.com

From: Rick.Stossel@thinkmag.com

Ms. Thorton, I hate to be the one to bring this up, but as someone who likes a fair fight, I just can't let you persist in the delusion that splitting an infinitive is permissible. Along the same lines, someone really should sit you down and explain the "that/which" distinction. As for Hillman's concern that cutting Social Security benefits will "effect" seniors, well, people are getting older no matter what.

Melanie had called her mom to get an explanation about that last one. At first she was too embarrassed to be mad, but then the day passed, and no one else seemed to notice the flub. What's more, her boss's talking points that day had argued that one of Hillman's primary challengers "could care less about keeping sugar subsidies," and Melanie realized that in the mad storm of messages, careful English was the first thing to erode. So fury overtook shame and she had considered writing Rick a snarky e-mail, something along the lines of "Well, I did learn to write from your magazine." If the note had been from some stringer or junior correspondent still congratulating himself on his upgrade from the city hall beat she might have been brave enough to actually send that reply; as it was, all she wrote was "Thanks."

When she asked him later why he had sent the initial e-mail, he laughed. "Sweet girl, I was just trying to get your attention." He winked at her. "And, of course, I needed to teach you a lesson."

The buzz of her Berry brought her out of her memory, but she ignored it for a minute. She deserved to savor this peculiar victory. *Nothing went wrong.* And the other campaign or at least their begrudging mouthpieces admitted it. Attacking Hillman's Ivy League activism was a knee-jerk response, and while it worked with some groups, the campaign had discovered that most swing voters found that message, on its own, insignificant. This surprised and disappointed Melanie: She had gotten interested in working for Hillman after seeing clips of his mid-sixties speeches, in which his slightly affected Kennedy accent had seemed charming and his words had seemed real and moving. That people could profess not to care one way or another about that pivotal time in Hillman's life was a mystery to her. *You really have to get to know him before you start to not care,* thought Melanie. She winced inwardly. *Do I really think that?* It wasn't that she didn't know Hillman or didn't care. It was just that he had become almost a complete abstraction—even in person he no longer seemed to exist as anything but a bundle of catchphrases and gestures. He had forgotten the knack of spontaneity. In fact, Melanie had just written a memo reminding advance staffers to "look for spontaneous moments" on the trail. The campaign was thinking of taping the spontaneous moments and putting together a clip reel of them for Hillman to review.

She breathed a "hmph" and started channel surfing.

Room service came, polite and silent. The waiter didn't bat an eye at the state of the room or of Melanie's hair—all of which to her seemed like it belonged on the cover of a porn video. He just wheeled his cart, burdened with silver and bacon, to the side of the bed. There was probably an etiquette class for hotel waiters about how not to look at the barely dressed women who appeared in the rooms of men who checked in alone. *Now if only there was a class for us, too,* Melanie thought.

Rick was engrossed in his papers still, and ate without really looking at his food, his fork stabbing the bone white plate blankly. He didn't always hit his food.

Melanie attempted to keep some kind of order, but failed. She buttered her rolls primly, and then dropped them in her lap. She cut her pancakes carefully, but got syrup on the sleeves of the hotel robe.

Her phone jingled again, this time with the theme from *The Godfather*. Karen Skoloff, her boss, was calling. She'd picked that one out herself.

"This is Melanie," she said in her most professional voice, knowing that Skoloff didn't really understand caller ID.

Skoloff's cigarette-scarred voice cut through the static: "Are you watching CNN?"

"Uhm, no . . . ah . . ." Melanie fumbled for the remote, spilling coffee down the front of her robe. *Shitshitshitshit.* Rick looked up from his laptop: "I'm not paying for that." Melanie blotted at the robe with one hand, gave him the finger, and changed the channel.

"I'm not sure what I'm seeing here, so I thought I'd ask you." Skoloff's clipped tone stabbed at Melanie's stomach.

On the screen, the camera panned and scanned black-and-white images of a mental ward, circa 1950 or '60. Patients in pajamas, an empty shock treatment room . . . then there were more artfully hurried cuts to rows and rows of blank-eyed soldiers in uniform. A male voice intoned ominously: "John Hillman says he spent his college years fighting for the rights of others. But what if the real fight was *in John Hillman's mind?*"

Melanie suppressed a laugh, relieved. "Uhm, what is this?"

"I assume it's some Republican bored with ruining the water table who wants to suck up to the president by killing Hillman. But I have no idea what their angle is, aside from alleging that Hillman is the Manchurian Candidate."

Which at least would give him some foreign policy experience, reasoned Melanie. "Ah . . ."

"You've heard nothing about this?"

Melanie squeezed her eyes shut and weighed her options. Her mental faculties still recovering from last night, she couldn't recall having heard about these ads before. There was a slight possibility that she had heard about them and said something to Skoloff and that Skoloff had forgotten, but this seemed unlikely. Accusations that the candidate was a product of a mind-control experiment—unlike, say, accusations that the candidate was a weak-willed opportunist indebted to special interests—did not happen every day. So: She had either not heard about the ads—which made her seem out of touch and incompetent—or she had heard about the ads and not said anything to Skoloff—which made her seem just incompetent.

"I think someone mentioned them to me a couple of weeks ago. They just didn't seem . . . plausible enough to worry you with."

Melanie could hear the squeak of her boss's cigarette as she inhaled. "Plausible," she murmured, enjoying the word's novelty. "That's not your call."

Melanie knew better than to argue the point. She watched the coffee stain set into the terry-cloth robe and waited for Skoloff to decide if she was going to ruin her day.

An exhalation on the other end of the line. "Fine. Fine," Skoloff said. "This is your baby now. I've got shit to do. Oh, and get that fucking spontaneous reel together. I want the shot of him playing checkers in Nashua, jogging with Clinton, serving ice cream in Davenport, and the fucking cow or beagle or llama or whatever it was he was petting at the state fair in Nebraska."

"Sure. I'm on it."

"Hmm." Skoloff clicked off.

Melanie stared at the dead phone in her hand, the remote in the other. Her mind felt scrubbed and raw, and the objects in her hands felt suddenly unfamiliar. What are these for again? Do I want to know? She had to fight the urge to throw her BlackBerry and cell phone across the room, just to see what would happen. Would they bounce, would they break, would they explode into a thousand tinkling pieces? Would there be flames? Would Rick stop reading the fucking paper? A sour hiccup of laughter escaped her.

"Hmmph?" Rick queried.

"Nothing. Nothing." Melanie got off the bed, stripped off the soiled robe, and started for the shower. She was switching into Business Melanie Mode, as Julie called it, and what had been formerly amusing—the messy food, the low-grade hangover, and Rick's focus—was now irritating. She had a problem to solve.

MELANIE TOOK A CAB back to collect her things at the Bayside Days Inn. Rick had kissed her good-bye in the room, opened the door for her, and not quite shoved her out. At first she wore her broken shoes, sort of half-tiptoeing to the elevator. Then she just took them off. The Four Seasons' carpeting was plush and warm between her toes. Then she caught a glimpse of herself waiting in the mirror. Her shirt was wrinkled, her hair twisted into a half-ponytail, she was carrying her shoes, and her underwear was in her purse. *But not so bad,* she thought. *Not so bad. My shoes are very expensive. I sort of belong in a hotel with people who have more than one home.*

But when she stepped onto an elevator filled with bleary-eyed delegates and satisfied donors, she was certain everyone knew. The underwear sent out a radio signal. She smelled like sex and bacon. She wasn't wearing any shoes. She looked up to avoid everyone's eyes and caught her own in the elevator's metallic ceiling.

Is that who I am? She saw the tops of her fellow passengers' heads. Bald spots, neat parts, the slightly slumped shoulders of people who know they're going back to work on Monday. *I am not tacky,* she thought. *I am just not wearing shoes or underwear. I am bohemian.*

The elevator let out in the lobby and she hung back. The marble floor chilled her flat feet and there were some glances. *There are lots of good reasons I could be here,* she thought to herself. *Lots of people I could have crashed with. Or even slept with! After all, I'm single!* She took a breath, held her head up, and walked out the lobby door.

The doorman who hailed her cab looked at her bare feet but didn't say anything. *Yes, I'm barefoot. So what. I'm Holly Golightly. I'm Edie Sedgwick. I'm Queen of the fucking Nile.* The cab seat was slightly sticky—and the floor was glazed with something slimy: She jerked her feet up and onto the seat almost as soon as her toes touched it. A twitch of disgust flew across her face. *But,* she thought, *yes. I'm getting away with this. Yes, I'm fine.* She took a deep breath of the cab's air-conditioning; it was sour and infused with the scent of car deodorizer: Wintergreen. It was like being forced to eat a cheap mint. Her stomach rolled. *I'm fine,* she repeated to herself, *I'm fine.*

The cab crawled along through highways she barely recognized, past supermarkets and dinky electronics stores with neon lettering in the windows. The day was bright and beautiful but something about the cab window made everything seem two-dimensional—like a movie set for a scene about taking a cab home. Or not home.

Melanie's hotel squatted anonymously in the near-flung suburbs of Boston. If she'd bothered to figure out the city's topography or had spent any real time in her room maybe she would have been insulted that Skoloff had stashed her there, so far away from the action. Well, she had been slightly insulted anyway, thinking vaguely, *So that's who I am to them*; and a flicker of that petulance came back to her when she opened the door to her room and was greeted with the slightly damp, lemony smell of accumulated unneeded maid service. She could see the parking lot outside the wide window directly in front of her, midsize American cars drifting in the milky haze of a sheer nylon curtain. She closed the door and the phony silence of ten-thirty A.M. in the suburbs folded in around her.

She had been in the room for maybe an hour a day but could have navigated it with her eyes closed if she needed to. Even though she'd only spent a few weeks on the campaign trail proper, she had quickly become an expert on the anonymous world of mid-range hotels. Places with "in-room coffee" but no minibar, where the staff wore polyester uniforms and the depressing hotel bars always made a big deal about their Irish coffee.

She looked around. There were the meaningless double beds with their plasticky quilted coverlets. When she first went on the road she was told never to touch them, because they don't get washed. Local news stations were forever doing pieces with black lights showing the stains left by careless salesmen and purposeful bachelors. A bedside table contained last year's phone book, dusty stationery, and an even dustier Bible. Next to the window, near the pressboard round table just big enough for a laptop and a cup of coffee, there was the chair upholstered in quasi-tasteful but ultimately misdirected chintz scratchy enough to sand a door. And on the wall . . . Wait. She wouldn't look. Generic country scene? Generic flowers? Generic "Main Street"? Ah, of course, this was Boston: generic seascape.

Clothes hung out of Melanie's suitcase like they had been shot trying to escape. She dimly remembered the hunt for a clean pair of underwear the night before. She was going through underwear fast lately. Today: commando style. Great for a plane ride. She tossed her things back inside the case, found a plain white T-shirt that didn't stink or have a stain and exchanged it for the wrinkled silk button-down that still smelled of smoke and sweat, champagne and sex. She frowned at her gloriously ruined suede stilettos, threw them in the case as artifacts if nothing else and pulled her flip-flops out of the suitcase as well.

She zipped up the case, packed up her laptop, and looked around the room. A half-empty cup of coffee from the one morning Melanie had woken up here still rested on the window, souring. Apparently anything that couldn't be conquered by lemon disinfectant wasn't actually cleaned. Melanie shrugged. She dug in her purse for a crumpled twenty and left it on the dresser, rewarding the maid service's consistency if not its thoroughness. Walking out the door, she glanced in the bathroom and saw a single tissue lying forlornly in the wastebasket, a kiss of dark red lipstick stapling its crease.

She shared a shuttle to the airport with a young reporter who worked for Gannett News Service. *Cute enough,* she thought. She delighted in not having to make a genuine observation, to decide if he was worth it and then work at the conversation. He was off to

South Dakota after this to cover a Senate race that, while important, was still in South Dakota. "Hey, that's rough," she said, trying not to let relief show in her voice: *So things could be worse.*

THE DELTA SHUTTLE TERMINAL did not smell quite as bad as the campaign's charter undoubtedly did, but there was no mistaking the scent of last call and bad coffee that hung over the heads of the journalists, delegates, and operatives seated there, wheelie bags and laptop cases gathered around them like children during storytime. Julie was lying down across a row of seats, one arm thrown over her eyes, the other arm dangling extravagantly, holding a pair of owlish Audrey Hepburn sunglasses. She peered up as Melanie approached.

"Who goes there?"

"The bearer of bad belts."

"Oh, yeah. Yuck." Julie sat up, placed the sunglasses expertly in her hair. Suddenly she seemed ready to deliver an annual report or give a policy analysis or maybe just convince a gaggle of company CEOs to part with several millions of dollars in exchange for being told they need to do more charity work.

Melanie collapsed next to her. "We're back in the cantina," she said, looking around.

"The cantina has closed. We're at someone's dreary cantina afterparty."

The shuttle was always a good place to catch the best of D.C. looking their worst. No one looks glamorous carrying their own luggage. And no one in D.C. looked very glamorous to begin with.

A cluster of Julie's colleagues from the Cleveland Park Group were sitting around a shabby table, wearing sunglasses and exchanging watered-down banter. The table was burdened with at least two electronic devices for every man present, and their eyes flicked back and forth from the men in front of them to their Berry indicator lights like they were following a tiny tennis match, each of them preparing for the moment when he would have to decide who was more important: the people there or the person trying to get in touch with him.

A couple of Democratic congressmen were drinking Bloody Marys and staring into space. Melanie could almost remember their names—she had memorized as many as she could before coming to Washington. She asked Julie, who didn't even glance up from her *Vogue* magazine: "Oh, please, congressmen? They're like interns. Why bother learning their names?"

JULIE AND MELANIE were friends because they had to be. Melanie had learned quickly that Washington is a town of many women and quite a few ladies, but very few girls. Girls in the almost pejorative sense—girls who could type and throw a ball, girls who worked until ten and stayed out until two, girls who would like to be played by Rosalind Russell or Katharine Hepburn in the movies of their lives. Girls who could read a menu and a bill markup, girls who never shied away from high heels or a fight, girls who had good restaurants and the House Former Members directory on speed dial. Maybe you could call them chicks. But "chicks" seemed too hard a word to Melanie's midwestern ear, bringing to mind images of fishnet stockings and cigarettes.

Both of which Melanie enjoyed on occasion, but when she thought about why she and Julie were friends, she knew it was because they were both girls.

They had met at a party thrown by one of Washington's more

fabulous bachelors, a CNN terrorism expert and foundation fellow whose personal wall of fame included pictures of him with both former presidents and Osama bin Laden. He affected colorful shirts and an English accent, but Melanie had heard he was actually from New Jersey.

The party was crowded and, by D.C. standards, it was raging. A bunch of people were dancing to the host's manically attended-to stream of Europop singles and everyone was drinking cheap red wine out of plastic cups.

Melanie had arrived late with some colleagues from the campaign who had abandoned her quickly after arriving. Left to her own devices, she proceeded as she always did, to the impromptu bar in the kitchen. Where there were no plastic cups left.

Scanning the room for replacements, Melanie had seen Julie in a corner with Hal Prentiss—a garrulous Clintonista and notorious political fixer who now worked with Melanie at the campaign— and a handsome blond guy. Melanie would later realize Julie collected handsome blond guys like pennies. They were contriving to pour some of that cheap red wine into empty beer bottles. Inventive, Melanie thought, if unsanitary. She spied a gaggle of guests leaving—conveniently leaving their plastic cups behind. Grabbing them quickly, she washed them out and walked over to the drunken Edisons and presented them with a flourish: "I don't know who you are, but I think I have something you need."

"You are our savior," Julie said.

"Hey, I just made the cups appear, not the wine."

"Still, excellent. Now can you do something with these loaves I have?"

"I don't know these men, but surely they deserve to be called better than that."

Frentiss and his companion, both clearly on at least their fifth cups, watched the exchange with puzzlement. Prentiss slurred: "You girls know each other?"

Melanie smiled at them: "Only in the biblical sense."

Melanie had a vague idea of who Julie was—Julie had confessed she had the same sketchy image: "Actually, all I knew was that you were from Iowa. I thought I'd recognize you from the hay in your hair." For her part, Melanie had heard that Julie was very good at what she did, whatever that was.

MELANIE TRIED to concentrate on the e-mail she was writing—it was a memo about the Nexis search she'd done on that wacky ad from that morning. Nothing about the ad or the group—"Citizens for Clear Heads"—made much sense. It had aired on all the major news networks that morning, and there had been a press release that, it turned out, Melanie had received. It had been accidentally sent to her spam folder, probably because it contained the words "prescription drugs" and "enlargement" and "penis"—the last in the context of some kind of electrodes hookup.

To: SkoloffK@hillman.com

From: ThortonM@hillman.com

Subject: Clearheads

As far as I can tell, these people are nuts.

She knew that probably wouldn't do it. They were going to have to deal with these Clearhead yahoos. The story had already started to float in the backwash of convention coverage and the deadly calm of August was still ahead, that time between the conventions when reporters write stories about campaign theme songs and a controversy about what the future First Lady might serve at a state dinner could take up an entire news cycle. The group seemed more likely to convince a small-town city council that fluoridated water was a communist plot than to influence an election, but their lunacy might not matter. The computer was making her lap hot. She jiggled it on her knees a little and started again.

> The group behind the Manchurian Candidate spot (you can watch the whole thing at www.whocontrolshillman.com) is "Citizens for Clear Heads," which bills itself as a grassroots effort to "inform America about John Hillman's links to ongoing Harvard University experiments in brainwashing and mind control."
>
> They *are* nuts.

An itch inside Melanie's head made her close her eyes and try to concentrate. But her fingers felt clumsy and her eyes kept drifting off the screen to glance down at the indicator light of her own BlackBerry. *Rick should have gotten into D.C. by now,* she thought. *He should know if his wife is in town with the kids for the night,* she thought. *There. Was it blinking? No. There?*

Melanie forced herself to look away. *Wait, there?* She grimaced. *I'm twelve,* she thought to herself. *I'm acting like I'm twelve.* To cure herself, she set her Berry on vibrate and put it in her holster. It would jiggle when a new message arrived and she could check it then. Until then, she'd concentrate.

When, five minutes later, she finally felt the feral cat purr of the Berry against her leg, she thought she might be imagining it. She had been doing that a lot. She admitted this to Julie over drinks once and

Julie had laughed: "Ah, yes, the phantom vibrator . . . brought to you by Stephen King in association with Penthouse Productions."

But that one was real. It wasn't Rick, of course; it was Skoloff.

To: ThortonM@hillman.com

From: SkoloffK@hillman.com

Don't go overboard researching those electrode-phobic freaks. Responding to an attack ad right now will waste our convention bounce and give them legitimacy. Find out enough to be sure they're off their collective rocker and then maybe soft-sell some off-the-record comments about how they're the fringe of the lunatic fringe. If we don't take them seriously, it's harder for your little reporter friends to.

And I want that spontaneous reel.

Well, that was quick, Melanie thought. But also not completely unexpected. She had suspected that Skoloff's phone call during breakfast was mostly about yanking her chain. Skoloff wasn't that concerned about the Clearheads; she was more concerned about keeping Melanie on the campaign treadmill. Skoloff had the tendency to confuse the momentum of the campaign workers with the momentum of the campaign—as though their internal poll numbers were a measure of pure energy expended. In general, the Hillman campaign saw more activity than progress, but then again, that seemed to be the case for most of the Democratic Party.

3

Friday, July 30

From: HillmanPool

On Behalf of Tom Vandenhauf

Sent: August 1

Subject: [HillmanPool] Pool report on a stick

TCH committed no news, but much color during his stop at the Minnesota State Fair in St. Paul this afternoon.

He was greeted at first by a small and rather silent crowd, then started what became one of the longest rope lines I have ever seen, walking several hundred yards down the main road cutting through the fair. Midwesterners appear to be a people of great patience, although several seem to have thought the candidate was a local faith healer.

After much handshaking and a surreptitious squirt of gel sanitizer, TCH bought one corndog, put a streak of ketchup and mustard on it, and took a bite. He took one more bite before handing it to an advance staffer. A few seconds later I spied such same staffer eating a corndog, which for the record he insisted was not TCH's.

Tom Vandenhauf, *Washington Post*

.   .   .

AS THE SHUTTLE taxied into National—Melanie could not bring herself to call it "Reagan"—she frowned at her BlackBerry to make it start receiving messages. She cradled it in her lap with both hands, head inclined toward it, willing the arrow in the upper right corner that signaled the arrival of mail to flicker to life.

Julie had her sunglasses on (she wore them for the entire flight, insisting that they were a subconscious cue for people to not talk to her. "I don't work in government anymore," she said. "I don't have to be nice."); she lowered them and looked over at Melanie: "Are you praying to that thing?"

Melanie sighed and straightened up.

Julie pulled out her own: "Let us worship together, sister."

Around the cabin there was the familiar frenzied plastic snap of cell phones being flicked open and the low squawk of dozens of voicemail boxes being checked at once. Two-way pagers were not, of course, supposed to be turned on until the plane was at the gate, but Melanie didn't know anyone who didn't just ignore this particular injunction. *If it really* were *a problem, planes would be raining down on the Potomac all day.*

Finally, as the plane approached the gate: information! Twenty messages gurgled into her queue, she scanned them quickly: campaign releases about energy policy, Viagra spam, and someone looking for a good place to take a date in Youngstown. *Where is it?* She flicked her nail over the dial to shuttle through the bulk delivery. Ah, there it was—one from Rick . . .

To: ThortonM@hillman.com

From: Rick.Stossel@thinkmag.com

Subject: Not going to the shore

Weather supposed to be bad, we're all staying in D.C. for now.

Melanie was angry and then heartbroken and then just annoyed. She had been counting on Rick's wife and kids being out of town this weekend. The affair was one more set of logistics she had to manage. She shoved her Berry in its holster, which hung on the outside of her bag, not even bothering to check her other messages. The light on her phone showed she had voicemail but she and Rick never called each other. Julie was with her, so how important could the message be? *Okay,* she admitted to herself, *it could be very important. Fate of the free world at stake and all.*

Melanie checked her voicemail while she and Julie slouched past the Cinnabon and the shoeshine booth in the terminal. There were a few calls from reporters looking for comment on the Clearheads. They'd bounced off Skoloff's brick wall and were pleading in the overly friendly yet pathetic way reporters do when they need fast help on deadline: "Mel, it's Dick here, trying to get some kind of on-the-record reaction to those tinfoil hat brigade ads. Off-the-record would be fine, too. It's a stupid story but we've got to do it and I've got to do a walk-up to the new ads before early deadline so I need something, anything. Even by e-mail would be fine."

Melanie didn't even bother to write their names or numbers down. She knew by heart the numbers of people whose calls she'd return right away. As for the lesser-known names leaving stilted and pushy demands, well, returning those calls wasn't going to help. That wasn't her skill. She didn't do dial-a-quote. She had friendships and they paid off over time. She'd just have to run into some people. Artfully run into them. Preferably after the drinking had started but before she was careening off the walls at Stetson's, breaking more shoes and running into people more literally.

The last message was from Skoloff herself, wheezing her third

reminder to work on the goddamn spontaneous reel already. *Crap.*
She really wants me to go in. . . .

Julie flagged down a skycap just before they went outside and
handed him a five-dollar bill and her bag, motioning to Melanie to
do the same. The skycap whisked them to the head of the line and
Melanie felt her hair go simultaneously limp and frizzy in the D.C.
humidity. "We sharing a cab?" Julie asked.

'Actually, I've got some errands to do. We'll catch up later?"

Julie got into the cab. "Sure, sure. I'm heading up to my folks'
summer house this weekend, but we'll talk when I get back." She
leaned her head out of the open window and shouted back: "Oh,
and that Clearheads thing is *hilarious!* About twenty people
e-mailed me the clip this morning! It's everywhere! So best!"

Melanie got into her own cab, frowning at Julie's parting words.
Twenty people. Everywhere. Huh.

She pulled out her cell phone and started returning calls: "Dick,
hey, it's Melanie . . . yeah, yeah, that's what I'm calling about. Off
the record? We're planning on handing out frequency jammers so
that the Clearheads can no longer receive messages from their
leader. I'm not going to offer you lots of 'What have we come to that
this is even a legitimate story,' but this isn't what Mom and Dad
back in Davenport are worried about, I can tell you that. On the
record? Can't say anything just yet; let me call you later. I just
wanted to give you a heads-up that it's bullshit. . . ."

MELANIE NEVER THOUGHT she'd be the kind of person who bought
her groceries at drugstores. She looked with a kind of mild surprise
at the contents of her shopping basket: a skinny quart of milk, a

couple of cans of soup, crackers, instant coffee, those unnaturally pink wafer cookies that were always on sale, and a three-pack of Hanes old-lady underwear. Melanie pressed her lips together at the thought of wearing the parachute-sized briefs in front of Rick. But it was the only kind Rite Aid happened to have. *But at least they had some!* thought Melanie. And laundry was not an option. No time. *If they sold wine here, I'd never have to go anywhere else.*

Even though she wasn't on the road as much as the advance people or the staffers who were on Hillman's plane, the late nights and long days had made even living in Washington seem like life on the road. Her small studio ("junior one-bedroom," the real estate agent had insisted) on the fringes of Dupont Circle still had boxes stacked in the closet and the "kitchen in a box" her parents had given her remained unpacked. She never shopped anywhere that wasn't within a block of home or work, and dinner was almost always the warm cheese and stale crackers left over from whatever event or television taping had happened that day. She couldn't remember the last time she'd done laundry. She just kept buying new clothes—disposable T-shirts and skirts from Old Navy, whose seams usually ripped about the time she'd get around to washing them anyway.

The Rite Aid clerk was monumentally unattractive. He had a mullet, angry patches of acne across his cheeks, thick glasses, and the kind of full lips that never seem to close all the way. He was here almost every time Melanie came in. His unsightliness embarrassed her. Her embarrassment embarrassed her. She felt bad about feeling bad for him, knowing somehow that it was wrong to think of a person the same way you'd think of the puppy at the animal shelter no one wanted to bring home, but she couldn't help it. At first she had tried to avoid having him ring up her purchases, but the clinch of guilt she felt every time she saw him didn't go away, and sometimes avoiding him meant dawdling in the back of the store for thirty minutes, pretending to read magazines about hairstyles or cars or bodybuilding.

So she had started to just get in line, but almost always found a place to rest her eyes that wasn't in front of her. She fiddled with her purse or searched for a very specific, nonexistent brand of bubblegum in the racks below the register.

Now she shuffled up to the counter and set down the basket. *Oh, the new* Us Weekly! She thumbed deliberately through the pictures of Pamela Anderson's pets as the clerk scanned her pathetic little picnic.

"Will that be all, Ms. Thorton?"

Melanie started. He knew her name? Was he hitting on her? "Uhm, uh." She was going to have to look at him. She dragged her eyes toward his face and let them rest there, realizing as she did so that the reason she had dreaded this in the past was that she was actually grimly fascinated by him. *What is his life like? Does he look in the mirror? Is he a virgin?* All these thoughts passed quickly as the weirdness of him knowing her name crowded them out. "How did you know my name?"

He smiled. It made his cheeks go red, which was not a helpful thing. But it was a genuine smile. Melanie couldn't help but smile back.

"Why, Ms. Thorton, you're a regular."

Her heart sank, but she forced a little smile. "Oh, yeah." She looped the plastic bags around her hand and started out, then stopped and turned her head: "Good night, uhm . . . what's your name?"

He practically burst from grinning: "Sandy!"

"Yeah, good night, Sandy."

The bags seemed very heavy as she walked out into the damp, hot twilight and turned down Florida Avenue toward home.

Sunday, August 1

ON SATURDAY, finally hangover-free, Melanie had tried to bat cleanup on the Clearheads, but the blood didn't seem to be in the water. Just a query here and there, and some blogs chatting it up. So Sunday she didn't go into the office, despite knowing that's where Skoloff would want her to be. The weekend after the convention was the only time she'd get to rest; she knew that both intuitively and because no one would shut up about it. Hal Prentiss had told the interns that "even if the candidate is caught with a dead girl or a live boy, get some rest. It's your last chance."

It would have been nice just to stay in bed. Shut the French doors that sealed off the alcove of her bedroom and run the AC on high until she caught cold. But she was taking a break, not slipping into a coma. So she got out of bed to get the *New York Times*, which could be hard to come by in Dupont Circle on a Sunday. She read the newspaper all week on the Web, and it was her one little attempt at maintaining sanity to actually get the real thing, with real money, from a real person. But that's the only effort she would put into it: She wore slippers, boxer shorts, and no bra to the Safeway, just four blocks away, where she also bought a single roll of toilet paper and bananas. At the Java Hut she bought a toasted bagel with cream cheese and an extra large coffee that she hoped would last her through lunchtime.

But then she went back to bed. She wiped away bagel crumbs,

listened to Oscar Peterson, and tried to focus on the paper. After a Robert Pear story on Medicaid reimbursement rates goes to the jump it's hard for any human to focus. She browsed the Vows section, a slightly masochistic detour that provoked a guilty pang. She wondered, not for the first time, if Rick's wedding had been featured in the *Times*. The urge to check Nexis and see was strong, but she buried it.

After a while the paper moved too slowly for her. She couldn't resist wading into whatever the chatter was online. She was fascinated by the blogosphere, though she had a hard time explaining why. She was unsure of how to summarize the adolescent, pseudo-sophisticated political sandbox that she had been observing with interest, mostly because it was, whether Skoloff realized it or not, her job. The fringiness of political bloggers made the Internet a kind of extreme focus group for new ads and new tactics. Their reactions wouldn't tell you how the country as a whole would react, but it was a way to take the temperature of the base. To do that, however, you did have to wade through pages and pages of text devoted to petty rivalries and to gleefully misinformed strategy memos on what the campaign should do next. There was something quaint and stupid about all the time bloggers put into these deconstructions. Sure, there were those who just flamed, but mostly the debate was surprisingly exhaustive and heavily footnoted. She had heard that bloggers called it "Fisking." Julie called it "fish slapping," after the Monty Python sketch in which two men took turns prancing up to each other, slapping each other with a mackerel, and prancing back.

But mackerel notwithstanding, blogs could be useful. In fact, unbridled by the antiquated concerns of the Hillman campaign chiefs, lefty bloggers were doing exactly the kind of oppo research that Melanie had been itching to do herself. Maybe they'd even lead her to Golden's Achilles' heel. She knew it was there; she could almost sense it.

Was it really only ten A.M.? she wondered. The only messages on her Berry were campaign spam about who was on what Sunday show and what the talking points were, along with the random announcement of new staff in Wisconsin or Missouri. Julie was at her parents'. The TiVo was set to record Rick's show at eleven, but suddenly it seemed important to make sure that happened.

Seeing Rick on TV could make Melanie pang or it could make her glow, depending mostly on how soon she would see him again and if their last meeting had left a good taste in her mouth. *As it were,* she nudged herself.

Collapsing onto her lumpy couch, she put her hand over her heart as if it would tell her in advance what the image of Rick would do to her this time. Aside from the discovery of a few more bagel crumbs, it gave her no clue.

She thought it would be okay this time. She smiled to think of his little signature look: "Smart take," he'd say into the camera. If he really wanted to emphasize a point he'd raise an eyebrow. It was the kind of theatrics people who play life-saving doctors in the afternoon would use. Melanie was certain that Rick had practiced it in the mirror.

But that's what made it possible to love him: He was faintly ridiculous and sometimes insecure. When you tease someone, that means the love is more real. It means that you're paying attention, he had told her. That's why he couldn't resist bringing up her complete reliance on spell-check, the butterfly clips she used in her hair when all else failed, and her fondness for movies starring talking animals.

Of course, Melanie reminded herself, Rick's favorite movie was the pseudo-deep Tom Cruise vehicle *Vanilla Sky,* which she had found so incredibly pleased with itself for showing that a rich man could, with enough money and time, learn to accept himself. Rick claimed to like it for the Dylan references and the lusciousness of Penélope Cruz, but Melanie suspected he might just be enthralled by the idea of being really, really rich.

He and Julie should get along better, she thought. Julie still didn't get what Melanie saw in Rick. Or, rather, she saw—the power, the high-threadcount sheets, and the nice wine—but she didn't approve.

Julie tried to bring up the topic once, not long after Melanie had first told her about the affair. They were sitting in Le Bar—it was across the street from the campaign. Melanie called it Le Lunchroom and she knew the menu by heart.

"He's just . . ." Julie was saying, swirling her chardonnay, looking toward the ceiling as though it were an interesting book. She slammed the book shut, looking right at Melanie: "He's an operator."

"If you weren't being so clearly hypocritical, I'd be irritated," Mel replied. "Besides, I like him."

"I can see that," Julie said, taking a sip of her drink. "Your blouse is misbuttoned, by the way."

Melanie put her fingers to her topmost button.

"Made you look." Julie grinned. "And you have just confirmed all my suspicions. During the day, even . . . I don't know where exactly you find the time. But you've recovered nicely, dear. No smudges, even."

"It's campaign season, which someone once told me is a time in Washington when you can get away with anything."

"Ah, right." Julie's face fell into a more serious composition. "He's a meta-operator," she announced.

"Meta? So your parents' money wasn't completely wasted," Melanie shot back. Julie's wealthy family and all its trappings—

boarding school, Yale, a habit of referring to "the help"—weren't her strongest assets when it came to advising politicians on how to reach out to middle America, and Melanie knew she could be surprisingly sensitive about it. "Again, why is that a bad thing?"

"It's not." Julie brushed off the insult. "Not at all. But it does mean that he can't be trusted."

"Please. We're both so careful about everything, I'm thinking I could run the CIA."

"Just make sure he's not a double agent," Julie said, signaling the waiter for the bill. "He's always after something."

"And I guess he succeeded." Melanie allowed herself a saucy toss of her head.

"Darling." Julie looked at her friend coolly. "You are nothing if not a prize, but a good fuck is hardly worth risking your career. He wants something more. You may be the cake, but he is always on the lookout for the frosting. Dirt about the campaign, maybe . . . Which isn't terrible or something to hold against him. I dunno. I don't have him quite figured out."

The waiter came with the bill.

"You are full of surprises today," Melanie said, reaching for the check. "Here, let me pay. You're always getting it."

Julie laid a gold American Express corporate card on top of the check. "Melanie, I don't think you understand: I'm rich."

"I knew there was a reason I liked you."

SHE SMILED TO HERSELF and clicked on the TV, suffering through some televised evangelical church sermon that was really an only thinly veiled endorsement of the Republican agenda before finally the booming theme of Rick's show began.

No one wanted to be on the show the week after the convention, that much was clear. Rick had booked Hilda Lott, or, as they called her, Hilda Talks-a-Lot. Rick had told Melanie that bookers for talk shows called her and those like her "street meat," for her willingness to go on air at any time. Rick had joked about what event Talks-a-Lot would leave for a five-minute hit on his show. Son's baseball game? Sure. Funeral? Depends how close the relative.

All of the cable news channels kept booking her because she was versatile. Hilda could argue any issue round or flat. Once, she had argued that Golden's standing was getting better among women voters because of his "manly straightforwardness" until Rick had stopped her, apologizing that he'd incorrectly recited the most recent poll and that, actually, Golden wasn't doing well with women. "Proves my point exactly," she had said without missing a beat. "The Republicans need someone more sensitive."

Melanie watched Rick tap dance, talking about Thursday's speech. She had joked with Rick earlier that no one but shut-ins and twine collectors would be watching. But the show was getting better.

She could swear he was sending her a covert message when he joked about the convention bounce, wriggling his eyebrow in the middle of the sentence.

She reached for her Berry: "The convention bounce joke is getting old. Time to develop some new material. Let me know if you have time. I'll offer you some ideas."

The show ended with Hilda referencing the Clearheads ad—but just referencing. She noted that "the blogosphere is buzzing with talk of one group's wild accusations. Who knows if the Hillman team will respond?"

Rick didn't react to Hilda's closer. Melanie relaxed just a bit with that. He looked into the camera and ended the show. "You're watching America Now, and this has been *Capitol Insider*."

After the show he messaged back: "Glad you were watching. I can have the car stop by for fifteen on my way home. That's how long I would usually chat in the green room. . . ."

"Since you booked Talks-a-Lot you can probably stay longer."

"I don't want to push it."

She started to make a joke about tying him down, but she worried that he'd take her seriously or, worse, much worse, think she was being clingy. Every once in a while, she had the adolescent fear that she was being too needy. She had a near-constant urge to ask someone—a friend, a therapist, a psychic—about this, but she worried what the answer would be. *If it's really love do you feel needy at all?*

Monday, August 2

THE NEXT DAY, Melanie locked herself in the campaign's editing suite from nine to five. There had been a short break for a greasy lunch and she had drunk enough Diet Coke to qualify for a sponsorship deal. But she thought the spontaneous reel might be done. Now she would have dreams about it, she thought—Hillman scooping ice cream, Hillman driving tractors, Hillman in various working-class-themed hats (construction, baseball, cowboy . . .), Hillman holding enough different babies that Melanie wondered if it looked like he was involved in a paternity suit.

Now she wandered out into the main room, blinking a bit in the brightness.

At five o'clock on a Monday afternoon, the Hillman-Langley campaign headquarters had the ambience of a fraternity house in those twilight hours between when the hangover dissipates and the drinking begins again. It pretty much was a fraternity house, except for the policy papers and week-old editions of the *Times* that competed with take-out cartons and empty bottles of Diet Coke and Budweiser for desk space. And sure, there were enough women present that it all looked fine on camera and even on paper if you didn't sort the list hierarchically . . . but the boys set the tone.

Prentiss was the model. He was tall and broad-shouldered, with a tangle of wavy brown hair beginning to go gray. His success brought him suits that would cover Melanie's rent, though they seemed to wrinkle the instant he put them on. Now, he was slouched over his desk at the far corner of the office, pressing a tiny cell phone into his jowls. It looked like it had grown there. Seeing Melanie enter, he winked lasciviously.

It was funny how easily the boys on the campaign had put away whatever weird Dukakis hang-ups haunted them and started acting with all the crotch grabbing and locker-room humor they once despised in the president and his party. On Sundays, they used the big-screen TV in the war room to watch football while they drank longnecks and spilled delivery pizza down their shirts.

Prentiss, off the phone now, stood up in his corner and maneuvered toward the bathroom. On his way, he picked up a copy of the *Post* and cleared his throat. "Gonna go lay some cable, folks. Be back when I'm back."

Melanie cringed. A new intern—some honors student from Smith with expensive clear braces and a Marc Jacobs handbag, who by all rights should have been creating PowerPoint presentations at Daddy's law firm this summer—giggled.

Melanie's solid flyover background—though her dad was an engineer, her grandfather had grown corn—meant that she was no stranger to fart jokes or lesbian porn. And maybe all the pants-hitching, pizza-scarfing, beer-pounding, and balls-scratching wouldn't bother her if it wasn't so . . . celebrated. Celebrated as only men who have too many facial creams for their allergic rashes in their medicine cabinets can do. *Maybe we're just supposed to be getting in touch with our inner red state,* she thought as she threaded her way through the maze of desks that, six months ago, had started out in tidy couples of two. Now they had given birth to misshapen Siamese twin deskchildren, hollowcore doors slapped on top of sawhorses, and file cabinets draped in campaign posters.

Interns drifted around, poking through piles of faxes and flirting with one another. The sound of some kind of strategy-planning meeting drifted out from the war room. She could have been in that meeting, but she had sort of wanted to get something done. The voices quibbled:

"No, we have to keep hitting on the economy. He should be at the factory gate shaking hands, at the unemployment office looking concerned, and surely there is a fucking community college in every swing district. This isn't that hard, people."

"But we can't have him talking to out-of-work widget makers while Lady Di fidgets with that fucking Hope diamond she has on her finger." *So that new nickname for Mrs. Hillman has really caught on,* Melanie observed.

She set her laptop bag on her desk and began a search for an open electrical outlet. The office had clearly never been intended to be home to fifty staffers, each with their own utility belt of gadgets that needed to be recharged and laptops that needed juice. And there were the five fax machines, four copiers (two color), four or five dorm-room refrigerators, and at least half a dozen televisions, ranging in size from the war room's drive-in theater model to the ten-inch relic that Skoloff had on her desk.

Melanie was on her knees, trying to figure out if the cord she was about to pull ran to the copy machine or to the mini-fridge where her quasi-assistant kept his mysterious collection of off-brand sodas and Kozy Shack puddings, when she sensed (which is to say, smelled) Skoloff's approach: menthol cigarettes and Coty cornsilk powder.

"And here I was thinking you didn't really work that hard," Skoloff croaked. "On your hands and knees, even."

"I was just finishing up the reel. Jamie and Andrew are in the editing suite looking at yesterday's Ohio footage." Melanie sat back on her heels and waited for the sarcasm to twist into an instruction.

Skoloff stared down at her, tapping her foot slowly. She held a cigarette with a precarious mile of ash between two bony fingers. Behind a pair of glasses with red rims and lightly tinted lenses her eyes were hooded. Her short gray hair capped her head like a cabbage leaf, and her high-waisted slacks and blazer obscured any suggestion of curves, making her look like a thick cylinder.

"I'm still thinking about this Clear Blue Easy fuckshit. We get too proactive and it looks like we're worried. We don't do anything maybe it blows over. But we have to get the cabal to agree it's meaningless." She sucked on her Virginia Slim and the ashy end of it quivered. Melanie wondered if Skoloff cared whether it fell.

Not like it mattered on this floor, which held a collection of tomato sauces, ground-in Oreo crumbs, and the dregs of any number of alcoholic beverages. *The family of an out-of-work widget maker could live quite well off the scrapings from this carpet.*

Skoloff continued: "You know Rick Stossel, right?"

Melanie's heart stopped.

"We're friends." *Oh, that sounded natural!* Melanie allowed a spark of self-congratulation to illuminate the bleak possibilities before her.

"Everyone's casting around for a story now. If he skips over this one . . ." Melanie felt Skoloff's eyes sharpen on her. "Why don't you see what he's thinking on this?"

Was the conventional wisdom so easy to game? More important: What the fuck was Skoloff really asking her?

"I'll, uhm, talk to him."

Skoloff nodded. "Right." She turned on her heel and walked back to her office. She tapped her cigarette, letting the ash fall.

We're never getting our deposit back now.

To: Rick.Stossel@thinkmag.com

From: ThortonM@hillman.com

I'm supposed to talk to you about the Clearfucks. Can you possibly meet for two minutes tonight? It's actually kind of important. We could do it in public even.

Melanie winced a little as she hit "send" on that one. *Should have joked about something,* she thought. This note had a whiff of desperation. Maybe more than a whiff. Perhaps a gale.

From: Rick.Stossel@thinkmag.com

To: ThortonM@hillman.com

Two minutes. I think. Let me juggle some things around. Supposed to have a drink with NBN's Karl Taylor, you know, the editor of The Point, The Most Influential Tip Sheet in Politics (cue music please) but no doubt he'd rather you were involved somehow, if you know what I mean. Want to meet

with me early then stick around for a drink with him?

Melanie felt her stomach tumble at the thought. *Christ, no. Nonono.* The last thing Melanie needed was a chance to be on display with Rick in front of someone as scandal-trigger-happy and as suspicious as Taylor. *He'd bust us before the drinks were ordered,* she thought. Back before she had taken up with Rick—which was when, exactly? Sometime last century?—she had thought that Taylor's preternatural ability to sniff out hanky-panky was part luck, part wishful thinking. Now she realized it was simply years of observation.

To: Rick.Stossel@thinkmag.com

From: ThortonM@hillman.com

Let's play it by ear. How about I meet you at DC Coast around 7? We can see what happens.

From: Rick.Stossel@thinkmag.com

To: ThortonM@hillman.com

Sure thing. You know I like to watch . . .

Well, at least I might get laid, Melanie thought, snapping the window closed and turning to the mountain of clips her interns had rounded up for a printed backup to the spontaneous reel—they were accounts of Senator Hillman being kind to small animals and children and generally appearing human. Proving *that Hillman is human is, of course, another matter,* Melanie thought. *Maybe if we could just perform some kind of medical exam. . . .*

. . .

D.C. Coast was plastically elegant and hyperconscious of its status as the officers' club of the Hillman campaign. The restaurant had some kind of vague seafood theme, but mostly Melanie focused on the wine list and who else was there. She didn't bother going there unless she wanted to be seen. Skoloff needed to know this meeting was happening, and sometimes it was necessary to be among the humans.

Melanie thought of all the times she had ducked around corners and bent down into wheelwells to avoid being seen with Rick. To avoid being seen with him *too much,* she corrected herself. Some socializing between the two of them wasn't just normal, it was beneficial. To Melanie probably more than Rick. Sometimes it seemed to Melanie that he had chosen her, swooped down off of some D.C. Mount Olympus and raised her above mere mortals.

Melanie told herself that she wouldn't watch for Rick's arrival. She would not, she told herself, keep looking out the restaurant's plate-glass windows, eyes peeled for his particular gait and profile. She would not devolve into Bridget Jones.

She looked out the window.

Ack, Melanie thought, and glanced around the bar.

Melanie was used to being early—"Time is the one thing you can never make up to people," her father told her—and, back before her life became a C-SPAN channel in a blender, she would carry a book around for occasions just like this one. Reading a good book at a good bar was one of life's great pleasures, as far as Melanie was concerned, though sometimes it gave strangers something to talk to you about, which was a mixed blessing. *Not a blessing at all, really,* she thought. *It's bad enough when people you* know *want to talk to you.* That wasn't fair. Melanie liked people. It's just that she now had to be so on guard all the time. She shook her head to clear it. Who would have the time for a book now, anyway? The last written work of any real length she had gotten through was *The Point*, and that's only because she was scanning it for a mention of Rick's latest piece.

On the other side of the bar, a small clique of campaign folks seemed to be forming. One of the girls waved at Melanie and Melanie smiled brightly and waved back. *Okay, they saw me, that's fine,* she thought. *Now, if I have to actually explain why I'm here . . .* She cocked her head in an exaggerated way, as though she felt her Berry vibrating. Melanie shrugged, pantomimed an oh-the-work-is-never-done sigh and pulled the device out. She was scrolling through the candidate's schedule for the next day when a voice interrupted.

"They're more addictive than cigarettes, should come with a surgeon general's warning." Rick was suddenly at her side, leaning up against the bar, smiling wolfishly. Melanie grinned.

"And they serve the same purpose in social situations—now all the Asperger patients inside the Beltway can just play with these instead of lighting up when they don't want to talk to each other."

"Asperger?" Rick raised an eyebrow. "Haldeman's aide?"

"Your age is showing. You know, like autism, but functional. You can dress yourself and whatnot, but you can't actually interact with people. It's what everyone here has."

Rick grinned, and Melanie felt herself go slightly swoony inside. It was a nice grin. "Now, let's get a table . . . by the window?"

Melanie frowned.

Rick raised his shoulders. "What? Who wouldn't want to be seen with the smartest woman in politics? Second smartest, at least . . ."

Melanie felt the narrative of the evening start to slip out of her hands.

"Just kidding. I'll take care of it."

Melanie settled up at the bar as Rick went to go talk to the hostess, and she realized how few of her own drinks she had bought in the past weeks. It was one of the reasons it was so hard to keep track of how much she drank. The other reason was, well, how much she drank.

Rick trotted over from the maître d's stand with the smooth dark-haired girl coming up behind him. "Come along, Nancy's taken care of us," he said, turning back to wink at the hostess, who giggled.

Huh, Melanie thought, suddenly not feeling so swoony. *Huh. Is he trying to make me jealous?.* She had created compartments for the unseen affection Rick probably showed his wife, but to see him working his charm on another woman right in front of her was disorienting, a feeling she wasn't supposed to be having at this "business" meeting.

They sat down, and Rick ordered an Amstel Light. He patted his gut as he did this. "Gotta make the trainer happy, you know?" he told the waitress. Melanie thought, *What part of having a personal trainer makes it obligatory to always talk about having a personal trainer? It's D.C.'s excuse for bling. I guess it's subtler than flashing a wad of hundreds or just setting the keys to your sailboat down on the table. Do sailboats even have keys?*

Rick looked over Melanie's head and did a quick scan of the room before coming back around to meet her eyes: "So, Dragon Lady's got her undies in a bundle about the Clearheads, eh?" He clicked his tongue. "Must be driving you crazy."

"Yeah, well . . . I don't know. I mean: She's driving *me* crazy. The

Clearheads *are* crazy and Skoloff . . ." Melanie wondered how much detail to get into. "She thinks there may not be a need to respond."

"Interesting."

Melanie tensed slightly, wondering if she had already said too much. "I mean, there's absolutely nothing to it. And there's a worry that if we spend too much time responding that we'll piss away the convention bounce."

Rick grinned. "Ah, yes, the convention bounce." He dropped a slow wink.

Melanie glared and under the table he brushed his leg up against hers. She pulled it away but let slip a smile. "Careful," she whispered. He smiled back. Her voice returned to a normal register: "But what do you think?"

"Hmmmm." Rick leaned back in his chair and crossed his arms. *Ah,* Melanie thought, *Business Rick.* He screwed up his mouth a little and cast an appraising glance at Melanie. It wasn't the same look he had laid on the hostess; it was something a little different. He looked like he was trying to decide whether to tell her something or not. She sat up a little on the edge of the chair before wondering if he was *really* deciding or if this little performance was just an excellent way to get people to think you were letting them in on a secret. *It's the kind of thing Julie would do.* Melanie thought. *Hell, it's the kind of thing I should do.*

Whatever Rick was doing, he was talking now. "Skoloff is fucked if she thinks this is going to blow over. It's a strategy that might have worked for Kennedy, but Hillman's negatives are already so high that it doesn't take much for something to stick. More important: It's fucking August now, and there's nothing else to write about. What, you have new ads coming? Great, more green lawns with playful dogs jumping on the candidate. Who cares?"

Tough love, Melanie thought, eyes widening just a little. He leaned forward, in full lecture mode now. She'd seen a variation of this on his show, when he laid out the week's must-reads or shot down a guest's theories. This was arrogance or confidence or maybe it was bullshit, but Rick said it with such authority it was hard not to believe.

"But beyond everyone's boredom, you've got to deal with how it doesn't *matter* if the Clearheads are loons. They've got a little money—from someone or somewhere, anyway. They've got an entertaining story, and they just did the most effective fifty-thousand-dollar ad buy in the history of politics. I think they paid for maybe—*maybe*—three hits of that ad, but between Web down-loads and clips on all the nets, anyone who knows or cares about the race at this point has seen the ad."

"And whose fault is that?" Melanie said, not quite able to rein a knee-jerk sense that Rick's lecture was also a lead-in to his telling her he would be doing a Clearheads story himself.

"Oh, ours, of course. Mainstream media. But it's a story, Mel, and it's now bigger than the Clearheads themselves. The blogs—left and right—are already making it a cause, and they can keep this story alive without our help. In fact, if we *don't* do a story about it, they'll make an even bigger fuss. 'Big Media refuses to look into Tinfoilgate. Blog at eleven.' "

"When you say 'if *we* don't do a story,' are you speaking collec-tively or royally?"

"Ah. Well. We'll see." Rick tried his grin out on her, again.

"Seriously. It's okay if you are, I'd just like to know."

"I wish I could tell you, sweetheart." He took a sip of his beer and glanced away.

"Well, if you *do* write a story, can you tell me what your angle is going to be?"

"I think I just did." That grin again. "Doesn't that get me something? Giving away a free preview of a *Think* cover story?"

"Cover?" Melanie fell back into the chair. "Shit."

"Just kidding," Rick said, gesturing for her. "Come back here. Really, I have no idea what we're doing yet."

"You must have some idea."

Rick frowned at her. "Yeah, some." But then his expression turned mischievous. "We're not going to let these guys get in the way of that convention bounce Skoloff was talking about, though, are we?"

Rick's hand was now on her leg, and Melanie was amazed by how quickly she forgot about the looming prospect of a damaging *Think* cover story. "Well, I guess not. . ."

"Screw Taylor," Rick said, under his breath. "Let's get out of here."

Heart racing, Melanie followed him to the parking garage.

The coupling was speedy and urgent and a little uncomfortable—a seat belt buckle had left an imprint on Melanie's knee. There was a delicious tension to these sessions, though. She loved the walk back to the car, the struggle not to touch or look each other in the eye. By the time they opened the backseat door, Melanie's thighs felt the prickly warmth of anticipation and she swore she would have an orgasm the moment he touched her. That didn't happen, but it didn't take either of them very long.

.   .   .

RICK AND MELANIE were pulling out of the garage in his black Mercedes SUV when his cell went off. He picked up the phone from between the seats and grimaced slightly. "Kathy," he said. Melanie nodded and tried to look serious but not sad. She was getting better at it after almost three months of being the other woman in earshot.

She pressed her forehead against the cool glass of the window and looked at herself in the side mirror. She was slightly flushed from their fucking—yes, *fucking*, she thought, *quick, efficient, effective*—in the backseat of a car parked in a deserted corner on the lowest level of the garage.

Rick was talking to his wife about dinner plans for that weekend. "Sure, if that's where you want to go," he said. "You confirm with Anna yet? I don't think Tracy's available."

Pause. He drummed his fingertips on the steering wheel.

"That sounds great. We haven't been there in a while." Pause again, a quick glance to Melanie. "Tell them Daddy will be home soon."

Melanie squeezed her eyes shut against the image of the Stossel hearth in Chevy Chase taking shape in her brain.

Rick used to excuse himself when his wife called. He would give Melanie a crooked grin and shrug—"What can I do?"—and then turn into a corner or walk into the hotel bathroom or go into the hall. He would lower his voice, and Melanie would put her head under the pillow to keep from hearing the conversation. Sometimes she thought it would be easier if he just talked. The quiet almost-whisper made his conversations with his wife seem all the more intimate, and if Melanie let her mind wander at all, she would find herself straining to make out a word, a thread of meaning. *That's just what you do when people are whispering*, Melanie thought.

Rick lied easily and well to his wife, though at the height of the campaign it wasn't that necessary. People's movements were simply unaccounted for. You were on the plane, you were on the bus, you were stuck in a meeting, you were filing, you were drinking yourself into oblivion. Marriages either stretched and bent to accommodate this or they broke. Rick's marriage had lasted through four campaigns—he and Kathy must have found some level of flexibility they could tolerate. Right?

Did Kathy know? Did she suspect? Did she care? These had been Melanie's cab-ride-home thoughts ever since it became clear that the affair would last beyond drunken fumbling in the Racine Hilton. She had no answers for these questions; they simply rang through her brain like clock chimes, regular and echoing in the hollow place she had cleaned out to accommodate her enormous guilt. Julie had once said she felt sorry for Kathy, but Melanie didn't know if pity was exactly how she'd describe the ugly swirl of emotions that dealing with the reality of Rick's marriage stirred in her. Pity was what you felt for someone who was helpless. Kathy was being taken advantage of, but she wasn't helpless. When she really was honest with herself, Melanie knew that the chief emotion Kathy raised in her was abject fear. It was more than just fear of getting caught—it was the history Kathy shared with Rick, the aches and pains they had nursed each other through, the joy they must have felt at bringing their children into the world. She knew that in the face of that shared past, she was small, and her time with Rick not just short but maybe empty, too. That's what scared her the most.

Cheating wasn't without its glamour, of course. They called it The Walk of Shame when you stumbled out of a strange guy's dorm room with a hangover and your shirt on backward, but sneaking out of a hotel and getting out of a cab at seven A.M. wearing a party dress and carrying your heels could feel more like a red carpet strut. While she was growing up in Iowa, the only people Melanie knew of who had affairs were characters on *Dynasty*. She had to admit there were times now when she felt like her new illicit hobby was just part of growing up, a part of coming to Washington, not that different from developing a taste for gin or foreign cigarettes.

But, much as with the gin and Gauloises, there was a price to pay the next day, and no matter what kind of *Breakfast at Tiffany's* thrill she got from those early morning exits from fancy hotels, there was a grubby quality to their actions as well: wearing the same underwear twice, and the sour taste of lying.

Rick was wrapping up the conversation: "No, I don't think I'll make it out Thursday."

Melanie opened her eyes. *So maybe we're on for Thursday,* she thought.

He continued: "Yes. Sure thing. Love you, too."

Melanie had already shut her eyes again by the time he got to "too." She bit the inside of her cheek.

I'm not this person, Mel thought to herself. *This isn't me.*

4

Tuesday, August 3

To: Senior, Senior Staff

From: SkoloffK@hillman.com

Date: August 3

Subject: Meeting protocol

It has come to my attention that some of the Senior senior staff have been sending "deputies" to Senior senior staff meetings. Senior senior staff meetings are for Senior senior staff. You may send deputies (NOT ASSISTANTS) to senior staff meetings and senior staff may send THEIR assistants to REGULAR staff meetings. All Senior senior staff must attend Senior senior staff meetings, unless they have a conflict with another meeting at which only principals or Senior senior staff are allowed, in which case, you may send a deputy.

THE DAYS HAD a different consistency now than before the convention. Everything seemed thinner, less substantial. Maybe it was the heat, and the way the sun baked the city until the buildings appeared to sag and the normally crisp monuments looked smeared. It seemed to Melanie that things should have more clarity now that there was less to do: The downtime should have put more air between everything, more white space around each event, making everything neater and easier. Instead, things seemed to bleed out more. Meetings that would have taken forty-five minutes two weeks ago sprawled into an hour; at a dinner that was supposed to start at eight people would just drink gin and tonics until they couldn't stand anymore at ten.

Melanie's datebook became wholly unreliable. It was full of cross-outs and arrows and sticky notes. Eventually, she just gave up and started organizing everything around the most recent e-mail in her inbox. It worked well enough for both the campaign and for her social life, but still, nothing was simple.

With the campaign, sometimes the most complicated task was parsing a single morning's worth of meetings.

To: Staff

From: SkoloffK@hillman.com

Subject: 8/2 Poll #s, Tuesday Conference Call

Hal has a breakdown on the absolutely newest poll numbers. Our post convention surge continues and we're strong with women and minorities. Only 38% of respondents were familiar with "attack ads" on H. It's great news, everyone, and we'll be excited to go over them in the senior staff conference call at 9AM.

To: Senior Staff

From: SkoloffK@hillman.com

Subject: Real 8/2 Poll #s, Real Tuesday Conference Call

The numbers are slowing down faster than expected. Someone fucked up and I want to know who. Tell me why it's not your fault at the senior senior staff conference call at 8:30AM.

To: Undisclosed list

From: SkoloffK@hillman.com

Subject: New fucking poll numbers, Tuesday senior executive senior staff conference call.

Is it the Clearfucks or was it that disastrous fake "home video" at the convention? Our inability to give a straight answer on gay rights or the fact that H failed to kiss a single baby over three days in Wisconsin? I'm either firing one of you or hiring someone to join you. Please have your resignations and/or recommendations ready at the senior executive senior staff conference call at 8AM.

The conference calls seemed to get more exclusive as they got earlier, but Melanie knew for a fact that Skoloff regularly convened an "executive senior heads of staff" conference call at ten A.M. some days just to throw people off. You could spend a whole day in conference calls if you played it right, which wouldn't be such a bad life, really. You could take a conference call from your car, in your house, on the john, or—as Melanie knew from experience—in flagrante. She smiled at this, remembering one July night when Rick ran his fingers over her bare stomach as Skoloff rasped out a new stem cell research position. It had been Hillman's fourth, for those who were keeping track.

The social call e-mails were often less vulgar than Skoloff's digital harangues, but they were just as desperate. On Tuesday, the e-mail came around nine A.M. like it always did:

To: Undisclosed Recipients

From: Hank.Lensky@currentmag.com

Anyone doing anything fun?

Julie called Lensky's social ritual "throwing chum in the water." It was Lensky's way of creating a scrum of sources, colleagues, and potential dates he could insert himself into. The move had the superficial appearance of socializing, and at first Melanie had assumed that Lensky was lonely. Julie set her straight:

"Well, he may be lonely, but that's not why he's always putting blood in the water," she had said. "He needs to feed. He's not afraid of being alone, he's afraid of not knowing what's going on."

"Has to keep moving or he'll die," Melanie observed.

Julie smiled: "I think through my metaphors very carefully."

The BlackBerry made such predatory socializing easier: No one called anyone to make plans because that would pin you down to a real-time answer. Instead, the chum was thrown and everyone would circle around it, sending out casual pings through the Washington ecosystem for who was where and doing the cost/benefit analysis for each possibility. Practically, the ritual made no sense. A two-minute phone call would settle time and place; instead, one created elaborate e-mail trees, full of forwarded invitations and private companion-wrangling (text messages and IMs would fly: "Are you going?" "Are YOU going?" "Who else is going?"). The system was not without its flaws, but it assured that you at least knew about what was going on, even if you had no intention of showing up.

The gatherings themselves sometimes showed the strain of their creation, at least until the second round or so. Melanie, often overly sensitive to that kind of strain, tried to get to the second round quickly. Especially, as was the case at the moment, when Julie wasn't there. It was early Tuesday night and Julie was on a conference call to coordinate the California Processed Foods Association Campaign for Healthy Kids. ("Isn't that like the tobacco companies campaigning for smoke-free workplaces?" she had asked Julie. "We handle that account, too," Julie replied.)

At first Melanie felt guilty for leaving work a little early, but the crowd gathered on the roofdeck of Local 16 held enough colleagues and contacts that it basically was work. *That's probably how we all justify it to ourselves,* Melanie thought. She fiddled with her Black-Berry to have something to do while she finished her first drink. Around her, the conversations were typical.

"Do you know what happened to Beth? Last I heard she was headed to Georgia for a Senate race," she heard one of the partners from the Cleveland Park Group quiz Hal.

"Unclear," came the reply, and Melanie smiled. No one said "I don't know" in Washington. Instead, everything was always "unclear." When does the meeting start? Unclear. Where did the insurance forms go? Unclear. What time are you coming? Unclear. How much did you drink? How did you get home? Does his wife know? Unclear, unclear, unclear. It was as much an incantation as an answer, implying that the speaker had full knowledge of the situation but that some outside force—you, perhaps—made making sense of the event impossible.

Melanie considered joining the conversation—she happened to know that Beth Wilcox was working oppo for the Senate campaign he mentioned—but without Julie as a buffer she needed things to become a little more unclear (or at least blurry) before diving in. She got another drink and considered her options.

She could talk to the Fox White House correspondent, who was surprisingly earnest and less surprisingly dull. Or she could schmooze with that hot consultant from the Bay Group—she had heard a well-founded rumor he might join the campaign. She could

lay groundwork for the campaign's response to the upcoming
Republican convention if she talked to an editor from *Hotline*, or
she could try to pry open the head of that blogger girl who always
seemed to show up at these things—what was her blog called?
Swamp Thing? Maybe she would have some insight into how to
fuck with the Clearheads—the Hillman campaign was in dire need
of blogger fu. She could do any of these things, and if she didn't
decide soon, someone would decide for her.

Her Berry buzzed; she was grateful for the interruption.

To: ThortonM@hillman.com

From: Julie.Wrigley@clevelandparkgroup.com

Subject: Call me

There wasn't a message. Melanie frowned and felt a combination of panic and pique. Ominous but empty messages were a pet
peeve, probably stemming from the first time anyone had ever told
her "We have to talk." She toyed with the idea of not calling back.
But it was Julie. It was probably important. And that annoying Fox
News guy was headed right toward her . . .

She flicked out her phone and edged to the border of the bar. At
the height of summer, the sun had only just gone down and she
could feel the warmth of the wood deck through the soles of her
sandals. On Julie's end of the line, the phone seemed to ring a hundred times.

Finally: "Sorry for the cryptic message," Julie said.

"It's okay," Melanie replied. "But why?"

"I didn't want to risk sending an e-mail astray. Where are you?
Can you talk?"

"I'm at that Local 16 thing. What is this about? You're killing me."

There was a pause. She could hear Julie take a deep breath. "I have an advance of Paul Lead's column."

Melanie waited for Julie to continue and then, as the pause grew longer, she realized that Julie didn't need to say more. The pieces fell into sickening place: Lead's column . . . urgent message . . . can't talk . . .

But she had to be sure. "It's not about the campaign, is it?"

"Not exactly."

"Oh, God." Rick. Her and Rick. Melanie felt a hiccup in her chest that could turn into a sob or a scream. . . . She looked around. Everyone was still clustered around the tall blond intern Prentiss had brought with him. Prentiss thought of the intern pool as a lending library. She swallowed. "Oh, God. How bad? What?"

"I don't want to read it to you. Can you get to a computer?—this is not something you should be squinting at your Berry for."

"Uhhm. Uh . . ." Melanie made a fist and hit herself on the thigh. *Straighten the fuck up. Deal, damnit. Deal until you can get out of the goddamn bar at the goddamn least.* "Ug."

"Mel? Mel, don't go Cujo on me."

A sharp intake of breath. "I'm fine. I'm gonna head home."

Julie's voice softened a bit. "Look, we'll figure this out. We will. Just get to a place where we can talk."

"Right."

They clicked off and Melanie looked at what was left of her drink. She finished it in two long pulls and walked toward the door, leaving behind the boys and their Swedish Bikini Team player.

. . .

"FUCK. SHIT. Fuck, fuck, fuck, fuck." Melanie's heart was seizing up in her chest. She could feel panic like a bull's-eye on her back. She paced the short distance through her kitchenette and the living room and back, standing at the farthest possible point from her cheap Ikea desk and the computer on it. She hadn't turned on any lights since getting home, she had just gone immediately to check out the column. Now, even from this far away, if she took her eyes away from the gray-blue glow of her laptop's screen, the darkness seemed total.

"Fuck."

She had called Julie as soon as she finished reading the column, and now her knuckles tightened to white on the cell phone. Julie broke in, her voice flat and slightly chilly: "So what you're saying is 'Fuck.'" Melanie fought back the urge to snap at her. The panic was spreading across her shoulders, and she knew she was on the edge of tears. She took a deep breath and waited for Julie to continue.

"Read it to me again," Julie said, in that same distantly thoughtful tone.

Melanie didn't have to look at the item again; she had it memorized. Another deep breath: "'Every conservative in town—and some liberals—believes that John Hillman's campaign is getting undeservedly good press. But do they know why? How close is the relationship between the campaign's decidedly inexperienced junior communications staff and D.C.'s media elite cabal? Sources tell us that at least one staffer has gotten so inside one capitol pundit's head'—ha! Ha! *Capitol Insider!* Get it?—'that she no longer even needs to make a phone call to get him information. . . .'"

"Mmmm." Julie clicked her tongue. "That is bad."

"I KNOW IT'S BAD!" Melanie gritted her teeth against the

welling of tears behind her eyes. She gulped air as images of her possible future formed in her head: Rick's certain furor at being found out, her parents' annoyingly quaint shame, and—perhaps most seriously—Karen Skoloff firing her with a smirk and a smoke ring. *And how the fuck did he find out? The header at the Four Seasons?* She couldn't believe it was all her fault.

"Someone told him, you think?" Melanie felt her voice go into a whine.

"It is strange he didn't try to call you . . ."

Melanie thought back to the barrage of phone messages she had deleted Saturday without listening to them. Her phone had some unfathomable recall for incoming numbers, and she scrolled through the screen. *Fuckfuckfuckfuck* Three calls from the *Post*'s 334 extension. Melanie heaved in a lungful of air. She could feel a wailing sob building.

"Calm down. Calm the fuck down," said Julie, in an unexpectedly measured tone. Melanie was quiet. For a time, neither of them talked; there was just Melanie's occasional sniffle. She had crossed the room again and was staring at the *Post*'s website, not really reading, just letting the words float and blur together in front of her. *Should I call Rick?* she thought. *Should I call Karen? Should I start sending out résumés? I am a crisis manager! How do I manage this?*

Julie cleared her throat: "Okay. Here's what I think: I think this is a nonstory."

"It's a nonstory that could get me fired."

"No, wait. It hasn't yet and it won't. I think I've figured this out. The only reason Lead even ran with this story is that he's desperate for items, right?"

"Maybe . . . I mean, it is Rick . . ."

"Don't flatter yourself or him, sweetie. Everyone *we* know knows who Rick is and maybe even cares about who he's fucking but . . . Put it this way: Does your mom know who he is?"

"That's not fair. My mom barely knows who Hillman is."

"Exactly. I'm guessing she shares that trait with many Americans."

"Okay, now you're just insulting me."

"No, no, you're not getting it. This isn't just about trying to convince you it's not a big deal. . . . I'm saying that there is something we *can do* about it." Julie was talking faster now, her voice was in a higher range. "Because you're right: The ten people who live here are going to be very excited about this item. But this wouldn't have made it into the paper at all if Lead had something that *more* people cared about. It's just that it's August. Not only is half the town gone, the people who are left here just aren't very interesting."

"Again with insults," Melanie said sharply.

Julie rolled along, ignoring her: "But what if something really exciting happened? What if there was a story big enough to push whatever meager crumb of gossip Lead has on you guys off the table? Are you two really important enough for him to stay on the story? We don't have the firepower for an Operation Lewinsky, bombing a milk factory in one of those tan countries we hate, but we can do something. There is tail involved, and it will wag the dog."

Melanie felt herself drift out of the panic that had gripped her so tightly, almost physically—Julie's idea seduced her away from the ledge of despair she had been ready to jump off of. "I see where you're going," she said. "But what story are you talking about?"

Silence on the other end of the line. Then, apologetically: "Still working on that."

Melanie knew better than to try to get in touch with Rick right away. And she also knew better than to face Skoloff (and the pack of randy young—and old—men) at the campaign the day that something like this hit—but unfortunately, it couldn't be avoided. Melanie shut her eyes tight and prepared herself for a day of lying low.

5

Wednesday, August 4

FELLOW SCHOOLMATES AND SCIENTIFIC SKEPTICS
BUY AD TO RAISE DOUBTS ABOUT HILLMAN
The New York Times; Section A; Column 1; National Desk
August 4

A group of Harvard classmates of Senator John Hillman and renegade medical researches have bought television time in three key states accusing the senator of having undergone experiments which, they claim, hamper his mental faculties to this day.

"I saw him with wires coming out of his head," says Edward R. Phillips, in the ad from the group, known as Citizens for Clear Heads: "Who's at the other end of those wires? That's what the American people deserve to know."

The group's founder and spokesman, Craig Donnelly, is even more blunt: "John Hillman will raise your taxes at the touch of a button. Someone else's button."

The advertisement, which layers snippets from recent interviews with familiar black-and-white photographs of Mr.

Hillman, along with stock footage of mental institutions, is one of the many being run by independent groups, known as 527's for the provision in the tax code that enables their operation to run attack advertisements this season.

Few potential voters interviewed for this article had seen the advertisement. However, it struck a chord. Told of the group's argument, Amy Trilling, 34, of Cleveland, Ohio, said she would have to see more to judge the allegations, but she acknowledged of the candidate, "He is awful stiff."

HER CONFIDENCE DISSIPATED with each step she took toward the office. She was about to walk into a room full of people who now thought they knew her secrets. Who, as it happens, actually *did* know her secrets. Julie tried to help her rally:

To: ThortonM@hillman.com
From: Julie.Wrigley@clevelandparkgroup.com
Where are you? Hiding isn't going to help. Head tall!

In the elevator, she began to regret her dawdling. She should have been the first person in, already busy and at her desk, doing something dreadfully important. *At least I finished that fucking spontaneous reel,* she sighed to herself. *Now we probably want the "proof he's not operating under mind control" reel. She longed to put together something—anything—on Golden, but realized there were more pressing matters at hand.*

She had her Berry in her hand when she walked into the office. Always the perfect excuse for not meeting anyone's eyes. She found her desk and sat down. She looked up briefly and swore that the entire room suddenly looked away. Except for Hal Prentiss. He was grinning at her like she had come in nude and carrying a steak. Melanie had not signed up for this kind of bullshit.

Her desk was covered in weeks-old newspapers and folders of outdated press releases. She never read either, so they just accumulated, an archaeology of the campaign. During her first week she had thought order could be imposed if she had enough trays and baskets and boxes to put things in. Now those optimistic purchases from the Container Store just gave the sheaves of paper a hilly topography. Periodic excavations turned up lonesome lip balm tins and half-filled steno books. Melanie resisted the urge to sweep the whole mess onto the floor. *Though,* she thought, *it's not like it's possible to draw* more *attention to myself.* She sat down and started instant-messaging with Julie.

Thortonology: Prentiss is looking at me like he knows his chances have improved.

WrigleyJules: Have they?

Thortonology: uhm, yeah. Because I'm probably now single.

WrigleyJules: ?

Thortonology: Even if he's okay with it when I see him, how long can the guy and I keep it together now that everyone is watching and that everyone knows?

WrigleyJules: the least of your worries, really. And I bet Mr. Guy probably doesn't care as much as you think. Rumors have been floating around about him for years. He's used to it.

Thortonology: How do you get used to it?

WrigleyJules: Just give it time, darling. By the next campaign, you'll be planting items about your affairs yourself. Btw, did you see the Times this morning?

Thortonology: Duh.

WrigleyJules: No, I mean, *see* it. Like, on paper. The Clearheads are on
    A1 . . . with pictures . . . and with a sidebar on "the role of the blogos-
    phere in this pivotal moment during the campaign."
Thortonology: Jesusfuck.
WrigleyJules: Exactly.

Melanie scooted out from her desk and began looking for an
actual, physical copy of the *New York Times*. The most recent one on
her desk was from July. She searched the massive pile of papers in
the middle of a cluster of interns' desks. She checked in the sad, drab
"waiting room" area at the front of the office, where she found a day-
old *Boston Globe* and single copies of *National Review* and *American
Cheerleader*. (*Guess Prentiss took the shuttle recently,* she thought.)
No one read the paper on paper anymore, it required too much sift-
ing. She was summoning the nerve to ask Skoloff for her copy, suddenly feeling the need to clear her throat, when Skoloff's insistent
rasp burst into the air. "Thorton! Meeting!" she called, standing in
the doorway of the war room, cigarette dangling from her lips.

"Be right there!" Melanie grabbed her Berry and notebook off
her desk and jogged into the meeting.

About a dozen staffers were scattered around the perimeter of
the room. Some were shuffling memos and clips, while others were
alternating expectant gazes between the two gurus in the room.

Prentiss sat at the head of the scarred and stained table,
hunched over a mammoth take-out cup of coffee and, of course—
there it was—the front page of the *Times*. "I can't fucking believe
this shit," he said. "I talked to this jackass yesterday and he said it
was a 'Notebook' item, not the fucking front page."

Skoloff took a long drag off her cigarette. "And what is the fucking 'blogosphere'?" she coughed.

Melanie's eyes widened involuntarily. Out of the corner of her eye she saw the shoulders of young Garrett Shnick crumple. He ran the Hillman-Langley blog. Prentiss was not so restrained: "You're shitting me, Karen. Right? You *do* know what blogs are, don't you?"

Skoloff glared. "They're those Internet . . . things, I know that, Hal," she said, stabbing out a cigarette. "But who cares what a bunch of shut-ins writing about their cats' bowel movements have to say about the Clearheads?" Clearly, the fuzzy convention camaraderie had worn off.

Hal leaned back in his chair and chuckled. "Well, they're the only ones saying anything about the Clearheads at the moment, Karen, since you decided we're not."

Skoloff's nostrils flared menacingly. "It's a nonstory."

Prentiss wriggled his bushy eyebrows: "Tell that to the *Times*."

"I would have, *if it had been my job to talk to them.*"

Melanie was concentrating very hard on tracing the outline of a box she had doodled. A quick glance around the room showed other staffers engaged in similarly important tasks. *No one likes it when Mom and Dad fight,* she thought. *Except Mom and Dad.* Skoloff and Prentiss sniped at each other as a way of keeping busy. They weren't pinning blame so much as merely sticking pins to see who would bleed first. Get in their way and they'd prick you.

Chuck Reed, the campaign's token Texan and a communications deputy with only the vaguest of job descriptions and a TV-friendly face, cleared his throat. "Perhaps we should consider, you know, bringing some of these 'blogs' around to our side."

Both Prentiss and Skoloff's heads swiveled to Reed and said, in near unison, "Shut up." Prentiss added "shit head," but, Melanie reflected, that could well be a term of endearment.

Reed's boyish face turned bright red, but he kept talking. "Look, what's important here? Is it who did or didn't shut down the *Times* story or is it figuring out how to get past the Clearheads issue so that Hillman can win?"

Melanie wondered which of the interns in the room Reed was trying to impress or, more likely, sleep with.

"We're trying to figure out how to shut the *Times* story down *so that* Hillman can win. The blogs don't matter now. The *Times* has run it. That's why it was on *Today* this morning. Now it's going to be on *Inside Politics* and then *Nightly*. They always follow the *New York Times*," Skoloff said, icily. "But welcome to Washington, Mr. Smith."

Chuck pouted and tossed a glance to Prentiss, who shrugged. Only ten minutes into the meeting and the room already had a sour feel, like they had been there all night. *We might well be,* Melanie thought.

The thought was singularly unappealing. She exhaled audibly. All eyes in the room swiveled toward her. Reflexively, she smiled. Then she realized that they were waiting for her to say something. She cleared her throat.

"Well, actually, Chuck has a point. The blogs aren't homogeneous," she started. "To the extent we're being helped by progressive bloggers, it's that they're attempting to punch holes in the Clearheads' claims using public records. They're looking at coverage of medical experiments at Harvard, Hillman's academic record, and also at the history of the Clearheads group. The founder appears to have, uhm, a colorful résumé. I believe he belongs to a 'scientific fraternity' whose newsletter once called into question whether or not we'd ever really landed on the moon."

Skoloff was looking at Melanie with something Melanie wasn't sure she'd seen before . . . respect? Surprise? Skoloff brought her cigarette to her lips and nodded. At the other end of the table, Prentiss crossed his arms. "And why aren't we using this yet?"

"Uhm. Ah." They weren't using it because Skoloff had given orders to let the story die of its own weight. They weren't using it yet because Melanie, now that she thought about it, wasn't sure that the story was true. *I guess that part doesn't really matter.*

The meeting dwindled to a close with no decisions made, just people drifting out in the reverse order they came in. They talked about seeding an anti-Clearheads blog, they discussed the campaign's blog—Skoloff had thought it was just for press releases— and then discussion veered to spinning whatever was to come out of the Republicans' convention.

Melanie left when they started discussing if the Hobbit guy would do a blog. She had a date with Julie, anyway.

THE MARGARITA MELTED in Melanie's glass. She stared at it glumly: "On top of everything, I'm still not sure about Rick. I'm supposed to see him tomorrow; I guess I'll find out then." She had heard from Rick, but the Berry message was cryptic. "Busy. Conversation not for e-mail. See you tomorrow." That was something. Melanie was irritated not to have more, but Rick had a paranoid James Bond streak that sprang up every time the affair came close to the surface. Melanie thought of the times he had left a hotel to call home from an office or a press-center landline, and then returned to the hotel.

"Really?" Julie fiddled with a straw. "You'd think it would at least be good for his ratings. . . ."

"Stop, okay?" Melanie looked around for their waitress. It was three P.M. on a Wednesday, and the Glover Park outpost of Austin Grill was deserted. Blessedly so. Melanie had only just barely resisted the temptation to come out of the campaign offices to meet Julie wearing Jackie O sunglasses and a long, brunette wig. Instead, she just slouched into the booth and kept her eyes on the menu. The restaurant's plate-glass windows offered a view of only vacant sidewalks, and for once Melanie was grateful for the emptiness of D.C. in August.

"At least you can be glad you haven't done much TV," Julie suggested.

Melanie glared. Julie, of course, had done lots of TV.

"Trying to be helpful!"

"You can be helpful by coming up with a plan to get me out of this."

The waitress came by wearing a tight Austin Grill T-shirt that Melanie would have almost considered demeaning had she not realized how much it could score its wearer in tips. Julie ordered another round. Melanie took the opportunity to check her e-mail on her Berry.

There was nothing more from Rick, but someone had finally forwarded her the transcript of that morning's *Today* show, which had featured the leader of the Clearheads campaign, Craig Donnelly. She had heard Skoloff mention it and had made a mental note to look into it, but she hadn't realized it would be this bad:

LAUER: So what you're saying is that the man who could be leader of the free world may not control his own thoughts?

DONNELLY: That's right, Matt. We're preparing to release documents indicating that Senator Hillman, when he was an undergraduate at Harvard, participated in government biofeedback experiments. These test subjects were conditioned, with the proper trigger, to redistribute wealth.

LAUER: Are you talking about class warfare?

DONNELLY: Yes. That's why the tinfoil cap is crucial. In fact,
I've brought one for you.

LAUER: Why, er, thank you.

DONNELLY: I know you don't think you need it. But that's
precisely why you do.

"Jesusfuck," said Melanie, not quite under her breath. "Jules, I need you to look at something. . . ."

"Is it the *Today* show thing?" Julie was not quite paying attention; her eyes followed their waitress as she returned to the bar.

"You saw it? What am I saying? Of course you saw it."

"Of course I saw it. And it's a good thing you asked me first because *of course* you saw it, too." Julie brought her eyes back to her friend: "Tell me that at least you TiVo'd it."

"Actually, if I didn't TiVo it on my own, the machine probably did," Melanie said, swishing her margarita around in an attempt to reincorporate the ice. "You know how people joke, 'My TiVo thinks I'm gay'? My TiVo thinks I'm a dork. Well, it thinks Rick is a dork because Rick programmed it, and he programmed it to record nothing but the morning and nightly newscasts and the Sunday shows. I got really excited the other day because it had recorded something called *Porn in America*, but that turned out to be a *Frontline* special."

"Yeah, mine auto-records the Spanish-language newscasts. It thinks I'm a bilingual dork."

The waitress brought their fresh drinks, and again Julie seemed to be looking at her a little too closely.

After she left, she asked Melanie, "So, do you recognize her?"

"The waitress? No, should I?" Melanie almost swiveled her head to look but caught herself. *I'm losing it,* she thought. *My mad skillz.*

I'm losing them. But she recovered, and found the waitress's reflection in the restaurant windows. She was medium height, with long, dark hair gathered in a high ponytail; she was a little skinny but had incongruously full breasts. In addition to the suggestiveness of her tiny T-shirt, her jeans rode very low on her hips; when she bent over to pick up a plate, a narrow slice of thong peeked over the waistband.

"Ah, the Monica," Melanie said.

Julie smirked: "Yeah, I saw that, too. Not sure how that's supposed to be sexy. It always just makes me want to pick my own underwear out of my ass."

The waitress turned around and Melanie saw that she wasn't quite as pretty as you'd want someone with that body to be. *Though I suppose with that kind of body, you don't have to be that pretty,* realized Melanie. However she looked, she didn't look familiar. Melanie shook her head: "I don't think I know her."

Julie took a thoughtful sip of margarita. "Maybe it was before your time. Were you here for Nick Burton's surprise birthday party?"

"Burton . . . covers the Hill for the *Post*, right? I think I may have gotten invited, but I didn't go." Melanie wasn't, in fact, sure if she had been invited. She was probably freshly arrived from Chicago at the time, still getting lost in the Metro system and struggling to get her head around the District's Byzantine parking laws. (Pink overdue notices still papered the front of her refrigerator.) She was figuring out where to have lunch and she took books to dinner so that it wouldn't feel quite so weird to eat by herself. The campaign office had seemed cavernous and Skoloff had appeared to actually breathe fire. Then she had met Julie, and Julie had swept her into every party since, but Melanie's pre-Julie social life in D.C. was more impoverished than she liked to admit.

"Mmmm. Well, you missed quite a party. I don't remember the last part of it myself and supposedly there are incriminating pictures of half the White House press corps on Olivier's hard drive. . . ."

"Yes, well, as a wire reporter, he needs more blackmail material than most."

"They may not be *that* incriminating," Julie continued. "In any case, this place catered it. There was a margarita machine, and that waitress was there to work it. But something definitely went wrong. At the end, everyone was convinced that the machine had been— and I quote—'tampered with.' "

"What, Diebold makes margarita machines? They're not satisfied with rigging polling booths in Ohio?"

"No, seriously, the word was that she or someone put in way too much tequila. All I know is that I don't remember much past the moment when she took her shirt off."

"I thought she was *working* the machine."

"She was working something. Maybe it was for tips."

"I can't believe I missed this."

"I can't believe you didn't hear about it."

"Yeah, why didn't I hear about it?" Melanie continued to watch the waitress out of the corner of her eye.

"Dunno. Too embarrassing for too many people?" Julie pushed her food away. "In any case, she put on quite a show and it's almost certain she fucked Ed Thompson that night."

"The MSNBC guy?" Melanie raised her eyebrows. "He sort of looks like a potato."

"Yeah, but he was in Iraq." Julie's mind was already somewhere else. This gossip was too old to hold her attention. "Some people will fuck anyone who's been on TV."

Melanie cringed, wondering just how pointed Julie had intended that remark to be. Julie didn't appear to notice and just continued: "So, has the campaign decided what to do about the Clearnuts?"

Melanie sucked in her breath and pushed her chicken enchilada around on her plate. "I don't know yet. Skoloff seems so certain that it won't amount to anything, but it's the only story out there right now. Or the only story that feels new. How can I get anyone excited about our new ads—one features that guy who played a hobbit!— when there's some genuine crazy people to write about? I'm even worried that *Think* is going to run a piece on them, and Rick can't do anything about it."

"They could always write about Lady Di."

"Are you trying to help?"

"Always, darling." Julie narrowed her eyes. "At least you realize the appeal of the story. I can't believe Prentiss and Skoloff are so naïve. You'd think anyone who worked for Clinton would realize that the only thing more appealing than a conspiracy theory is a sex scandal."

"I know. It would probably help if Prentiss and Skoloff could actually communicate with each other."

"You know, that's what you need: a sex scandal." Julie tapped the Formica table with crimson nails.

"Thanks, but I think I'm covered in that area."

"No, seriously . . ." Julie began, her fingers tapping slightly faster as her idea gathered steam behind her eyes. Melanie watched warily.

"You need a really *juicy* sex scandal. You remember what I was saying about your mom not knowing who Rick is? You need recognizable names. More than one recognizable name."

"I need the president's name, preferably."

"Well, yeah."

"I knew you were a creative problem solver, but I didn't realize that you actually just made things up to solve problems."

"Like the Clearheads didn't make their shit up?"

"What are you suggesting, exactly?"

"I'm suggesting that we can kill two nondescript birds with one giant, flashy stone." Julie was smiling wide now. She signaled the waitress for the check.

Melanie was unsure. "Wait a minute, we still have drinks left."

"We have to get to my office. There was an off-site for the principals today and no one else is going to stay past five. And we have work to do."

The waitress dropped the check on the table and Julie shoved a couple of twenties in the folder, grabbed her purse, and started toward the door. "I'm going to go head over. Pick up something to drink on your way."

Melanie looked at the check. Julie had left barely five bucks tip on a thirty-five-dollar tab. She had gotten used to Julie paying for most of their meals—but since she, unlike Julie, knew what it was like to work for tips, she hesitated to be a party to Julie stiffing a waitress, even a slutty one. *Maybe especially a slutty one,* Mel thought, shrugging off her suspicions that this particular waitress's male customers kept her in $200 jeans and glittery lip gloss anyway. She put another twenty in the folder.

THE OFFICES OF the Cleveland Park Group were airy and sleek with modern but nondescript furniture and lots of blond wood. There were as many televisions as at campaign headquarters, but they were all flat screens and tastefully and unobtrusively hung like artwork, rather than set haphazardly on rickety temporary desks and hooked up to jerry-rigged bootleg cable boxes. Their desk chairs had as many levers and positions as a *Hustler* sex swing, but they were much more comfortable and probably more expensive. Vague modern paintings lined the walls and the break room featured a Viking range and a Sub-Zero refrigerator with a seemingly self-replenishing stock of Diet Coke, Evian, and microbrew beer.

If it seemed like the offices were out of a television show about high-powered Washington lobbyists, that's because they were. One of the young firm's first accounts was consulting on a reality show about the election, and several episodes had been filmed there—that mix of consulting and theater, politics and popular culture was almost precisely what CPG's founders had had in mind when they stepped off the campaign buses and into the private sector. The firm's specialty was a service of its own invention—something Julie referred to as "Kabuki consulting," an artful and almost invisible form of lobbying that didn't involve actual appearances on the Hill at all. CPG told companies how to get the public on their side—the politicians would follow. The slogan on the CPG business cards said it all: "We were never there."

The offices were a bit off the beaten path, too, set down by the waterfront and underneath the overpass in Georgetown, where the bold concrete of CPG and the glittering glass of the Ritz stood out as bold flagships of civilization. Melanie pulled up in front of the offices in her puttering Reagan-era Oldsmobile—an old boyfriend had dubbed it "the lawn mower"—to find that parking was unusually plentiful. She was just in time to notice a custodial worker scrubbing graffiti off the building's face. Melanie squinted and saw that it read: THE NEW TRICKLE-DOWN ECONOMICS: GOLDEN SHOWERS.

Melanie found Julie already at her desk. "What's the offsite about?"

"Some meeting about our 'class trip' to Vegas at the end of the year."

"And you'd rather work?"

"No, this is play—and it's not like I can bill you," Julie said, swiveling in the chair. "Though I probably should. I have already started on the solution to your problems." Julie turned back to the computer and gave a voilà gesture of her hands, pointing Melanie's eyes toward the website she had apparently been working on for the ten minutes before Melanie came in. It had a ten-minute look about it. It was based on one of the tartier off-the-shelf templates from Blogger.com. The color scheme was pink and black and gold, and it said in large, girlish script at the top, "Capitolette."

Melanie combed her brain. All the political blogs had names that sounded either like high-school gifted-class newsletters ("Instapundit," "Daily Kos") or military operations ("Hit and Run," "Little Green Footballs"). She did not recognize this one. And she'd remember a girl—the only one she knew of was that gossip blogger she always saw at Stetson's and she'd seen the other night at Local 16, "Swamp Thing." "Capitolette?"

"Read on, Macduff."

JULY 28

T. came over last night. I was tired from going out with H. the night before (not to mention sore!), but he practically begged so I told him ok. I didn't bother really getting dressed—I mean, I didn't bother putting on something nice. He's used to seeing me in a short skirt and heels but if he's demanding to see me on a Sunday night, I figured he could get what he paid for.

But it turns out that I should have been more generous. He was.

He wanted to see me because he's stressed about his job. The campaign's not going well, he thinks—that's not what the papers say but I guess he knows more than I do—and he worries he'll be out of a job come January. He says he's not sleeping. He thought getting some head would relax him. I told him that knowing I had rent money would relax me.

We both were pretty relaxed by the end of the evening.

Melanie sat back in her chair and looked at Julie, who was beaming. "Well? What do you think?"

"I think you must not be as rich as you claim," said Melanie. "And I think you should *not* be one to talk about me and the Big Boy." Melanie smiled. "*And* I think you should teach a seminar on time management."

Julie rolled her eyes. "Please. It's not me. You know it's not me. It's . . . Capitolette! Washington's latest Capitol Hill call girl. She's like that other one, but hotter and with real dirt. She knows about the margarita mix-up at Nick Burton's, she was in a threesome with Morgan Black from NBC, she's fucking someone in the Golden campaign."

"And she doesn't exist."

" 'Exist,' 'doesn't exist,' these are technicalities. It's the Internet! It's a fucking blog"—Julie caught herself and half-laughed—"a very hot fucking blog indeed. We're going to make it 'Penthouse Forum' meets 'Roll Call.' "

"I thought that's what *The Point* was," said Melanie.

Julie sighed: "Darling, people use those tip sheets to score points and fuel rivalries, but no one really plays dirty. There's nothing about sex or drugs or even rock and roll. Nothing really explosive. That's why I feel sorry for poor Plead. . . ."

Melanie glared, but Julie continued, happy to be instructing. "No, seriously, the 'Reliable Source' gig notoriously sucks. Not only do they make you triple-source everything, but you can't play people off one another like you can in New York. No one in this town can afford to go nuclear."

"Because everyone has to work with everyone else . . ."

Julie tented her fingers like a comic-book villian. "But Capitolette doesn't have to work with anyone. . . ."

"Do you have plans for anyone in particular?"

"No one worth naming," she said curtly, and swung back to the desk.

Melanie felt a shiver of frustration—her life was laid bare to Julie; who was she to keep secrets now? *But then again,* she thought, *I have enough secrets to keep already.*

"I'm so glad you could figure out a way to use my misfortune to settle your own personal scores," she scolded. But Melanie was intrigued. She admired the careful imprecision of Julie's first entry. The lover in question could, really, be talking about either campaign (though it was true that the press reports tended to portray Hillman's as floundering *more*). Even the prostitution—*It was prostitution, right?*—was only hinted at.

"Hey, darling, in Washington, other people's misfortune is the *only way* you can settle a score. Sorry it had to be yours, but . . . I think this is going to work." Julie crossed her arms and settled into herself, ready for the next question.

"Is it plausible, though?" Melanie twirled a strand of hair, examined it for split ends. "I mean, anything this hot, would there be talk floating around by now?"

"Yes and no." Julie took on the aspect of a schoolteacher, her syllables clear and slow. "You have to remember, no one here will ever admit they don't know something. It's considered a major faux pas to admit being uninformed. You tell anyone here the hottest, freshest gossip you have and only the most green intern will say that it's news. Everyone else is all, 'Oh, right, I heard that, too.'"

"True enough. But come on: fucking a campaign person for cash?"

Julie shook her head, still explaining to a recalcitrant child: "Not just a campaign person. She's fucking a lot of people."

"Even more reason to think it would have blown up by now."

"You're still not getting it. It's even more reason that *no one will admit they don't already know about it*. I mean, come on. Even you didn't want to admit you didn't know about the margarita thing."

Melanie froze up for a second. Julie was right, she realized. Julie was exactly right. . . .

Julie pushed herself up out of her chair and gestured for Melanie to get in front of the computer. "Now, your turn." Julie leaned over and clicked a tab on the screen, opening up a black form. "I'm going to make us something to drink."

Julie picked up the plastic bags and headed off to the break room, slim hips swinging, a bounce in her step. She was practically whistling. *Now that's a born crisis manager,* Melanie thought.

She swung herself in front of Julie's computer, marginally intimidated by its flat screen and impressive purr. But she was even more intimidated by the idea of making up a sex scandal juicy enough to distract the Washington press corps from, well, her own sex scandal, not to mention the burgeoning Clearheads debacle.

Then again, how hard could they be to distract?

"She needs to be sluttier." Julie's voice came from behind Melanie. She turned. Julie had come back from the CPG break room bearing a cut-glass pitcher filled with the light green goodness of fresh margarita and carrying two coffee mugs. Melanie noticed the mugs and gave her a quizzical glance.

"It's all that was clean," said Julie, setting down the drinkware. "And you can drink frozen beverages out of coffee mugs, just not *cold* beverages. Besides, drinking margaritas out of coffee mugs is acceptable on campiness grounds." Julie's good breeding had bestowed her with an elaborate taxonomy of what kinds of glasses and plates could be used on any given occasion. She had once forced Melanie to leave a party where the host was serving martinis out of wineglasses.

"At least they're not empty beer bottles, right, Martha Stewart?" Melanie took a mug. ("Gore-Lieberman: Prosperity & Progress" it read, and Melanie grimaced.) "What do you mean by 'sluttier,' anyway? I have her fucking on the copier, for chrissakes."

"Fucking in the office doesn't make you a slut, darling," Julie cooed. "At least, for your sake, I hope not."

Melanie gave her a tight smile. Julie sat on a desk space opposite the computer and sipped at her margarita. She thoughtfully looked at the computer screen over her mug (emblazoned with "51 percent is NOT a mandate"), and stuck out a long leg, pushing Melanie out of the way for a clearer view.

"You know what makes you a slut?"

"Fucking in a parking garage," Melanie said, not hesitating.

Julie looked at her sideways. "We'll table that for a second, though location is definitely part of it. What's that old story about *The Newlywed Game*? Something about 'the strangest place you've ever had sex'?"

Melanie finished the joke, donning a good ol' boy accent: " 'That'd be up the butt, Bob.' "

'Right. I swear, that alone will have more people talking than fucking anyone on a copier," said Julie. "Unless, of course, she is making copies at the time."

6

Thursday, August 5

To: PRESS.RELEASES@lists.whitehouse.gov

From: PRESS.RELEASES@lists.whitehouse.gov

Sent: Thurs Aug 5 13:36:15

Subject: POOL REPORT #2, 8/5

After leaving the estate where the two fund-raisers were held in Raleigh, the Golden motorcade stopped about a mile later. The President had stopped at a children's lemonade stand by the side of the road outside a modern, suburban home. By the time your pooler hurried up to the scene, the president was drinking some pink lemonade from a cup and praising the girl who was ostensibly running the enterprise. "Trying to help the local economy," he quipped, and invited reporters—including your pooler—to join him. "You're a little tart," he said. "I mean, it's a little tart." Your pooler took Mr. Golden at his word.

Cheryl Reiss, *New York Times*

MELANIE'S EYES WERE OPEN long before her alarm went off at six A.M., her stomach clutching, her head wrapped in a dull ache.

There had been much tequila the night before, and even some

genuine laughter. Julie's plan to distract D.C. from the Clearheads and Lead's column with Capitolette was far-fetched *but,* she thought, *not as risky as, say, having an affair with a married man.* Melanie tried to roll her eyes but the wet concrete sloshing around in her skull prevented her from doing so.

She stepped gingerly to the floor and navigated around the growing pile of dirty clothes that engulfed one corner of the small bedroom. *I think there used to be a chair under there somewhere. There's at least six or seven dozen pairs of underwear, that's for sure.* She wondered how many pairs of Old Navy string bikinis—and Hanes old-lady briefs from the drugstore—she'd have by the end of the campaign. Rick had been threatening to buy her some more sexy lacy things with complicated closures and, more likely than not, no crotch, but he hadn't gotten around to it yet. And unless this Capitolette ruse went well, he might never.

In the bathroom, Melanie looked through the water-spotted mirror to her reflection as she brushed her teeth. The toothbrush was new and it hurt her gums a bit. She thought about Rick's morning habits, the ones that, as a mistress, she would never get a chance to get fully used to: the way he laid out all his toiletries on a washcloth as soon as he got to a hotel, his thick-lensed, hideous glasses with aviator frames that he only wore for the short trip from bed to sink. A pang shook her. Even if Capitolette worked like a charm, her relationship with Rick was still a campaign fling, and those came with very short life expectancies. *I'm gonna lose him,* she thought. *I'm going to lose him. And soon.*

She sat down on the edge of the tub, hard. Had she ever *had* him? Did she really *want* him? It all started out so casually and so stupidly. *And,* thought Melanie, *that's the way it's going to end.*

The toothpaste barely made a dent in the tequila deposits that clung to her teeth and tongue, and the coffee she made turned sour in her stomach almost on contact. Of course, she hadn't actually made coffee at home since June or so, so if it tasted as though something had crawled into the pot and died, there was a good chance that it had in fact happened.

Melanie's BlackBerry blinked at her from the kitchen counter. An almost knowing wink, she thought. She wondered how many messages there would be from Skoloff, and how many from Rick, if any. His wife and kids were around, so they were in semi-blackout, and it was never clear if his silences during those periods were chosen or imposed. She knew. She *knew* he had seen the Lead item, he just wasn't responding to it yet. *Is he going to be like Skoloff and the Clearheads about this?* Melanie wondered. *Ignore it until it won't go away? Will I find out tonight?*

Maybe, she thought, *Rick will be really impressed by how I'm handling this.* She grasped onto this idea like it was tip money. *Maybe! Sure! Julie may have come up with Capitolette but we wrote the site together, and he loves that kind of randy shit. More to the point: He loves the game. Capitolette is the ultimate wag-the-dog scenario. . . . There is, in fact, no dog involved. Just tail.* Melanie sniffed a shirt and smiled.

Before leaving for work, she gave herself one last look in the mirror. *No visible stains, toenail polish only mildly chipped, hair . . . well, I'll deal with the hair later.*

THEY HAD AGREED to meet at the Mandarin for "drinks" that night and despite his assurance from the day before, Melanie needed to be reassured that he would come:

To: Rick.Stossel@thinkmag.com

From: ThortonM@hillman.com

Still on?

To: ThortonM@hillman.com

From: Rick.Stossel@thinkmag.com

Yes.

They talked about it as soon as Rick got there. He walked in, his head down in that sheepish way he had when he was the one to knock on the hotel door, they kissed, and then she asked: "So it's not the end of the world?"

She was holding both his hands, standing a step back from him. They could be about to dance or about to play ring-around-the-rosy. It didn't feel, however, like they were going to fight.

Rick's gaze narrowed at her. *Angry? Reproachful? Curious?* Melanie couldn't stop the reflexive temperature taking. She could barely concentrate on what she was feeling herself; every ounce of energy poured outward. "The Reliable Source item, you mean."

"Of course that's what I mean."

"Well . . ." Rick took a step, breaking contact. *Oh!* Melanie thought. *Bad sign, right? Right?* He sat down on the edge of the bed. "Clearly, I'm here. So it's not as though he's ended *our* world."

Good sign! Melanie was getting vertigo from the switchbacks in her emotions.

Rick bent over and started untying one of his shoelaces. *Great sign!* He continued: "I guess, well, I guess it's something to keep an eye on." He levered his shoes off with his toes and leaned back on his elbows. "Look, I read the item and I admit that I was a little surprised to see it got such placement, but you can't tell me you didn't suspect it was coming at some point."

"Oh, well, of course." Melanie's response was automatic, though she wasn't sure what she was agreeing to, specifically. People had been whispering about her and Rick for weeks, sure. And Lead had poked into the rumors at the convention. Should she have known about *this piece*? Suddenly, Melanie was certain she should have. *It's my job to fucking cock-block shit like this,* Melanie thought. *I was too busy eating the $100 breakfast at the Four Seasons.*

"I should have been able to spin Lead," Melanie said, shaking her head. Rick reached over and put his hand on her knee. He was smiling slightly.

"Hush. You can't beat yourself up over this," he said, his fingers massaging her lower thigh. "The point now isn't what you could have done—I just wish you'd paid closer attention. Maybe we could have headed this off at the pass. But it's too late now."

Melanie's skin felt a little heat at his touch, but her mind was still processing the conversation: *Don't beat self up. But it's my fault. But it's too late. Where's he going with this?* Melanie found herself mesmerized by Rick's fingers. He had his hands on both of her knees now, his fingers played just under the hem of her skirt.

"What do you mean, too late?" Melanie said, thinking of the plan she and Julie had hatched the night before.

Rick smiled without looking up, his concentration focused on her legs. "I mean, there's nothing we can do now. Trying to bat down something as insubstantial as the blind item he printed would only give it more weight."

Melanie tried to parse the metaphor and failed. She shook her head. "You sound like Skoloff about the Clearheads."

Now Rick looked up. His fingers stopped their gentle circles. "This is very different." He squeezed her knees. "Completely different. You understand that, right?"

"Suuuu-re." Melanie cocked her head and squinted at Rick. "You mean because the Clearhead accusations are false and, well, you and I are in fact fucking?"

Rick snorted. "Cute." He took his hands off Melanie's knees and walked to the large window and pulled the curtains shut, a little viciously, and turned back around. His arms were crossed in front of his chest. *Lecture mode,* Melanie thought, and wondered if he would be offended or flattered if she actually were taking notes. "As I explained: The Clearhead story has an entire media machine behind it, and it's being dropped into the news desert of August to bloom like a weed."

Weeds bloom? Melanie wondered.

It will survive on the bullshit bloggers spread. The Reliable Source item about us, on the other hand, is like a bit of pollen on the wind. It hasn't landed anywhere. People have noticed it and they wonder if other people have noticed it. But—so far—there's no one breathing life into it. No one has a stake in keeping the story alive except for Lead."

Melanie nodded slowly. The man loves his metaphors. But she kind of got it. Neither of us is running for president and the story didn't, it was true, come with the kind of hyperbolic sleaze factor or whiff of perverseness that made affairs into multiday media stories. It was, when you got right down to it, a pretty generic campaign fling. Melanie wondered if its ordinariness depressed Rick. It sort of depressed her.

He continued: "I know this town. This isn't gonna stick." Rick walked over to Melanie and pulled her up off the divan, his hands sliding down her back to cup her backside possessively. He grinned down at her. "Never apologize. Never explain."

They kissed. Rick's tongue played lightly over her teeth.

When they pulled apart, Melanie said just one thing: "Did you just quote Karl Rove to me?"

Rick began unbuttoning her shirt: "Turns you on, too, does it?"

Melanie didn't answer, choosing instead to fall back onto the bed and pull Rick with her.

AFTERWARD, Melanie lay sideways across the bed, her head propped up on one hand. Outside the large window of their room she could see the Fourteenth Street bridge, sluggish with rush-hour traffic. The room was cool and spacious, spare, providing such contrast to the rest of her life at the moment. The chaos of the campaign and her apartment, and maybe her life in general, drained her. The sheer messiness of it tugged at her sometimes, the way a flicker at the edge of a television set can make you jumpy or how clashing patterns can make your eyes hurt.

Rick, however, was being fastidious—putting his clothes on hangers to steam out the wrinkles while he took his shower. Melanie watched him out of the corner of her eye.

"You're not mad," she said, not sure if it was a statement or a question. It was a statement that needed an answer. It was a statement in search of confirmation. It was a statement of interest.

Rick didn't answer right away.

"I'm not mad," he said, finally. Now that was a statement. Or was it? Was he asking her, maybe, if he should be mad?

. . .

SHE HAD OPENED the curtains back up while Rick was in the shower. Shutting them against an empty courtyard, seven stories up seemed overly cautious. Of course, that's probably why they hadn't been caught. Rick was overly cautious. *Probably the wisdom of experience,* Melanie thought, then pushed the idea quickly away.

She heard humming just above the whoosh and patter of the water. It sounded like . . . could it be? *The Indigo Girls? I'm having an affair with a lesbian,* Melanie thought.

The sun glinted off the cars on the bridge and suddenly Melanie wanted Rick to be gone. She wanted to be here, alone in this feng-shuied room with a plate of new-wave sushi and a bottle of wine. Or maybe not alone. Maybe she'd invite Julie. *What does it say about this relationship that I now want to share my postcoital moments with my best friend instead of my lover? It means I'd rather talk about my lover than talk to him, I think that's what it means.*

And now he was getting ready to leave. He knotted his tie smartly and went to go take his suit jacket out of the closet. "The soaps here are so fruity," he said. "It's a good thing Kathy's not around tonight. I don't think I could explain smelling like this."

"Couldn't you have showered at the gym or something?"

Rick shrugged his jacket on and turned back to the mirror. "Good point. But still. I look forward to seeing if the Ritz's soaps are less . . . faggy." He turned around to Melanie.

"Now, how's my girl? You gonna just spend the night?"

She smiled up at him. "That's what I was thinking. Order some room service. Maybe watch some LodgeNet porn. . . ." She rolled over and got onto her knees, the sheet falling away as she reached over to embrace him.

"Whoa there, sweetheart. I may not like smelling like patchouli or whatever it is they have in there, but I also can't very well meet the boys for drinks smelling like freshly sexed you. Though it is," he said, leaning down to give her a peck on the forehead, "a much preferable scent."

Melanie smiled a small smile and sat back down on her heels. "Good point."

Rick chucked her under the chin. "Don't be sad, pal. I'll see you soon." He turned and gave himself a final check in the mirror. "Do you see any Melanie hairs?" She shook her head. "Okay, I'm off."

"Bye."

Before he went out the door, he looked out of the security peephole. Maybe it wasn't overly cautious, Melanie thought, maybe it was just smart.

SHE FILLED JULIE in on everything. Julie hadn't been able to come over—she had a dinner—but she called Melanie from her car and quizzed her, expertly, on Rick and his reaction to the scandal.

"He actually quoted Karl Rove?" Julie laughed so hard the mike on her cell phone headset picked up as pure buzz. "I love him. I have to say, I hate him and I love him. You have such extraordinary taste, my friend."

"I don't actually think he was doing it as a come-on."

"But it worked, didn't it?"

"Ha. Say what you will, I feel okay about things. He convinced me."

Julie laughed, not nearly as loud or long. "You mean he *spun* you. Tsk-tsk. That should be your job. And Rick's not what should be making you feel okay about things. Capitolette is."

"You think?" Melanie played with her expensive sushi. The best part of eating sushi alone, as far as Melanie was concerned, was playing with it. At the moment, she was constructing a tuna-roll fort.

"Oh, I don't know. Maybe he's right. Maybe we don't even need the blog. It's true I haven't heard anything further about you two since the piece. I mean, there was some minor buzz, and about twenty people forwarded it to me. I think you also made a blog or two."

"Shit, really?" Melanie frowned at her tuna fort. "I should have looked for myself but . . ."

"It's okay," Julie said. "You shouldn't have to. I'll filter this crap for you for now. And this dinner should actually be good for finding how much people actually care, too. If these people aren't talking about it, no one is. On the other hand, if they are talking about it, everyone will be. It'll be like a focus group!"

"Are you going to dial test?"

"Only if you have some negative ads coming out. Okay, I'm here. Talk to you later, darling."

"Later."

Melanie stuck a chopstick into the top of her sushi masterpiece. She wasn't hungry anymore.

7

Monday, August 9

Just got back from my date with M and boy is my ass tired! Kidding, kidding. Though, really, you'd think M grew up on a farm with the way he knows what to do around a barn door. We screwed for a while and all he wanted to talk about was "candidate this and candidate that" and something about how Air Force One is the only plane left where you get real silverware. It's amazing how he can work "Air Force One" into conversations. He brought me some M&M's from there once and I guess I was supposed to be impressed before I started eating them. Well, he can eat them out of my ass.

Actually, I think he'd like that.

MELANIE SENT THE SNIPPET to Julie to post, wondering how she'd react to Melanie's using a tidbit she'd heard from Julie's semi-regular hookup in the entry.

WrigleyJules: I can't believe you're using the David story about AF1!
Thortonology: You think I shouldn't? It adds a touch of vérité, I thought.
  Also, surely someone else somewhere has made the same joke. That's
  the whole point of that joke. Everyone's made it.

WrigleyJules: Yes but only David is so impressed with himself that he has
  to keep repeating it.

Thortonology: We can take it out.

WrigleyJules: Eh, why bother. It's not like anyone is reading the thing yet.

Thortonology: Yeah, I know. I thought you'd say this would take right off!

WrigleyJules: Give it a couple of days.

Thortonolgy: What else am I going to do?

WrigleyJules: I hear you have a little Clearhead problem.

Thortonology: Oh, *that*. Haven't you heard? We're not going to respond to
  these baseless attacks while real Americans with real problems are
  suffering thanks to the incumbent's tax cuts for the rich and a foreign
  policy that has lost us respect abroad and made us weaker at home.

WrigleyJules: Do you have a macro for that yet?

Thortonology: Control-fuck-you.

WrigleyJules: Ikfjadklsjflajskd

WrigleyJules: I have lost control of my fingers I am laughing so hard.

Thortonology: Just please maintain dominion over bladder. Wouldn't want
  to ruin that Aeron chair.

WrigleyJules: Control-fuck-you. Just kidding. Hey, have meeting.

Thortonology: bb.

WrigleyJules: bfn.

Melanie looked around the office. Sunlight streamed in
through the greasy windows and you could almost watch the
threadbare carpet begin to fade. With Hillman at his ranch in
Montana and the incumbent in New Mexico, the staff often dwindled to hard-core lifers and the two interns who didn't have anywhere else to go. They were getting really, really good at "Double
Klondike" solitaire.

The sounds of the new Clearheads ad drifted out from the war room: "In a world where your identity is your most precious commodity, how can we trust a president who doesn't even know who he is. . . ." It sounded more like the trailer for a straight-to-DVD action flick than a campaign ad, but that's probably why it had been downloaded approximately as much as the new *Star Wars* trailer. "They would have to get Hillman fucking Paris Hilton to make it more popular," Julie had said.

Melanie had nodded: "Yes, but at least that would help the campaign."

As it was, the ad relied as much on Democrats' outrage as it did on any Republican scheming for its heavy play. Republican bloggers posted the video file for free just for laughs, while Democratic bloggers showed it to rile up their party and maybe even evoke some real passion and support for Hillman. No one in the conference room could admit there was another reason for the ad's resonance: Hillman did act like a robot sometimes. *Anyone who needs to be taught how to be spontaneous . . . ,* Melanie thought.

The Clearheads were probably generating donations for both sides, but for those Americans just starting to pay attention to the race, the ad was almost certain to cancel out—if not wipe out—all the carefully choreographed infomercials that had run on the big screens at the convention. Melanie herself had spent fruitless hours one day in an attempt to get the Hillmans' elderly yellow lab to romp as photogenically as the president's dogs always seemed to. She tried treats, she tried toys, she was tempted to use a rolled-up paper. Unfortunately, the dog was about as excited about the Hillman campaign as most voters were. In the end, she had offered to get the family a puppy. "Voters love puppies," she told Skoloff.

They used a still shot.

A new instant-message window popped up on Melanie's screen.

PointMan123: Hello hot stuff!

Melanie rolled her eyes. Her keyboard felt dirtier just from having to type responses to Karl Taylor's nudge-nudge banter. She rolled with it because she had to, because Taylor's daily cheat sheet to the campaign could torpedo a new gambit out of the gate or could crown a new leader in "the image race." Melanie held out hope that Hillman had a chance in that kind of contest because it didn't poll actual voters, just journalists.

Thortonology: Hey. I don't think I have anything for you today.

PointMan123: You wound me! I was just dropping in to say hello.

Thortonology: But as long as you're here . . .

PointMan123: Melanie, you wholesome Hawkeye, it's not what you have for me, it's what I have for you. It's big, it's juicy, and it will give you lots of pleasure!!

Thortonology: If it isn't either a foodstuff of some kind or a photo of the president fucking an intern, I'll be very upset.

PointMan123: Close on the latter. Check it out: http://capitolette. blogspot.com

Melanie thumped back in her chair. Capitolette in *The Point*. Of course. They should have started lobbying Taylor earlier. Melanie bit her lip and wondered how long she would need to wait to respond to make it seem like she hadn't read the blog. Then again, if she really had never seen it before, she'd respond immediately, most likely with something along the lines of "Oh, that?"

She took a more moderate but typically Washington approach:

Thortonology: Omg. Am I in it?

PointMan123: Not unless you're ass-fucking some intern I don't know about. . . .

PointMan123: Are you? That would be kind of hot.

Thortonology: You know about all of the interns I'm fucking.

PointMan123: The interns in addition to . . .

A chill seized Melanie's back and she waited to see if Taylor would continue.

PointMan123: Oh, never mind.

Melanie thought, *He's letting me know he knows. Well, fuck. Can he be distracted?*

Thortonology: Those rumors about me and Wrigley are just rumors.

PointMan123: I'd like to hear more about them just the same.

I bet, thought Melanie.

Thortonology: Isn't the new site enough for you?

PointMan123: Too much is never enough. But, seriously, check it out. She knows her shit and, uhm, more. The sex stuff is also good. Heh.

PointMan123: Later.

Thortonology: B.

Melanie cut-and-pasted the transcript of the IM conversation into an e-mail and sent it to Julie. Her phone rang a minute later.

"Oh. My. God," Julie said, half-whispering.

"I thought you had a meeting."

"I did, I did!" Julie's voice became a little shrill. "I ducked out because this is such fantastic news. Should have known that prick Taylor would go for this. But so soon . . . He may be a better reporter than I thought."

"I wonder if he was just ego surfing. Didn't we put a link to *The Point* in Capitolette's blog roll?"

"Yeah, that might be it. Still . . . this is great. You know the next step, of course."

"Well, getting it actually in *The Point*."

"I don't know if we even have to aim that high," Julie said. "You know Karl's network. I'm guessing you're the twentieth person to have the exact same IM conversation with him today."

"Right down to the insinuation about us having an affair?"

"Well, you and *someone* having an affair."

"Please."

"Okay, okay. But, hey, kid: light at the end of the tunnel, you know?"

"Yes, but it's just another train."

"People loooove train wrecks, darling. It's going to be great."

"I hope you're right. I'll call you before the party tonight."

Melanie felt fidgety, though. She unhooked her laptop and took it to a deserted conference room. Building on a success of some sort would ease her mind. She logged into the blog:

We fucked at Local 16, can you believe it? The doors in the stalls in the ladies' go all the way to the floor, so he just followed me in. It was a bit of a tight fit. In more ways than one! The shorter guys, I'm telling you, do not underestimate them. That hand-span-dick-size thing is a total urban legend. Dreamed up by a tall person.

Anyway, he wouldn't shut up about some piece he's writing, some poll about "security moms" or "patio dads" or whatever the fuck they're calling the suburbs these days. The suburbs are only good for one thing, I told him: luring men out of them. Mr. T, who wound up going back to Virginia himself that night, just pinched my ass and gave me another 50 to buy the next round.

Melanie sat back and looked at her work. Surely, some journalist in town was writing about security moms. Who hadn't? *But, oops, better make that Maryland.* She posted the entry and smiled smugly to herself, not resisting the urge to pat the laptop like a dog who had done a neat trick.

EARLY THAT EVENING, Melanie dialed Julie as promised.

"It starts at seven? You can't be serious. They can't be serious." Julie's voice cackled over the speaker on Melanie's cell.

"We'll show up at eight," Melanie said, lowering her eyelids to put on mascara.

"And we'll still be the first people there. Hey, where are you calling from, anyway? You sound like you're at the bottom of a well."

"Close. I'm in the bathroom. And you're on speakerphone."

"How . . . intimate."

"Just putting on makeup for the party."

"Makeup, really? What's the occasion? Will Mr. Wonderful bless us with his presence?"

"Not going to dignify that with a reply."

"Sure, Skoloff."

"No, really—I just feel like dressing up a little."

Julie's laughter rang against the slightly grimy white tile. "What does that entail, exactly, for you? Pants instead of shorts?"

"You're mistaking me for a blogger. In addition to pants, I wear underwear."

"So Mr. Wonderful definitely isn't in town."

"Ahem. Anyhow." Melanie pursed her lips and smoothed on dark red lipstick. "Also I found some clothes I bought in Boston but didn't even get around to taking the tags off until thirty minutes ago. Nice clothes. You would approve."

"When did you go shopping in Boston? And how come I didn't go with you?"

Melanie straightened up before the mirror, squared her shoulders and smiled. *Not bad,* she thought. "The day before you came up. I just barely had time—at that stage, I had this fantasy that I'd actually be going out, so I went to Newbury Street and splurged." She was lying. Rick had bought her the clothes and given them to her before she went to Boston, though they were bought with the idea that she'd be going out. She never even actually brought them to Boston, which was the only reason they were still clean.

"Well, I look forward to judging them," Julie muttered. "And it's a party for who?"

"Whom. Unclear," Melanie said. "Wait, let me look at the invitation."

Melanie stepped over to her laptop lying open on her bed and scrolled for the eVite, then shouted over her shoulder. "It's a book party!"

"Are you still in the bathroom or in Maryland?"

Melanie took the three steps from the bed to the bath. "Sorry. Had to look at the computer."

"Tell me right now how many pieces of electronics equipment are open and running in your bathroom."

"Does the vibrator count?"

"If it has a microchip," Julie pronounced. "Mine does."

"I doubt if there's anything micro about your vibrator."

"Hmmm. Well, I am a girl of significant appetites. You know, I should loan it to you sometime. Mr. Wonderful would pale in comparison."

"Bring it along tonight."

"I just might. It's possibly the only thing that could make the party interesting," Julie sighed. "What book is it anyway? And who has a book party in August?"

"Someone who's afraid of competition," said Melanie, running some "volumizing hair wax" (that's what it said on the label) through her roots. "Actually, it's someone from the last administration . . . Assistant Deputy to the Secretary of the Interior or Third Ambassador to Latvia or dogcatcher or something. Has a radio show now on Air America."

"Air what? Oh, never mind, I have a conference call. Talk later."

"Later."

Melanie picked the phone up off the sink's edge to click it shut; as she did she had an idea: Rick was out of town but she could still show off the outfit. She'd never had a reason to use her camera-phone before.

She stood in front of her full-length mirror, phone held slightly awkwardly in front of her. Getting her whole body into the frame might be tricky. *Top then bottom?* she thought.

She did look good. For once. The black pencil skirt slid easily over her curves and the white shirt nipped in just enough to show off her waist. The skirt was J. Crew—just simple and nice—but the shirt was some French label that Melanie had never heard of before, and it felt luxurious, its material so fine that it almost snagged on her cuticles when she put it on. It had French cuffs. *Of course it had French cuffs,* she realized. But Melanie had never had a shirt with French cuffs before. In fact, she hadn't really been aware that women's shirts could have them. Rick had included cuff links, thank God. The shoes were hers, a pair of green lizard pumps that matched the cuff links, or matched them well enough.

Melanie smiled to herself and wondered if undoing another button would be gilding the lily. Or showing the lily off. Something. Rick had bought her the bra, too, a few weeks back. She undid a button and snapped a picture.

She sent the pictures to Rick's AOL account and put the phone in her purse.

On her way out she glanced in the mirror again. *So this is what it feels like to dress up.* She wondered if her colleagues would recognize her. Then looked down and decided to button her shirt back up again.

IT WAS A short cab ride to the downtown hotel where the party was to take place, but Melanie had already heard from Julie.

To: ThortonM@hillman.com

From: Julie.Wrigley@clevelandparkgroup.com

   Flee

Oh dear, thought Melanie.

Julie was standing outside the restaurant, smoking a cigarette.

"That bad, huh?" Melanie asked. Julie only smoked antisocially, when she wanted to be alone or when it provided an excuse to leave a room.

"You have no idea," Julie said, taking a long drag. "We could leave now, you know." Julie raised her eyebrows and brightened her face like a mother getting her toddler excited about a trip to the park.

"And go where?" Melanie plucked the cigarette out of Julie's hand and inhaled.

"I was going to suggest Stetson's, but you might be too well dressed for that." Julie took a step back and looked Melanie up and down. "That shirt is a Seize sur Vingt, and if you bought it for yourself I'll buy you another one. You certainly didn't buy it in Boston."

Melanie blew a thin stream of smoke out of her smile.

"I'll take another one in pink," she said. "Now, what's so terrible about this party?"

"Oh it's not that bad, it's just . . . dregs."

"Dregs who won't appreciate exquisite French style?"

"Just wait till you see the book—they barely appreciate English."

They went in.

"You know," Julie said, "the last time I had drinks here, there were hookers standing outside and needles in the alley."

"Today, there are no needles and all the whores are inside."

"They're just as unattractive, though."

They wound their way through varnished wood and frosted-glass partitions to a semiprivate area. A placard blowup of a book jacket announced the publisher's congratulations for Wiley Stone, author of *Please Let's Make America Better: One Man's Thoughts on Rescuing Our Country from Religious Bigots, Blood-Thirsty War Lords and Women-Haters.*

Melanie stopped in front of the sign. "Oh."

Julie nudged her on: "I know. 'Women-haters.' I love how the title manages to combine both the pussy and paranoiac aspects into one unattractive lump."

Melanie recovered a bit, shaking her head: "Should I even be here? We've already had a hard enough time distancing the campaign from Michael Moore, and at least his book titles are coherent."

"Incoherence is probably the book's saving grace," whispered Julie. "Oh, and speaking of unattractive lumps . . ." She gestured forward. "Check out your three-o'clock."

It was Leslie Doherty, publicist to lefty types and professional big mouth. Her full figure was wrapped in a too-tight dress with a camouflage pattern and she teetered on high-heeled espradrilles. Turquoise earrings dangled to her shoulders and her hair was in a sort of *I Dream of Jeannie*–inspired topknot. Her husky voice boomed: "I'm SO glad you girls could make it! How ARE you! I don't think I've seen you since the convention!"

Julie smiled and gave Leslie a polite air kiss. "Has it been that long?" Her well-bred sarcasm was so subtle only dogs—and Melanie—could hear it. "My, time certainly does fly."

"Hi, Leslie. Good to see you." Melanie successfully completed an air kiss, too, mentally congratulating herself. She usually only just barely navigated the city's varied kiss-hello culture—the higher the social status, the more likely you were going to have to give up some cheek, but the lack of a stable aristocracy meant no one was trained in that kind of thing. So some people did total air, some people brushed lips, some people just grimaced and kind of knocked cheekbones. Usually, Melanie left greeting Leslie with a bruise to prove it.

Leslie's bangles jingled as she gestured hello. "Welcome to Wiley's party! Copies of the book are over there." She pointed to a Cheops-high stack. "And help yourself to the bar. There are some fun drinks!"

"Fun drinks?" Melanie asked. "Aren't all drinks fun?"

Leslie sighed exaggeratedly and ignored the question, turning to Julie: "Can I introduce you to the author?"

"I may need a fun drink first," Julie replied. "But if you're making introductions, maybe you could just fill us in on who's here."

Leslie did a quarter turn and tapped her finger on her cheek: "Well, it's early yet. But over there, that's the assistant CNN bureau chief. There's the assistant deputy manager of the *Post* op-ed page. Next to her is the associate producer for *Fox Sunday Live*. And over on the right is the deputy associate assistant to Chris Matthews. Oh, and that girl over there, the one with two drinks in her hands? She does the Swamp Thing blog." Leslie turned back around. "Great party, huh?" She jingled her bangles in good-bye and walked off.

Melanie looked at Julie: "Assistants, associates, deputies, and bloggers. Oh, my."

"It's a veritable Who's Not list." Julie shook her head sadly. "I did warn you."

"And the drinks? So are they not fun?"

"They're so not fun they ought to come with a tax bill. Come on." Julie led the way to the bar.

In front of it, a sign announced drink specials.

The Pina-COLA-raise: A dash of rum, a dash of pineapple, and a helping of economic justice!

The Single-Payer Scotch: This Scotch and soda makes for preventative care!

The Filibustermaker: No pro-life Supreme Court nominees can get past a beer and a shot of minority party legislative rights.

The Blue State: A martini, but blue.

The Rainforest Crunch: Midori and wheat grass, on the rocks!

"Those are the drinks you have to *pay* to drink?" asked Melanie. "Shouldn't they be giving them away? Preferably to those who need them the most?"

"Yes, but at least they're subsidized."

"But so inaccurate," replied Melanie. "Liberals only drink white wine and light beer."

"Or," observed Julie, "Kool-Aid."

Melanie approached the bar. "Can I get a martini?"

The bartender looked pained. "Not unless you want me to add curaçao to it. . . ." He shuddered.

"This hurts you more than it hurts me, eh?"

The bartender smiled. "You're the one who has to drink it."

Julie chimed in: "Touché." She set two twenties on the bar. "Surely there's some Bombay Sapphire back there somewhere. . . ."

The bartender eyed the bills: "You're sure you're at the right party, ladies?"

Melanie smiled at him: "Oh, we're sure we're at the wrong one. But we might have the right bartender."

The bartender grinned at them both. Melanie put her hand on his wrist as he grabbed the bills. "Oh, and, when you make mine? Three olives, please. . . . I haven't had dinner."

He winked at her and moved around the bar, pocketing the bills.

Melanie turned to Julie: "That's a lot of money for two drinks."

"Eh, I'm allergic to bad puns. It's worth it."

Melanie found the bartender's figure in the crowd, returning with the gin not-so-well-hidden under his jacket. "He's cute."

Julie brightened: "And probably not married."

"Mmmmm."

He made their drinks and Melanie let her eyes linger on his before they both turned away.

"At least you practiced your flirting muscles," Julie said. "You know they atrophy if not used regularly."

"Oh, sweetheart, those are the only muscles I do use regularly."

Julie smirked. "Reporters don't count."

Melanie sighed.

They stood in classic Washington party stance—a kind of three-quarters turn that had more in common with how actors let an audience in on a conversation than how real people stand and talk. The stance meant two things: that the conversation was meant to be interrupted and that those having it were more interested in the rest of the room than in each other. At least for the moment. Julie and Melanie each regarded the crowd over each other's shoulders, wary and excited, like snipers.

Julie raised an eyebrow, a signal either to duck and cover or to lock and load. Melanie sought clarification: "What?"

"Plead's here," Julie announced.

Melanie resisted the urge to look. "Where?"

"Behind you. He's talking to Leslie. My God, what is that she's wearing? She looks like an armed-forces Hummel figurine."

Melanie kept her eyes forward. "What should I do?"

"As your communications adviser, I can only advise you to stick to core competencies. Unbutton your blouse, give him a hug, and talk about how you miss his reported pieces in the Style section."

"I thought flirting with reporters didn't count."

"You're not flirting, you're pumping."

Melanie took a slug of her drink. "For that I expect at least cab fare home."

"Shhhh . . . here he comes."

Lead grinned below his incongruously hip glasses. He wore a sharply tailored jacket and garish tie. He looked at Melanie with a raised eyebrow. "How's tricks?"

Melanie dutifully took to her task. Charming people was easy, really. Mostly it involved not contradicting their own view of themselves. And being just a little bit slutty.

"Paul!" Melanie led. "Where's the notebook? Or can I wag my tongue freely tonight?" She smiled sweetly in counterpoint.

"Oh you can use your tongue however you like around me." He smiled. "As long as you tell me where it's been."

Melanie felt a twinge of panic. Was he getting at what she thought he was getting at?

"Oh, we're going to start a blog devoted to that very subject," Julie interrupted.

Lead cocked his head.

Melanie nodded: "Wheresmytongue-dot-com."

Julie took a bite of an olive: "Findmytongue-dot-com."

Lead interrupted with faux authority: "You're going to try to compete with Capitolette?"

Melanie's heart jumped. So good. So very good. Her smile turned real. "Maybe we'll have pictures."

"Promise?" Lead rocked back on his heels. "You two definitely have your work cut out for you if she's your template."

Julie put down her empty glass. "She's not a template. She's an inspiration."

"She's inspired, that's for sure. Now, what are you girls up to, really?"

Melanie felt the pang of anxiety again. He could be digging. . . .

"Nothing, Paul, really."

"That's not what I hear."

Melanie gulped. Was that audible? she wondered. She cast about for a reply, her mind curiously blank. "Ah . . ." she started.

Julie interrupted: "Well, Paul, we *actually* were just about to tear ourselves away from this fabulous party. Top secret. Shhhh. Don't tell *anyone*. It was great to run into you, though."

Lead looked confused. "I, uhm . . ." Julie took Melanie's arm and started steering her off. Lead called after them, "Later, I guess . . ." Julie nudged Melanie quickly and whispered, "Say good night, Gracie."

Melanie glanced across Julie: "Good-bye, Paul! It was great to see you!"

He waved a couple of fingers and raised an eyebrow.

Julie maneuvered them across the room. "Another round? I think I've got another twenty somewhere. . . ."

"I thought we were leaving," Melanie said. "And in a hurry, it seemed."

"We were leaving that conversation."

"Why?"

"I haven't known you that long, darling, but I know that look. The my-midwestern-charm-is-about-to-crumble-and-I-may-inadvertently-reveal-what-really-frightens-me look."

"Oh, *that* look," Melanie said.

"Hey, you have something personal at stake here. If you didn't get a little freaked out I'd worry."

"I wasn't freaking out."

"You went from zero to sixty twice in the space of that conversation. I don't know what Paul thinks, but it was best, I thought, to leave him on a high note."

"Yes, that was good news about Capitolette," Melanie looked around. "Don't you think he'll notice that we said we were leaving and we're not leaving?"

"Of course not. In Washington, you're allowed at least thirty minutes of 'I'm about to leave' time. I know one woman who tells people she's leaving as a way of saying hello."

"I think that was Katharine Graham's method," Melanie said. She looked her friend in the eye. "Now, Julie, stop party scanning. There's no one here."

Julie nodded in agreement. "Maybe if I stop paying attention someone will show up."

Melanie agreed: "A watched party never roils." Julie rolled her eyes but Melanie continued: "Seriously. You say I went from zero to sixty, but you didn't say if you thought it was justified."

Julie's face hardened into something like seriousness. "Sweetheart, it's probably going to be justified for a while. I just didn't want to see your panic blossom into full flower right in front of our pal Plead." She saw Melanie's eyes narrow and was ready for a response. "If you're annoyed with me, that's a good sign. Really. Means you've got enough self-respect to be angry."

"I was annoyed, but now I'm just impressed with your spin on my anger."

Julie smiled. "It works even better on boys."

"I bet. Especially if you're naked."

Julie laughed. "Speaking of naked boys . . . Want to ask our helpful bartender when he gets off?"

"That seems a little personal."

Julie scowled lightly at her.

Melanie laughed. "I know, I know. Good idea, though. Why

don't you do it?" Julie smiled in anticipation and began to walk off. Melanie called after her, "I'll just stay put. Say good-bye to some people, maybe."

Julie stuck out her tongue.

8

Tuesday, August 10

To: ReedC@hillman.com

From: PrentissH@hillman.com

Subject: FW: It's raining in Montana

Date: Aug. 10

Got this from Jake—apparently he's writing from the back of the plane . . .

To: PrentissH@hillman.com

From: HowardsJ@hillman.com

Subject: It's raining in Montana

Date: Aug. 9

Hope things are looking up from your point of view, because things are shitty here. Whole place smells like piss and failure. A heads-up: Don't know if you're getting in on the conference call with principals tomorrow but DO NOT try to tell them fuck about the Clearheads. I did that last week, complaining that John sounded like an idiot dancing away from the allegations, and now, thanks to Taft, I have a better chance of fucking Paris Hilton than I do of getting 5 minutes with the candidate.

Sent wirelessly via BlackBerry from T-Mobile.

. . .

CAPITOLETTE MADE *The Point* the next day. Just as an aside, really, but it was up there in the first three paragraphs, which was all anyone ever really read:

> In these lazy, hazy days of summer, conventional wisdom watchers rest their eyes from must-reads, but before we make you eat your political spinach, allow us to Point you to one wonkette whose fine print is hotter than the roof of Lauriol Plaza. She's captured the imagination of the Gang of 500 even more than a double-bylined Dan Balz/Mike Allen article laying out the hurdles for Golden's intergovernmental affairs portfolio. See for yourself: capitolette.blogspot.com.

The e-mails started coming in almost instantly after that, and most of it was probably typed with one hand: "Capitolette: I'm thinking of u and your creemy center. Exchange pix ok?" Maybe twenty percent or less expressed outrage: "Dear Whorebag: It's skanky chicks like you who give all of us a bad name! I'm a Hill staffer and I have never once spread my legs, ever!" (Melanie had forwarded that one to Julie with a note: "I understand Senator Santorum raises virgin staffers in vats.") Then there were the media inquiries. No one was offering Barbara Walters specials yet, but they had heard from television, radio, and all the national dailies except for the *Wall Street Journal*, and Melanie suspected they were just trying to figure out a financial angle.

The reporters were uniformly fawning in a way that Melanie found familiar.

"Mrs. Capitolette: Well, you sure have everyone's attention here in Washington," wrote one of the *Washington Post*'s political reporters.

A general Washington assignment reporter from the *Times* tried to play girlfriend: "You're a girl after my own heart. So brave and funny in the face of the Capitol's overwhelming sexism. I'd love to buy you a drink."

And one of the Fox guys tried cozying up with his own anecdote: "I know what you must be going through; when I wrote my story about having dated the young Miss America, I thought the media would never leave me alone."

She and Julie shot the media requests back and forth all day, mainly commenting on the tactics used and wondering how many of the men who were writing from media outlets were also sending thoughts about Capitolette's "creeminess" from their hotmail accounts. Indeed, they spent the better part of an hour trying to figure out who had written the solicitation from anchorguy123@ hotmail.com, which ended with a request for a picture, the promise that the sender was "as well hung as rumor has it," and an offer of a room at the Mandarin Oriental should "you and I find each other acceptable."

"I'm certain he's just local," Julie had insisted. "I only have heard one rumor about what's in the pants of any national anchor and that's that Chris Matthews keeps Nilla wafers in his. People just don't talk about the penises of anchors very much. I think they like to think of them as neutered. All smooth down there, just like Ken dolls."

"Now, *that* would be a rumor."

"I actually think I did hear that about Andrea Mitchell."

"Shush."

They were sitting at Tryst in Adams Morgan, reading the e-mail on Julie's PowerBook via the café's wireless Internet connection. Melanie had worried that it was too public, but Julie pointed out that everyone at Tryst would be too busy reading their own e-mail to pay that much attention.

The affair had made Melanie more attuned—some might say paranoid—about privacy issues, but it also made her feel more like a native. Her Berry was password protected—standard operating procedure—as was her cell phone, which was a little more unusual. Rick had taught her how to erase the list of "calls received" and how to call out without showing her own caller ID. She kept meaning to implement something she'd noticed about the *Washington Post*'s campaign correspondent: He never forwarded e-mails, just wrote new ones with the old text pasted inside, a safeguard against sending a missive to the wrong "john" in your auto-complete address book. At the Starbucks that was equidistant from campaign headquarters and the *Post,* the first chairs taken were those with their backs against the wall. People in town and on the campaign were obsessive about secrecy, in a way that only people who like to gossip can be. Melanie had heard more than one person boast about being "the most discreet man in Washington," an unverifiable claim that would seem to suggest the opposite was true.

But the ten people who populated that world were not at Tryst. Though Adams-Morgan served as dormitory area for staffers who wanted some distance from the Hill, their presence wasn't felt at Tryst. Tryst was too cool for that. Melanie found it annoying. The mugs tried too hard to be big and whimsical. The music sounded like cell phone ringtones and the grumpy waitstaff thought bringing you a menu was a favor. The clientele was no less aloof. Artful loafers instant-messaging and working on their novels or something. It didn't look like work, and there were people there doing it for *hours*. Such in-your-face idleness offended her midwestern sensibility. *Don't these people have jobs?* she wondered. *Shouldn't they at least pretend to have jobs? If this is our unemployment crisis, I'd vote Republican myself.*

"We have to start responding to some of these," Julie said, scrolling through the inbox.

"I know," said Melanie, taking a sip of lemonade. "But which?"

"Some print interviews first, I think," said Julie, clicking open a few of the more promising supplicants.

"First?" Melanie squinted at her friend. "What kind of media blitz do you have planned?"

Julie sighed and leaned back in an overstuffed couch they had commandeered. She curled her perfectly exercised calves up underneath her. Melanie frowned down at her own legs, whose pale softness seemed to spread even as she looked.

"Unfortunately," Julie started, "I don't think we can do the kind of media blitz I'd like to do. You know, Gennifer Flowers at the Waldorf-Astoria, a blowup of the cover of *Star* magazine, audiotapes. . . ."

"You're getting that faraway look in your eye," Melanie said. "It reminds me of the time you wrote the speech for John McCain accepting the veep slot."

Julie smiled ruefully. "A girl can dream, can't she?" Julie set her attention back to the laptop. "In any case, we don't need the Waldorf-Astoria. We just need to figure out how to play this out for a few more weeks. We'll work with what we've got."

"Maybe," Melanie said. "Maybe it's not so terrible that we're not starting big. Maybe we shouldn't start with the *Times*. The new chick they have there would bust us, anyway. I think we should start with someone big, but gullible."

"By gullible, of course, you mean, eager to get a scoop," Julie corrected. "Zealous, perhaps."

"Yes," agreed Melanie. "Very zealous. Horny would help."

Julie ran her finger down the list of e-mail addresses. "Too bad we can't bring a TV person in. . . ."

"How would we do the interview?"

"I know, I know." Julie was lost in thought. "I got it. Who is less likely to dig too deep on a scoop than the number-two gossip column in town?"

"You want to give this to Plead?" Melanie blanched, feeling betrayed. Her voice dropped several registers: "After what he did to me?"

"*Especially* after what he did to you, darling." Julie had already hit reply, her fingers were poised over the keyboard. "First of all, he's clearly desperate. Second, if he thinks this is a hotter sex scandal than yours . . ."

Melanie nodded, beginning to catch on. "Right . . . And third . . . won't it be awful for him if it turns out it's a big hoax?"

Julie grinned, "Well, I wasn't going to try to appeal to your base instincts, but now that you mention it. . . . It works on many levels."

Melanie grinned right back and slid the keyboard off Julie's lap and onto her own. "Well, speaking of appealing to base instincts . . ."

IN THE END, it took several e-mails to get Lead to agree to their requirements. His smug but clever wordplay belied a reporter concerned that violating the rulebook would jeopardize his scoop.

To: Plead@washpost.com

From: Capitolette@gmail.com

I wasn't going to write back, but I am a big fan. And I've always wanted to be a boldfaced name! Can you do that? I'd love for you to be the one to plump my persona, as it were. Unfortunately I can't do a sit-down interview. As much as I'd like. And really, I'd like. Can we do it over e-mail? I, personally, can do a lot over e-mail. And sometimes it's better if you use your imagination, if you know what I mean.

To: Capitolette@gmail.com
From: Plead@washpost.com
You flatter me, Capitolette. I would be happy to participate in the darkening of your appellation. And I have read your blog, so I know exactly what you can do over e-mail. But I will need to get some proof that you are who you say you are.

To: Plead@washpost.com
From: Capitolette@gmail.com
Would some gently worn underwear do?

To: Capitolette@gmail.com
From: Plead@washpost.com
Ahem. Ms. Capitolette, I don't know where you learned your manners but I'm keeping my children away from there and from you. I may, however, send my wife. In any case, I spoke to my editors and they're willing to run a Q&A on my say-so though it will have the kind of disclaimer language at the top that usually runs with infomercial weight loss ads. So, you up for it?

To: Plead@washpost.com
From: Capitolette@gmail.com
I thought you'd never ask.

9

Thursday, August 12

SEX AND THE SINGLE BLOGGER:
WASHINGTON WHISPERER TELLS ALMOST ALL
The Washington Post; Reliable Source; August 12

The Hill's latest raunchy rumor grist is an anonymous Web log—"blog"—by a woman who claims to have intimate knowledge of Washington's political players. Is she this year's Monica Lewinsky, a "Newinsky," as one wag put it, or is she a bimbo version of all those Nigerian millionaires who keep wanting me to help them get their cash out of the country? The Reliable Source had the extraordinary pleasure to conduct an e-mail interview with an entity who claimed to be the already infamous "Capitolette." Regarding her emergence onto the Web, she told us that the site started as a lark, "something to take my mind off the itching and the burning." We expressed concern about these symptoms, but Capitolette assured us that the "soreness was temporary." As for who she is and where she works, the mysterious maiden is cagey: "I wouldn't say that I'm a familiar face, but I've seen lots of familiar faces. And they've seen a lot of me.

Some more than others." We can vouch for neither her identity nor her website; we can say she left us wanting to know more.

ALMOST AS GOOD as the Reliable Source interview was getting picked up by the Swamp Thing blog:

> We've mocked Plead in the past, although it's true we're fascinated by the comings and goings of Park Service officials and by who is the speaker at the vegetarian association dinner. To be fair it was the *national* association dinner. Wasn't it a Baldwin? The one who narrates that cartoon about the train? But it seems like a blind squirrel can find an acorn every once in a while and Plead has stumbled on some gossip—ass fucking gossip, no less. We can hardly sit still. This Capitolette girl he talked to is a dame after our own heart, and other places. We hope Plead was gentle. She sounds ter-ific. But what the fuck does she look like? Her face, we mean. While the other end is more engaging of course, next time we're at Stetson's we want to know whom to buy a drink.

Now Capitolette had popped onto the radar of a hundred thousand of Washington's most connected and sex-obsessed. Capitolette's flooded inbox suggested that this was a redundancy. They'd had to upgrade their mail server to accommodate the heavy breathing since they obviously couldn't use a spam filter. In fact, they wanted the reverse: a filter that moved the most prurient writing to the top. They learned that when an anonymous account was being used, Washington had an inverse relationship between power and prurience. The more juice you had the more you were likely to think like Larry Flynt.

. . .

MELANIE SHOULD HAVE stopped working when she got home. Instead, she dialed the remote until she settled on *Law & Order*, and opened her laptop.

She had little use for ego surfing. Much of the city had inboxes full of personal Nielsen ratings: Google News Alerts, automatic television news transcript searching, TiVos set to auto-record and websites that combed the blogs to signal the most lowly staffer or intermediate pundit to media mentions of their names. But Melanie's job was to stay out of the news—if not her entire person then at least her name. To the world at large, to reporters, to editors, she was mostly a "senior campaign official." She was the source scribes turned to for background sniping, catty mudslinging, and between-the-lines readings of whatever Skoloff was telling them.

Her alerts always heralded something depressing. She used them to troll for Hillman's weak spots. Her list of search terms looked like the opposition's hit file. "Hillman and draft dodger"; "Hillman and flake"; "Hillman and zombie"; "Hillman and wooden"; "Lady Di." And now, the most recent one: "Hillman and Clearheads."

So it was an unfamiliar pleasure to finally have a reason to look forward to the News Alerts and the instant transcripts—a tickle of excitement every time the e-mail program bonged and she saw that she had gotten her, or rather, Capitolette's, name into the papers or on the air. Ticking through what had come overnight, she saw that the Washington correspondent for the *India Times* had compared her to Mata Hari. The *Grand Rapids Herald* mentioned it in their "Overheard in Washington" column. Imus had quipped about setting up Capitolette with one of his producers, and Joe Scarborough thought the whole thing showed the depths to which Washington had sunk.

Indeed it has, Melanie thought. Yet the flacking of Capitolette was so much more satisfying than any of the work she was doing for Hillman. *Doing for Hillman directly,* she corrected herself. And Capitolette gave her another reason to look forward to her Black-Berry's vibrations besides just waiting for Rick to get in touch from the shore or for Julie to declare it was cocktail hour. And it was certainly better than waiting for Skoloff to harass her about whatever conference call was coming next.

Melanie drummed her fingers on the keyboard. She stuck out her lower lip and blew her bangs upward and out of her face. She typed in the URLs for alt.country music festivals and cooking blogs. She watched the minute hand move from forty to forty-one minutes after the hour. Her energy was fading, and she eyed the half-bottle of Basil Hayden on top of her refrigerator as she weighed whether or not to do something about it.

When had she decided it was okay to drink alone? *Had* she decided? Or had it just happened, a smooth slide from one side of a line to the other that occurred either so gradually or amid so many other changes—she didn't floss anymore, she jaywalked all the time, she carried a balance on her credit cards—that she never noticed?

One day you were a normal college student who went through a gallon of orange juice every couple of days and then joined a campaign to change the world and then you were that woman who brings her own mini-bottles of booze onto the plane.

I will look at the Clearhead crap. Then I can have a drink. I will deserve it by then.

Melanie took a deep, steadying breath, noticing for the first time since coming home how dank the apartment smelled, like dirty clothes and cold pizza.

Cold pizza sounded good. Melanie remembered that back in

May, when she had first started seeing Rick, they had ordered in all the time, way too much food. They'd balance plastic take-out tubs from Heritage India on the sofa and watch the news. She dutifully scraped the uneaten bits into a consolidation tub and took them home. There they languished. Takeout is halfway to leftovers anyway, and in campaign life, fresh takeout from Cashion's was the one luxury she afforded herself.

Maybe the pizza wasn't such a great idea. She opened a window and breathed in again. The air conditioner in her small bedroom hummed. She could hear her mother accusing her of trying to "cool the whole outdoors." But the night was lovely and the fresh air made her feel better. More . . . clearheaded. She grimaced.

Just do it already. She went back to her computer and double-clicked the message that held the coming day's trickle, or stream, or flood, or possibly Armageddon-inducing tidal wave of Clearhead stories.

Reading the summaries, Melanie started to relax just a bit. Nothing major, it seemed: a press release, "voters undecided on the merits of the group's claim . . . poll finds increasing dissatisfaction with 'negative tone.'" *Sky blue, puppies cute,* Melanie thought. Something about bloggers "having claimed a victory in forcing the mainstream media to address . . ." *Grass green.* Absolutely nothing unexpected . . . until the end: "Wife of former gubernatorial candidate Gene Gusting admits undergoing sixties mind-control experiments, calls for Hillman to 'come out of the closet' so that others can 'heal.'"

Melanie closed her eyes and shook her head. *That drink is going to taste so good.*

She clicked on the link to the complete story. It was wire service, dated ten P.M. West Coast time, which meant it might not have made the early editions anywhere important. It was also short:

POLITICAL ACTIVIST CONFESSES TO "MIND CONTROL" PAST,
CALLS ON HILLMAN TO HELP OTHERS "HEAL"
AP, August 10, 10:33:14 PST

Teresa Altamont, talk-show host, political activist, and the former wife of a one-time California senator and former child star, today revealed that she had personally undergone the type of medical experiments at the center of the allegations launched against presidential candidate Senator John Hillman (D-Conn.). Speaking to a crowd of therapists, educators, and "communication facilitators" gathered for an anti-bullying conference here in San Francisco, Altamont said she had tried to suppress her own memories of the experiments until the ads run by the group "Citizens for Clear Heads" (see related story) triggered her to speak out. "I was young and it was a time for experimentation," Altamont said, referring to her college days during the 1960s. "I thought I would simply be expanding my perceptions, but instead I let the government into my brain."

Altamont's admissions were met with gasps and sympathetic applause, which grew to thunderous when she called upon Hillman to "come out of the closet" on the issue. "Only when we face the truth about these terrible abuses can we all heal."

Craig Donnelly, president of Citizens for Clear Heads, praised Altamont's openness: "She certainly isn't embarrassed to bring the subject up and we welcome frank discussion of this important issue." However, Donnelly said that Altamont seemed to be referring to a different sort of procedure than the kind his group alleges to have been performed on Senator Hillman. "We believe that the candidate was implanted with specific instructions—redistribute wealth, for instance, and to encourage others to become gay—Mrs. Altamont said something about the *government* being involved . . . now that's hard to believe."

An instant-message bubble popped onto the screen as she finished reading.

WrigleyJules: yt?

Thortonology: Of c. thought you had hooked up with that bartender again.

WrigleyJules: you think I'd let him stay? I have An Early Meeting.

Thortonology: you have A Problem Committing.

WrigleyJules: oh but I'm committed to you. For example . . .

Julie sent her the URL for the AP story on Gusting.

Thortonology: I'm reading it right now. Trying to decide how fucked I am.

WrigleyJules: I thought R was at the shore?

Thortonology: ha.

WrigleyJules: sorry. I haven't read the whole thing but I think you're just medium fucked.

Thortonology: that bad, huh? I mean, the Clearheads are backing off.

WrigleyJules: true, but it keeps the story alive and the pack luuuvvvvvs to write about Teresa. She's a quote machine. Also, I bet she has some stunt planned: she'll start a support group for "recovering mind control victims" . . .

Thortonology: Like Scientology?

Wr gleyJules: Like Democrats. Anyhow: I'm beat. You should get some
rest too.

Thortonology: Sort of wired.

Wr gleyJules: Just get into bed. Unless there's someone already there . . .

Thortonology: I would never cheat on my married lover. The only person I
am sharing my bed with tonight is Mr. Hayden.

Wr gleyJules: Your taste is improving. Night.

Thortonology: Night.

Melanie was tempted to find out which blogs had already
picked up on the Teresa story. But when she really considered it,
running through all the necessary steps—raising her arms to type
on the keyboard, for instance—her keyed-up feeling evaporated.
She felt like someone had yanked the plug at the base of her
spine.

She sighed and summoned the energy to close the laptop. It
clicked but something was wrong with the catch—it wouldn't close
properly and the screen continued to flicker and cast a pale green-
gray glow over the edges of the keyboard.

My candlelight, Melanie thought.

She went across the living room to the triangular kitchen area
and the moonlight paid compliment to her thighs. There was no ice;
just empty ice cube trays from—she thought she remembered—the
last time she and Julie made margaritas at home. She glanced at the
blender at the top of the fridge. *Remember? I was going to use you to
make smoothies.*

The bourbon was next to the blender and Melanie grabbed it. A
little branch water would have to do. She poured a half-inch into a
cleanish glass and waved it under running water. With the faucet

turned on, she thought about filling the lonesome ice cube trays, but didn't.

She took the glass—it wasn't *that* full, she told herself—back to the living room and pulled her desk chair around to face the window. She sat down and put her feet on the ledge; the not-quite-cool night air tickled her toes.

Her view was not very good. The apartment's one exposure faced northeast, toward the interior of the trapezoidal block. She saw mostly other apartments. There was a certain *Rear Window*–ish pleasure to keeping up with her neighbors, every story lived out in a window frame. But there were too many still lifes for it to be that interesting. Too many other people living alone whose apartments were empty from just after dawn until when the bars closed.

Melanie turned this thought around in her head and looked at the face of her cell phone on her desk to check the time. It was closing time.

She sipped at her bourbon, its warmth ran jagged down her throat. She had to crane her head a bit to get the other view her apartment offered: a stretch of Sixteenth street coming down off of U Street. At two A.M. on a warm night it became a highway of clumsy traffic as patrons poured forth, heading home from the bars.

Melanie took her feet off the sill and leaned forward, resting her elbow on the sill and her chin in her hand. The crowd moved in broken clots of two or three or four . . . but mostly two. Squinting, she tried to pick out the figures of people she knew.

The barrel-chested guy whose salt-and-sand-colored hair glinted in the lamplight was probably Prentiss, his arm around some girl whose name was not entirely worth knowing. Behind him, two men stooped and held on to each other like wounded soldiers. Were they laughing too hard to walk? About to be sick? Knowing how heavy the pours were in Dupont Circle's bars, probably both.

The shapes were almost all familiar—Stetson's had somehow morphed into a Democrat bar in the past few years; she remembered reading that Jenna and Barbara Bush got underage kicks there, but it was a solidly blue hangout now. U Street in general was still too scruffy for GOP types. They trolled Georgetown's more reliable reaches—Smith Point, The Tombs. College bars with cover charges.

Melanie let her eyes go unfocused. The figures blurred and moved down the street in their random, jagged walks like rain down a window. She took another sip of bourbon, found it less fiery, and let it linger on her tongue.

Then she saw Rick.

The bourbon swirling in her mouth choked her. She coughed and sat up straight, pounding her chest.

The shape was at the top of her view; he hadn't progressed much since she saw him. And he wasn't alone.

Hands in pockets, he walked beside a woman in a short skirt and tight top. They were talking. They were *deep in conversation*.

There were tears in her eyes from the bourbon's burn down her windpipe, but real hurt threatened to push them aside. Melanie watched the couple.

The walk, that half-slouch of someone who had grown tall too fast, the cock of his head . . . Could she see the TAG Heuer watch on his wrist? She squinted some more.

I'm seeing things, she thought. *Or trying to. I can't tell if it's his watch from a block away. And his hair is wrong. His pants are too tight.*

She watched some more. Her breath got easier. They stepped into the full light of a streetlamp at the closest corner. It wasn't him.

And what right would she have to be jealous anyway . . . right? She couldn't answer.

She lifted her glass to take another drink, then stopped. The taste of the last sip was still in her mouth.

She set the glass down on the sill and went to bed.

10

Friday, August 13

To: Julie.Wrigley@clevelandparkgroup.com

From: tina_kerry@americanow.com

Subject: Your 2:50PM hit tomorrow

Date: Aug 12

Hi Julie, thanks for agreeing to come on. We're thinking we're going to talk about Hillman's and Golden's competing policies on at-risk youth, or we might talk about the disappearance of the convention bounce or we could talk about the role blogs are playing in distributing information—not all of it true!—about the candidates. I've attached articles on all these subjects.

The town car will pick you up at 1:45.

I've left messages repeating this information on your voicemail at work, at home, on your cellphone and with your assistant. Please call me to confirm you've received it.

THE BOOKERS at America Now loved Julie. She was pretty, gave good sound bites, and she was an easy book. You could dial her with just a few hours' notice, leave a message, and she would even call back from the dentist's chair to say yes. They also loved her because she was a liberal who didn't hate the network for being an arm of the Republican Party. America Now was, in fact, a corporate client of CPG, though the bookers had no reason to know that, nor, Julie thought, should they really care. There was probably something unethical somewhere in the arrangement, but as long as Julie continued to just do unpaid segments, popping up to debate whatever neo-con blonde they'd pulled from her pod at the GOP opinion farm, she didn't think there was a problem.

Besides, she loved doing TV. During her years as a Senate aide, Julie had accompanied the boss to countless tapings, prepared reams of talking points, and handed him landfills of post-segment baby wipes to scrape off the pancake and the eyeliner that men always complained about having to wear during tapings but hardly ever refused. She had even managed to get on air a few times herself, though there were few opportunities for a junior press person to a junior senator from a solidly blue state to do anything bigger than C-SPAN.

Now she was a regular on most of the cable news channels and she still got the same little jolt out of each successful performance. It was like walking a high wire every time—there were a million ways you could screw it up, and the trick was to not think about them while you were in the middle of it. That was the way she explained it to clients: "Don't look down, you'll be fine."

And they usually were. As she had discovered, being *okay* on television was easy. There were a lot of little things to remember— *don't gesture with your hands, close your mouth when you're not speaking, stick to your talking points*—and one big thing to forget: that lots and lots of people—some of whom paid your salary—were watching.

It was being great on television that was impossible to teach and hard to even try to explain. Julie had come to believe it was genetic, something you could either do or not do, and there was no way to know if you could until you tried—like rolling your tongue or yodeling. Julie had discovered she could yodel, and it had landed her in every booker's contacts file under "Presentable Dems," or, as they called it at America Now: "hot not GOP." And that was why she was in a town car right now, scrolling through a list of talking points from the Hillman campaign on her BlackBerry and wondering what verbal jujitsu she was going to have to perform to get from "Are the Clear Heads putting Hillman out of the race?" (the network's newest proposed topic) to "Senator Hillman is a new voice for a new America with bold plans and record of leadership" (the campaign's current non sequitur response).

Teresa Altamont's overnight admission had given the Clearheads another breath of life with the cable networks, eager for anything mildly juicy to fill airtime during August's dead calm. Julie hoped it would die down, and she thought there was a shot it might. It was hard to change the subject once it had picked up steam, and this one was picking up steam. Former advisers to Altamont's loser husband now worked for Golden. They dished as "senior GOP operatives" about how the wife's headline grabbing explained why her husband lost. Reporters couldn't resist resurrecting tales of her loopy experimentation with Kabbalah. Grassroots activists were blogging away with the new information, the inevitable result of HTML soapboxes and minimal demands on their time.

Ever the taxonomist, Julie had begun to classify the cable news networks by their choice of car service. CNN always used the same set of drivers, and the cars came stocked with a cold bottle of spring water and the *Washington Post*. Fox's service was really polite and called to let you know they were there, but tended to have nothing to read in the back but three-week-old copies of *Think* and those glossy tourist-porn magazines that you get free in hotel rooms (*Jamaica on Parade!*). America Now sent cars with nothing in them but a withered mint.

Julie scrolled through the Hillman talking points again:

To: [Undisclosed list of recipients]
From: SkoloffK@hillman.com

Good day. As the Citizens for Clear Heads begins to distribute tinfoil hats, we need to remain focused on the issues important to the American people: John Hillman is strong leader with fresh ideas and a proven record.

Latest polls show that only 53 percent of Americans trust Golden in matters of foreign policy. That's a very vulnerable number. Americans have had four years to come to know the Golden's strategies, and they are unsatisfied. Golden cannot run on his record. John Hillman has a plan to renew respect for America at home and abroad.

A majority of those polled believe John Hillman "understands what it's like to work for a living."

Pabulum. Julie stopped reading and threw her head back against the seat. "Fuck," she muttered.

In the rearview mirror, the driver raised his eyebrows.

"Nothing," she said, smoothing her hands over her skirt. "Sorry."

She pushed her thumb into her speed dial for Melanie at the campaign: "I can't believe this dogshit your boss is giving me to work with."

"I know, I know. I tried to take out one of the times she mentions 'Americans' and she almost bit my head off. I don't know if she thinks *we* don't know what country we're living in or she thinks viewers don't. She probably read some book on subliminal persuasion sometime in the fifties and it's stuck with her."

"Also, she's as looney as the Clearasilfaces if she thinks that we can leap like a gazelle from 'Hillman electroshocked into submission' to 'strong ideas from a fresh leader with a new record' or whatever madlib slogan she's plugging in today."

"Oh, sweetie, if anyone can do it, you can. Hold on a sec, another call . . ."

Julie looked out the tinted windows. They were on Mass Ave., only a few blocks from the studios.

The driver cleared his throat. "Do I know you, miss?"

"Maybe you've driven me before?"

"Ah, yes, of course." His reflection smiled at her. "You are very pretty."

Julie smiled back: "I bet you say that to all the girls."

Melanie clicked back on the line: "I thought you were on your way to four hundred North Capitol. I didn't realize you'd be picking up company along the way."

Julie whispered: "The driver just told me I was pretty."

"Oh, yeah, he does say that to everyone," said Melanie. "But only Howard Fineman believes him."

"Fineman doesn't need to hear 'you're pretty' from anyone. He has it programmed as his ring tone. Anyway: Back to the talking points. Or what seem to be passing for talking points. They're really more like talking *blobs* . . . talking goo . . . talking thing-that-is-the-opposite-of-having-a-point-and-is-destined-to-destroy-fledgling-campaign."

"Talking craters?"

"We're getting there. But . . . oh, here we are. I've gotta go sign in. If you think of something brilliant, Berry it to me. I need it or I'm going to make it all up."

The driver turned around in his seat: "I wait for you here."

Julie grabbed her purse and opened the door: "I will count the seconds," she said to herself.

Going from the icy cool of the car to the August heat to the lobby's refrigerated calm was the full-body equivalent of an ice cream headache. As Julie signed in at the building's security station, she could see goose pimples on her forearm. She shivered and handed the guard her driver's license. The urge to look at who had signed into the building before her was not worth resisting, but she tried to be subtle about it. The squat, U-shaped building took up an entire block of prime Capitol Hill real estate and was home to the D.C. studios of Fox, MSNBC, C-SPAN, BBC, and America Now. Anyone in Washington with anything to say—and many without who just happened to be available at the right time slot—walked through here at some point. At the height of a major news event, the xeroxed sheet on the guard desk in the lobby of 400 N. Capitol read like a Bob Woodward book, crammed with the neat signatures of Senate aides signing in for their bosses, the scrawling script of White House correspondents, and the prim Palmer method of graying opinion writers whose longevity had freed them from the necessity of knowing what they were talking about.

On a weekday in August, however . . . Well, who was there? Let's see: Skoloff had gone on Fox around eleven, John McCain looked like he might have signed in for both MSNBC and America Now. Fred Barnes and Bill Kristol had come in one right after another and Julie wondered if the "Beltway Boys" had carpooled over from the *Weekly Standard* or if they took separate cars as a show of support for drilling in the Arctic Wildlife Refuge. Julie saw that Nigel Cooke, the red-faced but eloquent British pundit, had been in for a BBC hit and smiled to herself: *We're not the only ones taken in by hawkish opinions in such a civilized accent.*

Julie took her temporary pass from the guards and set out for the studio. Waiting for the elevator, she checked her Berry:

To: Julie.Wrigley@clevelandparkgroup.com

From: ThortonM@hillman.com

Subject: Talking rounded mounds

They're going to ask you something like, "These charges draw into question not just Hillman's credibility but also his fitness for office. If his campaign can't recover from such a damaging charge, how can they govern?" That's what Fox asked KS this morning, anyway. She basically ignored the question, which is par for the course but it did give Matalin a chance to re-ask it and make some kind of joke about how "the frequency must be jammed." We can't play at all and you shouldn't either, so say: "The campaign has been smart enough not to get distracted from Hillman's message of hope for the powerless and opportunity for all." Then, if you want, add what Skoloff won't let me say: "This is what happens when Republicans get bored with buying up riverfront property: They write checks to muddy the reputation of a good man who is trying to help the lives of people who don't have private planes.'

Julie stepped onto the elevator and read Melanie's e-mail again. She was already dialing Melanie when she got off on the fifth floor: "This is really good. Wow, look at you. I want you in the private sector."

Julie turned to the big glass doors and waited for the guard to buzz her in. The elaborate security measures that news organizations had instituted in the wake of 9/11 now served mainly to make guests feel like hired help.

"Thanks," said Melanie, who felt herself glowing a little. "I do, occasionally, do my job. You hiring?"

Julie laughed: "Wouldn't you rather work in the White House?"

"Shhh, you'll jinx it."

Julie stayed on the phone even though an assistant producer was now coming into the front area to get her. She motioned Julie toward the green room and Julie smiled icily toward her. Two can play at the hired help game, she thought.

"Ah, yes. What's the Technorati count on Capitolette today?"

"Two hundred links from outside sources. We're getting there, but pebbles have yet to amount to an avalanche."

"We just need to keep pushing."

Melanie got the transcript of Julie's America Now appearance later:

(BEGIN VIDEO CLIP)

TERESA ALTAMONT: We are all victims of mind control! The mainstream media, the crooks in this White House—John Hillman is a better man. Let us help him and help ourselves.

(END VIDEO CLIP)

LEIGH GRACE, America Now anchor: Is Teresa Altamont putting wind into the sails of the Citizens for Clear Heads? Or will her admission allow the stumbling Hillman campaign to finally get moving again?

Democratic campaign consultant Julie Wrigley joins us now. Julie, today's big question is will Altamont help or hurt Hillman?

JULIE WRIGLEY, Democratic campaign consultant: Good to be with you, Leigh. Well, look, obviously this campaign has remained focused on the issues at hand—and Teresa Altamont isn't one of them. Neither are the Citizens for Clear Heads. Hillman's message is hope for the powerless and opportunity for all. The only issue the campaign cares about relating to these ridiculous allegations is who's paying for them, and why are they getting the attention they are? This is what happens when Republicans get bored with draining wetlands and taking away government services from working people: They write checks to muddy the reputation of a good man who is trying to help the lives of people who don't have private planes.

GRACE: That's quite a charge.

WRIGLEY: It has more basis than the ads the Citizens are running. And these vicious attack ads just demean the debate and distract voters from the issues that matter to them. Why won't the president distance himself from these ads?

GRACE: I know you all that run these campaigns like to plan and plot, but some Republicans have said the reason that campaign ad came out was so that John Hillman could distance himself from it.

WRIGLEY: Ah . . . That would be a brilliant strategic move. But Leigh, I know the people on this campaign. They don't think that way.

GRACE: All right. Julie Wrigley on the Hillman campaign. Thanks a lot.

WRIGLEY: Thank you, Leigh.

Saturday, August 14

THE NEXT DAY they wound up at Stetson's again, with the bartender from that awful book party who Julie had added to her rotation, some other campaign staffers, the matching blond correspondent boys from *Time*, a surly *New Republic* essayist, a couple of Julie's colleagues, and that Swamp Thing blogger girl, whom they couldn't seem to shake. At that moment, the blogger girl and Julie were in the corner, apparently comparing the size of their breasts. Julie's colleagues stared, gaping.

"This is too fucked up to actually be a random collection of people," Chuck Reed drawled in Melanie's ear. She turned to look at him. A smidgen of makeup had flaked off onto his unbuttoned collar. *They loooooove to put our Texan on TV,* Melanie thought.

Chuck continued, "And what's your girlfriend doing over in the corner? Breast exams?" His eyes lit up. "Can I help?"

"Oh, please. She's just celebrating the successful America Now hit she did for us the other day with a few extra cocktails. And that blogger girl, well, she'll drink anything if someone else is buying, right?"

"I'm just observing it's a strange Saturday night here in Hobbittown."

"Hobbittown?"

"Where the little people live. All the big people have fled for the weekend, no?"

"And you thought that up all on your own?"

A momentary lapse in total cockiness passed over Chuck's face. "Ah, no. I think I read it on one of those blog things you're always talking about. Actually, I think that blogger girl who is groping your friend came up with it."

"Brilliant."

"Hey, I've been reading this new blog. Capitolette? Have you heard of it?"

Melanie smiled. "Yeah, yeah. I think I have."

"It doesn't have anything to do with the Clearheads, but it, uhm, well . . . there's definitely head in it."

Melanie laughed in spite of herself. *Hey, Chuck was kind of cute.* She smiled at him more fully. He had high cheekbones and smooth blond hair. His forehead was a little high and his nose slightly off, but his blue eyes and his grin pulled everything together nicely. Then her Berry went off. Her hand flew to the holster clipped to the side of her purse. She just stopped herself—only slowed, really, realizing Chuck was still standing right there. She smiled sheepishly at him and sort of gestured to the device, now in her hand. "Uhm, you know . . ."

Chuck smiled. "No problem. I'll just go get in line to perform one of those breast exams now."

Melanie watched him take a few steps away. He was actually sort of adorable. And he was single. *Why can't my life be more normal?* she thought. *Why* . . . She looked at her messages.

It was Rick, but it wasn't good: "You're not going to like this. Clearheads are our cover."

This news at eleven P.M. on a Saturday? The night's drinks felt heavy in her stomach. The messages flew:

To: Rick.Stossel@thinkmag.com

From: ThortonM@hillman.com

What the fuck? Why didn't you ask for comment or something? It's the cover?

To: ThortonM@hillman.com
From: Rick.Stossel@thinkmag.com
Yes, they did it in New York. A fucking kid up there wrote it. They only really let me in on it at the last minute.

To: Rick.Stossel@thinkmag.com
From: ThortonM@hillman.com
Bullshit.

To: ThortonM@hillman.com
From: Rick.Stossel@thinkmag.com
I'm serious. Look, it doesn't make me look very good either to have a cover story about politics that I didn't write and one that is, even for our standards, completely loony.

To: Rick.Stossel@thinkmag.com
From: ThortonM@hillman.com
Can you call?

To: ThortonM@hillman.com
From: Rick.Stossel@thinkmag.com
No. I'm surrounded.

Melanie felt a dart of pain shoot through her.

To: Rick.Stossel@thinkmag.com
From: ThortonM@hillman.com

Is it online yet?

To: ThortonM@hillman.com

From: Rick.Stossel@thinkmag.com

No. Not till tomorrow morning.

To: Rick.Stossel@thinkmag.com

From: ThortonM@hillman.com

Don't you have a copy?

To: ThortonM@hillman.com

From: Rick.Stossel@thinkmag.com

No, they kept it out of the system. That's how little they wanted me to read it. Wait, here, I've just gotten a copy. Don't hate me.

Melanie blew past whether Rick might be lying. *Think* was a legendarily twisted organization, so maybe it was true that its editors would think it was clever to cut their chief political reporter out of a cover that would ruin their reputation in the political community for ten years. She was so consumed with the exchange that she didn't even realize she'd piloted herself downstairs and right out of Stetson's. She would have walked into the middle of the street if the text of the story hadn't caught her dead in her tracks:

Jackie McDonnell had never heard of a blog last February when she voted in the Republican primary. In fact, the mother of four from Vernal Heights, Michigan, only used her computer to keep in touch with her scrapbook club and to e-mail her daughter serving in Iraq. Now though, McDonnell calls herself a "blog fanatic," checking in on the irreverent, sometimes saucy—and often wrong—"Web logs" as much as two or three hours a day. "I've stopped watching television and knitting," she says, petting her Dell keyboard. "Forget scrapbooking. I'm hooked."

Meet the new "blogger mom": They may be this election's most potent political force. McDonnell and her ilk have whip-slashed to every twist and turn of this year's dramatic presidential race in the new public square known as the "blogosphere." Like the pamphleteers of Colonial times, bloggers trade wild accusations for partisan gain, but unlike those limited nineteenth-century street arguments, the blog has plugged into homes all across America.

There are no statistics on how many Americans read blogs and little hard evidence that they are having an impact on political discourse. Further, analysts for both parties agree that traditional strategies—from door knocking to heavy paid advertising—still determine how races are run. Still, blogs are here to stay—and they're changing politics as we know it forever.

No story has consumed the bloggers more than the charge that Democratic presidential candidate John Hillman took part in mind-control experiments while a student at Harvard. No proof has come forward yet that Hillman engaged in such activities, but that hasn't stopped the bloggers. Their charges are chiefly four:

"Oh. My. God," Melanie said as she thumb-flicked the Black-Berry's tiny wheel scrolling the story in warp speed by her eyes. The writer then listed each of the Clearheads' charges in bullet points with a paragraph of explication for each one.

"They've handed the fucking magazine over to them," she said out loud. She flicked her finger looking for, praying for, the paragraph somewhere that would call their claims bullshit.

Reminiscent of the electric shock treatments that caused Tom Eagleton to drop himself from the vice presidential ticket in 1972, the Citizens for Clear Heads . . . .

Her cell phone rang.

"Hello." She flicked it open without thinking.

"Mel." It was Rick.

"How are you calling?"

"I'm smoking a cigar on the beach. I only have a few minutes. Listen . . ."

"You handed over the goddamn magazine to the Golden campaign. There's no comment from our side? Just some limp quote from a 'Hillman adviser.' I can find one of those at the Rite Aid. What the fuck happened?"

"I know," he said as waves crashed in the background. "I'm sorry."

The apology rocked her back a bit. *That was quick,* she thought. *Was it too quick?* Never mind, never mind . . . She was angry.

"We are so fucked," she said, trying to figure out whether she was more angry at being sandbagged by Rick and the magazine or Skoloff's asinine strategy of not taking on the Clearheads story in the first place. Whatever had gone wrong, it was her problem now.

"I've got to go."

"We are so fucked."

"Fuck me, fuck me, fuck me," she said a little too loud.

"Please," said a passing pedestrian.

"Fuck you."

THE COVER WOULD BE all over the morning shows Sunday. The story could no longer be ignored. And that meant she was going to have to interrupt Skoloff at whatever Georgetown dinner she was commanding with her steady pedantries. And she'd have to call Prentiss.

She Berried Julie upstairs.

To: Julie.Wrigley@clevelandparkgroup.com
From: ThortonM@hillman.com
    Clearheads on Think cover. I'm fucked. I've got to get to my computer and start typing. Call me when you're out of there. I need your help.

By the time Melanie had finished walking to her apartment Julie had already sent a reply.

To: ThortonM@hillman.com
From: Julie.Wrigley@clevelandparkgroup.com
    You'd better check Current too, these guys travel in packs.

Current, fortunately, had a cover on supermodel cuisine, but messages to the producers of the morning shows confirmed that all three cable news channels and the networks were going to talk about it. But no bookers had called to get comment or someone from the campaign to come on so the bleeding might not be that bad. But then again, the story wasn't actually *out* yet.

Melanie steadied herself on the counter and poured herself a glass of stale white wine. It was going to be another long night.

11

Sunday, August 15

To [undisclosed list]

From: ReedC@hillman.com

Subject: Trying something new

Date: Aug. 15

Don't know what anyone is doing tonight, but I've discovered this delightful little bar on U Street with a Western theme. Stetson's. Maybe you've heard of it? Seriously, guys. Can we find a new clubhouse? They're taking calls for me there now.

MELANIE HAD NOT slept well. In addition to everything else, the night had been warm and sticky. Her pillow had developed lumps. The sheets were itchy. Also, the twin focal points of her life were crashing together with hideous speed. There would be no survivors.

At five A.M., she gave up. She took a shower and hailed a cab. She was tired and bare-faced and she wore yoga pants and flip-flops. There was a suit folded up in her desk in case she was called upon, but somehow she doubted that would happen. The office was empty. Not for long, of course. She had maybe ninety minutes before the crisis team stumbled in. Would she catch shit for not having been able to use her "connection" to Rick to avert the disaster? What good was it to compromise one's principles if you couldn't get anything out of it? She clenched her jaw and didn't know whether to give in to bitterness or despair. *Or,* she thought, *might as well work.*

Standing at the office door, she took in the view of the deserted room.

In the dimness of early morning, you couldn't see the stains on the carpet or the crumbs on the desks. The haphazard layout seemed more orderly without the constant movement of staffers dodging desks. Skoloff loved it when the office was busy—everyone had to be doing something, even if it meant assigning people duplicate tasks (Melanie had once seen five interns gather together to xerox an itinerary) or inventing problems for them to solve ("Female Hispanic pharmacists 25–35 living in the exurbs don't love us! Do something!").

But Melanie liked it like this. Empty, expectant, and full of potential. The posters were bright and the televisions quiet and in Melanie's imagination, the campaign was staffed by boys in crew cuts and big smiles who handed out oversized buttons to men in hats. And the girls would wear skirts and pearls to do their phone banking.

She realized that she was channeling an image from a page on the campaign's website, the "Life Stories" section that featured pictures and anecdotes from Hillman's career: him going door-to-door for Kennedy, speaking at a civil rights rally in Alabama. She wondered what it would have been like to be a part of those history-making battles, if the people campaigning in them felt the peace of knowing you were fighting the good fight, in a good way. Of course there were payoffs and dirty tricks in the past, but the issues themselves weren't so thin and packaged. They played the game back then, too, but it somehow seemed more worth winning.

She sighed and considered turning on the overhead lights, but decided against it. Let the office linger a little in soft-focus. She wriggled around the tight maze of desks and turned on her laptop. She had seen most of the e-mail already, but there was something new from Julie:

To: ThortonM@hillman.com

From: Julie.Wrigley@clevelandparkgroup.com

    I have an idea. Meet me at Austin Grill for brunch? Promise it'll be worth it.

Melanie frowned. There was no fucking way she could get out of the office for brunch; she'd be lucky if she could get out for dinner. And Julie knew that.

She was about to reply in the negative when Julie's screen name popped up with an instant message:

WrigleyJules: Up early?

Thortonology: didn't ever go down

WrigleyJules: sorry sweetie. Need ambien?

Thortonology: have some. Couldn't risk not getting the 8 hours tho. You ever read the warning label on that thing? "may cause memory loss" or somesuch. I have enough to worry about.

WrigleyJules: I may be able to help.

Thortonology: Does it involve setting up a fake website?

WrigleyJules: no comment

Thortonology: jim golden and 14-year-old boy scout?

WrigleyJules: no comment.

Thortonology: whatever. I was going to reply to your email: there is no way I can get brunch. No way.

WrigleyJules: I figured. I just got excited. I can probably handle this by myself, tho.

Thortonology: handle what?

WrigleyJules: I really don't think I should say yet.

Melanie groaned softly with frustration. Even talking to Julie felt like trying to squeeze information from an uncooperative colleague. Why was everything so fucking hard? The calming effects of the empty office were wearing off.

Thortonology: don't dick me around.

WrigleyJules: I don't mean to, really. I just want to be sure about things before I involve you.

Thortonology: you're scaring me a little.

WrigleyJules: don't be, don't be. It's all fine and it could be great.

Thortonology: why am I having trouble believing that?

WrigleyJules: I think I would be having some trust issues if I were in your position right now.

Thortonology: that's very understanding.

WrigleyJules: hey, I didn't say I'd ever *be* in your position . . .

Thortonology: that's not as understanding.

WrigleyJules: I really am trying to help.

Thortonology: then go help. I'm going to figure out if I'm content to color inside the lines on this clearheads thing.

WrigleyJules: inside the lines versus . . . ?

Thortonology: no comment.

WrigleyJules: that's my girl. Ttyl.

Thortonology: bb

Actually, Melanie didn't really know if she had any ideas for what a more unorthodox approach to the Clearheads mess would be. Start a rival 527 to make outrageous claims about Golden? The campaign couldn't legally have contact with independently funded groups, but there were ways around that. . . . Was there something legal maybe but still outside the lines? Something that would get attention but not incur an investigation? *Put my experience to good use,* she thought. But beyond that, Melanie's thoughts kept running into empty corners.

She thought of those stories of Golden going off script while out on the trail. In a speech to a nurses' association, he had become tripped up in a litany of laudable duties and wound up extolling how those on the medical front lines "give patients the human contact they desperately need, including conversation, company, and tongue baths." He seemed to have bad luck with open mikes: He'd been caught telling his wife he needed to go "poo poo" and asking an aide how many nursing home residents would still be alive before election time.

During his first campaign, they had gotten more play. As it was, they were just lovable "Goldenisms," as *Slate* called them, fodder for late-night comedians that provided yet more proof of the incumbent's gritty, down-to-earth candor.

Maybe instead of the "Spontaneous reel," we should just have Hillman curse into a mike. Lord knows the campaign staff itself cursed enough. Any sentence that didn't have "fuck" in it no one would listen to. Chuck joked that no one on staff could get married during the campaign, because the vows would come out: "I fucking do motherfucker."

She willed herself to focus.

She opened a Web browser, intending to get a fresh look at what, if anything, had turned up in the Sunday papers. Instead she found herself on the campaign site, looking at the pictures of Hillman as an eager young volunteer. You could practically see his scalp shine, his crew cut was so short. Melanie wondered briefly if it would be possible to use just such a close-up to disprove any of the Clearheads' allegations. Maybe if they got a scientist in . . .

She clicked to the next page in the album. Here he was at a sit-in, a pale face surrounded by stern dark ones. In the background, other white faces shouted, ugly with rage. She recognized a few faces in the photo—a handful of Hillman's colleagues from those days had come forward to campaign for him, quite on their own, during the primaries. It was what probably helped them win. They were some of the best speakers the campaign had—passionate and compelling— but they had stopped doing photo ops and joint appearances because Hillman seemed uncomfortable with them now—maybe it was the mind control that made the difference, she joked grimly to herself.

THE SENIOR EXECUTIVE STAFF started to trickle in around seven-thirty. Skoloff walked through the office doors with her cigarette clenched tightly between her teeth, set to eat it, not smoke it. Every new arrival ratcheted up the ambient tension. It became too much at some point and when an intern nodded hello to her, she blurted out: "And here I thought I'd never see another *Think* cover I hated as much as the Ann Coulter one!"

His look turned puzzled, but he smiled—the way you would at a street person. Melanie turned back to her desk and fought the desire to bang her head against it.

She spent the day monitoring the television and trying to draft a memo about Donnelly that would be appropriate for real writers and not just bloggers. The television took most of her time.

The Sunday chat shows had taken Prentiss and Chuck eagerly, which suggested that the campaign wasn't being shut out, but also that the shows were moving slowly. Between the two, they'd be doing all the broadcast networks as well as half a dozen cable hits. Prentiss had been pushing to do all the broadcast shows himself— what was known in Washington as "pulling a full Ginsburg," after Monica Lewinsky's lawyer did such a tour. But *This Week* had been held out for Chuck. He was more telegenic, and they were trying to pick up an audience that cared about something a little more zesty than adult diapers and early morning fiber drinks.

By the end of the day, there was a dim silver lining around the bleak Clearhead cloud. The shows went pretty well. Hal and Chuck parried and even scored a few points. Only a few reporters called, and most, like the Sunday show hosts, were treating the *Think* cover the way they did newsmagazines in general: relics that were fixated with fad diets and exercise crazes but had stopped doing real news.

To: Julie.Wrigley@clevelandparkgroup.com

From: ThortonM@hillman.com

Where are you? I want to talk to you about something, but I am finally getting out and I *need a drink*. Will tell you more f2f.

To: ThortonM@hillman.com

From: Julie.Wrigley@clevelandparkgroup.com

I want to talk to you too. I've been researching all day. Finally have head above water. Meet me at my place? I'll get you that drink. . . .

Melanie could feel the back of her thighs unpeel from the chair. She hadn't been out of it since the post-morning-show meeting, but there had been some progress. She was optimistic about the campaign to draw blogger attention to Donnelly's flat-earther past, and at least the campaign was engaged with the Clearheads issue now. She grabbed her purse and laptop. Her back ached.

A cab dropped her at Julie's place in Dupont. Julie opened the door holding a glass of wine. Her smile was blurry and her eyes sparkled.

"You *already* started drinking?" Melanie cocked her head. "It was *my* tough day, you know."

"Mine has had its ups and downs, too, darling." Julie gestured for Melanie to come in. "How you holding up, girl? After a day like that your boyfriend owes you roses and a massage, at the very least. . . ."

"And a massage! I want a massage, too!" An unfamiliar woman's voice, twangy and high-pitched, chimed in from the back of the house.

"And company, too?" Melanie raised her eyebrows. "I thought you said you had been working all day."

"Trust me, it was work." Julie shook her head as though Melanie was unable to comprehend what she had been through. "You'll see."

Melanie followed Julie through the gracious town house, feeling, as she always did, a slight twinge of envy for all the comforts civilian life had given Julie. The interior designer who had found a couch with a "pure nook-fit," as he put it; the paintings by up-and-coming artists that accented the walls; the large Art Deco bar that took up one end of the dining room . . . and a blond girl in Daisy Dukes and an Austin Grill T-shirt.

Julie stepped in with an introduction: "Melanie, meet Heather Mason. Heather, this is Melanie, the co-conspirator I was telling you about."

Heather smiled broadly, and Melanie recognized her: the slutty waitress that Julie had been dishing about the day they had invented Capitolette. Melanie's mind whirred. The. Day. They. Had. Invented. Capitolette. Oh, Jesus, what had Julie done. . . . Melanie's head swiveled to Julie, whose smile widened as her eyes made a "Go on, go on" gesture. Melanie straightened up: "It's a pleasure to meet you, Heather."

"I'll say," Heather said, extending her hand. "I never forget a good tipper." It was Julie's turn to be thrown off a bit. Melanie mouthed, "Tell you later," as Heather approached. They shook hands. Heather's nails were long and painted hot pink. *Very impressive to keep that up while also slinging salsa,* Melanie thought.

"Well," said Melanie, "I've been there. It's a sucky job and tips make it bearable."

"Oh, I don't know," said Heather. "You meet a lot of interesting people. " She winked, and Melanie tried to figure out if "interesting" was code for "rich," "famous," or "available." "But, anyway: twenty bucks on a thirty-dollar tab. You must be a Democrat. I like Democrats okay. Republicans are better in bed, though." She laughed. Giggled, really.

Melanie now understood all the research Julie had done. And, she had to admit, Heather seemed perfect.

"Hey, Heather, you want to pick out some music while I get Melanie here a drink?" Julie interjected. "I think she needs to catch up with us."

"Sure thing," Heather said, wandering over to the racks of discs next to the stereo and unselfconsciously squatting down. Her ass peeked out a little from under the hem of her short, short shorts. Melanie couldn't help but stare.

Julie caught her and whispered: "Yeah, I know. I didn't know girls like that existed in D.C. . . ."

Melanie answered as they both turned to the bar in the dining room: "I think congressmen must import them."

"So, what do you want?"

"An explanation would be nice. You told her about everything, didn't you?" Melanie could feel irritation rising in the back of her throat. She closed her eyes. "Wait."

She could hear Julie filling a martini shaker. The clang of ice on metal jangled her nerves. She was starting to panic. And she had left the office feeling so . . . okay. This didn't feel like Julie pulling her feet out of the fire; this felt like she had started an even bigger fire somewhere else. *And why not tell me? I wasn't in a bunker all day, damnit.* The anger growled in her head as she thought about being cut out of the loop about her own life.

Melanie looked Julie in the eye: "Back this up for me. I mean, I think I get it, but just tell me what you were thinking."

"Look, honey, I don't have time to roll through the entire process—Miss Daisy in there will probably start pocketing my boxed sets, if she can find a place for them—but the very fact that you already figured out what my idea is means that it's a good one, right?"

Melanie tried to think through the logic of that assertion. It was flattering but . . . Julie moved on: "How much luck did you have fighting back the Clearheads today?"

"Ah. Well. It's not as bad as—"

"Have you seen the numbers yet?"

"No. They'll be coming in soon, though."

"Brace yourself," Julie said, with rough finality. "I hear they suck."

Melanie started to retaliate, but the words evaporated as she remembered Chuck's chilly predictions and Skoloff's infuriated chain-smoking. It was possible Julie had heard something she hadn't. It was, Melanie had to admit, actually pretty likely. She started to get angry all over again, but tried to put a leash on it.

"So Capitolette goes public?"

Julie rattled the martini shaker like a maraca, grinning: "And how."

HEATHER WAS STILL LOOKING through Julie's CDs, apparently unmindful of her ass waving in the air, when they walked in.

"Anyway, I couldn't decide. Do you have any hip-hop?"

Melanie jumped in: "Fuck it. I want to hear more about the plan anyway."

Julie widened her eyes at Melanie; it felt good to put her on the spot.

Melanie scooted around Heather, getting a close look for the first time. Melanie was somewhat disappointed to realize again how truly magnificent Heather's breasts were. High, firm, but with enough droop that they had to be real. Her eyes were green and heavily lidded—"bedroom eyes," naturally. Lips sort of thin, though they always seemed on the verge of parting. It worked. She also wore a lot of perfume. Opium, if Melanie's memory could be trusted.

Sitting on the couch opposite Heather, Melanie noticed that it really did feel like an interview. But the last part of one, after the candidate has met the entire staff twice, been out to lunch with half a dozen people, and been walked to the basement to see the boiler. The health care plan has been reviewed, there's been chitchat about last year's Christmas party, and now both sides have the feeling that it would be nice to find out one more thing about the other before making a decision.

Melanie took a sip of her martini. "So, Heather . . ."

She was usually much better at this.

"Yes?"

Melanie looked to Julie for guidance. Julie leaned back against the couch. "I think Heather and I have gotten to know each other pretty well," she said. "You just go ahead and ask anything you feel like. As long as Heather doesn't mind repeating herself."

"Oh, no. Of course not."

Melanie nodded. She wiped the condensation off the glass's base. Then the obvious question occurred to her: "Well, Heather . . . why do you want to do this?"

Heather looked like she'd just been asked to define "tort reform." She screwed up her face, her nose going scrunchy. She knocked back a gulp of wine. "Well, you mean, besides the money?"

Melanie sat bolt upright, "Huh?" *What? Julie offered her cash?* Melanie was just starting to do the math to calculate what if anything they could afford, and if it would even be legal, when she realized Heather was smiling at her.

"Gotcha," she said, and took another drink of wine.

"Funny."

Julie was amused.

Melanie continued: "I'm serious, though: especially since it's not for the money."

Heather shrugged. "Honestly? I'm bored."

Melanie let out a little half-snort, part laugh, part sigh. *Oh, to be bored again,* she thought. "Bored, you say."

"Well, yeah," Heather said. "No one's in town, the restaurant's half-empty most of the time, and my dealer has totally split. He's at the shore or something."

Of course drug dealers in Washington would go to the shore, Melanie thought.

Julie interrupted: "What sort of dealer?"

"Oh, nothing major. Just coke and some pot and maybe ecstasy every once in a while," she said. "Though, obviously, it's been a longer while than I'd like." Heather's eyes brightened: "Do *you* know anyone?"

"An, no. No," Julie replied. Melanie realized that it had been years since she'd done an illegal drug. Washingtonians traded prescription pills like candy—during a campaign the press plane was like a pharmaceutical trade show—but no one could or would risk inhaling anything more suspect than a Costa Rican cigar.

Heather nodded to Julie's demurral. She didn't actually look surprised; it would take a considerable amount of imagination to look at Julie's sleek professional exterior—even on a Sunday her jeans looked ironed—and see someone who had a lid of Acapulco gold on her person.

"So, anyway," Heather said. "I'm bored and this sounds like fun. I like to meet new people." She winked as she said this, pronouncing the word "meet" so it sounded like it was something described in damp paperbacks sold in truck stops.

Melanie pressed on: "And Julie's told you what we need from you?"

Heather seemed to intuit that another egregious display of sexuality wasn't needed for this question and she put on a soberish face:

"Yeah. You want me to play Capitolette." Her face broke into a perhaps more natural, less sober expression: "She sounds awesome."

Melanie let herself smile. "She is pretty awesome. . . . But she's also kind of a slut."

"That's okay," Heather said brightly. "So am I."

MELANIE LEFT JULIE'S EARLY, soon after they had wrung several assurances from Heather that she would (1) be available for "media training" Tuesday, and (2) not tell anyone. Anyone. Ever.

Julie had gotten completely soused by this point, smug and blurry in her satisfaction. Julie was high on taking Capitolette public as the solution to all of Melanie's problems, but Melanie was stuck on the realization that such solutions usually contained the seeds of new problems. *And bringing in a third person . . .* Melanie shuddered. Their risk of exposure had just increased exponentially.

Julie would have none of it. "She's perfect, she's perfect—she's a slut! She doesn't care about politics! She'll probably sleep with anyone who writes about her and everyone who doesn't will wonder if they could have."

"Written about her or fucked her?"

"Either. Both." Julie sighed. "You're focusing on what could go wrong."

"That's sort of my job," Melanie said. "Yours, too, if I remember correctly."

Julie glared. "My job, increasingly, has been to keep you from losing yours."

Melanie blanched. She didn't know whether to feel livid or embarrassed.

Julie's face softened. "Oh, shit. I didn't mean that. I'm sorry."

Melanie wasn't sure how to respond. The grain of truth in what Julie had said made her wince and twist inside. But thinking of all that was at stake, she summoned resolve: "It's not just about my job."

Julie came around and put her arm across Melanie's shoulders: "I know. I know." She squeezed. "It was a stupid thing for me to say, okay? I'm drunk and it's been a long day."

"Of drinking."

"Excellent point."

"I should go."

"Don't go away mad."

Melanie started putting her stuff together. "I'm not," she said. "But I do need to go."

MELANIE WALKED FROM JULIE'S, her laptop bag cutting into her shoulder and her balance just a little unsteady after a couple of martinis on an empty stomach. She was going to have to sober up and work more, too, she thought. Maybe she'd take a disco nap and then do some research.

She smiled to herself. It seemed like a sin against the party gods—there were actual party gods, Greek ones, right?—to call it a disco nap if you were going to work afterward. But something was bothering her about the campaign's inability to strike back at Golden; there had to be something, something in all those video clips. . . .

The work would also be penance. She knew that about herself. It would be a way of putting weight against whatever it was she and Julie were doing with Capitolette, convincing herself that her devotion to the campaign and fighting the good fight was what motivated all of it. Capitolette was a cul-de-sac off the main road.

Julie. Melanie stumbled a little on a crack in the sidewalk, stubbing her toe slightly. *That would never happen to Julie. Or maybe it had but she's learned something from it. And now was billing clients $400 an hour on how not to do it again.*

Melanie laughed a little, despite the stubbed toe and the ache in her shoulder. Her Berry went off.

To: ThortonM@hillman.com

From: Julie.Wrigley@clevelandparkgroup.com

Subject: In addition to being drunk . . .

Also, I'm having my period. Really. Call me when you get home and I'll even apologize again.

(Though I shouldn't have to. That period thing always worked in gym class.)

Melanie rearranged her bag and popped the Berry back in its holster, wondering if she'd be able to stay mad. She wasn't sure.

12

Tuesday, August 17

To: staff@hillman.com

From: SkoloffK@hillman.com

Subject: District smoking regulations

Date: Aug 17

I would like to thank the anonymous office staffer who posted a copy of the District of Columbia smoking regulations on my door. I am having it dusted for fingerprints now, so that I can thank you personally.

WHEN MELANIE GOT to work Tuesday, after a day's silence, there was a gift basket on her desk. More of a box, really. It contained trendy chocolates ("green tea" and "chili pepper" truffles), an untrendy box of wine, and a twelve-pack of perfectly sensible but not unsexy plain bikini briefs. The note read: "I'll waive the restocking fee if you can meet tonight for a high-level strategy meeting—Julie."

Melanie gave in and called Julie: "It's almost worth staying mad at you just to get some better wine."

"The beverage industry is making enormous strides with atypical packaging. Screwtops aren't just for Thunderbird anymore. The 'wine cube' is next."

"Client, eh?"

"Now, now: You are my most important client." Julie's voice was straining to be light, but Melanie felt the spin.

"Tell you what," she said, "I'm not mad and I promise to just forget the whole thing, but I don't want to be considered a 'client.'" Something in the way Julie's breathing changed signaled a release of tension on the other end of the line.

"What are you then?"

"Unindicted co-conspirator?"

Julie laughed. "We'll get better lawyers. I have to run now, but pick you up at eight? I think we should meet Heather at her place."

"She's included in the high-level meeting?"

"She's the agenda. We have to make a plan. I've already told America Now she'd come on tomorrow."

"Fuck, Julie—"

"You said you weren't going to get mad."

Melanie closed her eyes. She had that first-car-of-the-roller-coaster feeling, the weightlessness just before you rocketed down the hill. She shook it off: "I'll come," she said.

LATER, Julie sent an e-mail outlining the plan for the evening. It would be quick-and-dirty media training, with a side course in how to be Capitolette.

• If they ask you how much of what's on the blog is true, say, "It's based on my experiences."

- If they ask you to name your dates, say, "If my friends want to be as famous as I am, they can come out and name themselves."
- If they ask you about how much you got paid for your dates, say, "My friends are generous. I have a lot of time. They had a lot of money. It seemed like a fair trade."
- If they ask you about ass-fucking (or, as they might call it, "adventurous sex"), say there are several how-to books available if the anchor is curious about the technique.
- Please wear a bra.

Julie picked up Melanie at the office. As she climbed into Julie's Jetta, Melanie noticed a package in the backseat, wrapped in pink and black with a lace ribbon. "You got her underwear, too?" she asked.

"A Berry," Julie said, pulling into traffic. "But I thought I'd appeal to taste."

"Generous," Melanie said. "Did you expense it?"

Julie smiled: "No, but maybe I'll write it off. . . ."

Melanie shook her head.

HEATHER LIVED on the Hill, in an old row house that had been sliced into a hive of apartments. She let them in with a chirpy hello and then padded off to the bathroom. "Gotta tinkle," she said.

Her studio had the bones of what was once a small but elegant parlor: two walk-through windows looked out to the street; there was a wide plank floor and a nonfunctioning fireplace. It was really kind of lovely. But it was a complete mess. The futon, shoved into a corner, had a quilt of women's magazines and dirty clothes, and across the mantel of the fireplace slumped a line of dirty glasses and an array of candles. Mardi Gras beads dangled from the door to the bathroom. An army of beer bottles stood watch in the kitchenette, and on a stained and pitted coffee table stood a bong made out of orange glass. Out of the corner of her eye, Melanie watched Julie take it all in—she winced when she saw the bong.

"Do you think she did this all by herself?" Julie whispered.

"It's impressive, actually."

"I somehow don't get the impression she's going to be offended if we seat ourselves."

They walked over to the improvised living room area in front of the fireplace. When they sat, the foam sofa sank to the floor. Julie wrinkled her nose: "I think I'll just stand."

Melanie looked around some more; a poster from Madonna's *Like a Virgin* tour was tacked up over the bed. The poster was the first suggestion Melanie had seen that Heather didn't live entirely in the present. Now Melanie wondered where Heather was from and how she had gotten to Washington. Did she have a mother somewhere who was having to explain all this to the bridge club or reading group? Melanie cringed. Julie nodded toward the Madonna image, reading into it something else entirely: "I think we're gonna be fine," she whispered.

Heather bounced in. "Wanna drink?" she offered, brightly.

"More than anything," Julie replied.

PERHAPS IT WAS the lubrication that eased the rest of the evening, and when Julie handed Heather the box with the BlackBerry in it, her eyes lit up in a way Melanie, at least, found endearing. She could barely sit still while Julie explained how to check e-mail with it. "That is sooooo cool! Lemme see!" She snatched it out of Julie's hands.

Julie rolled her eyes. "Oh, like you didn't act that way with your first Berry," Melanie reminder her.

The media training hit a snag only once: "But I *never* wear a bra. I don't like feeling confined," she had explained.

Melanie's appraising eye looked over the nipples popping out of the thin material of Heather's T-shirt. "Clearly," she tried to explain. "It's just . . . the studios are cold, and, well, let's just say we don't want anyone to be distracted from what you're saying." Melanie stopped herself. What the fuck? *Of course* we want people to be distracted from what she's saying.

"You know what?" Melanie continued. "Never mind. Just be comfortable."

Heather grinned. "Well, then I'd have to do the show naked."

Julie broke in: "Maybe next time."

ON HER WAY into work the next morning, Melanie called Julie. Her stomach was in a nervous tangle: The town car was scheduled, the training was done, the Berry was programmed. There was no backing out now.

"Think I made the right call about the bra?" she asked.

"Let me put it this way: Would we rather people pay attention to her titty hard-on or to what she's saying?"

"Good point."

"You were totally right," Julie said. "Also, it guarantees she'll be picked up again in *The Point*."

"If not by *Playboy*."

"I think they already e-mailed. That account's mailbox is so full—the poor porn-spam filter just gave up, I think—I need to do a more thorough check."

Through the dirty windows of the cab, Melanie saw her office looming a few blocks away. She had a panicky rush of adrenaline shoot through her as she remembered the several different balls she and Julie were tossing back and forth. And then of course, there was Rick. *That ball is all mine,* she thought, sighing.

"What's that?" Julie said.

"I'm just worried. Is there a way you could show up at the studio?" Melanie wondered. "Like, I don't know, could she have hired the firm?"

Julie barked a bit of laughter. "CPG wouldn't touch her with a ten-foot pole."

"If you had a ten-foot pole I don't know how you'd keep her away."

"Ha. The point is that we can't risk going with her to the studio ourselves, and we sure as hell can't ask anyone else to do it. We're going to have to . . ." Julie paused for dramatic effect. "Trust her."

"You can't be serious."

"We don't have a choice. We need a Capitolette. For what it's worth, I think she needs the attention she's getting just as badly as we need her to be Capitolette's body," Julie rationalized.

"Mutually beneficial. Not unlike the relationships we made up for her."

"I don't think it's unlike her actual relationships," Julie said.

"I'm here." Melanie simultaneously held the phone between her head and shoulder and dug in her bag for bills. "I should go."

"Ping me when she's on."

"Right." Melanie handed over cab fare and uncrooked her neck, slapping the phone shut.

SHE WALKED UP to the building's glass doors and paused. Heat came up in waves from the sidewalk; she could feel her pores getting larger. She could feel rivulets of sweat run down the back of her neck and under the fabric of her shirt. *The mere prospect of air-conditioning should excite me,* she thought. *That should be enough to get me to the office.* The truth was it was getting harder and harder to muster the will to actually go to work. It wasn't burnout. She still could look at her collection of credentials from the convention and feel a little thrill. And when she watched Hillman give a speech, if he hit the lines just right, she could feel herself shiver as she imagined him as president. What had changed?

I have, she thought. *I've changed.* The office wasn't just a place she went to for work, and it wasn't just the opposition party that set traps . . . *It's that every time someone mentions Rick, my blood pressure rises. It's that every time someone mentions Capitolette, my ears prick up.* In a job that already required a paranoiac's attention to detail, she was moonlighting. *Lying,* Melanie thought, *is much harder than it looks.*

She took a deep breath of the oven-hot air and pulled her shoulders back. *I made it this far,* she reasoned, and opened the door.

The chilled air gave her goose bumps. She walked in.

SKOLOFF WAS OUT. Prentiss was in the corner, hunched over his monitor. Melanie could see that he was reading Capitolette. *Well, of course,* Melanie thought. She wondered if he was one of the many men who had propositioned Heather before she was Capito-

lette. She wondered if actually seeing what Heather looked like
would dissuade him.

Probably not, she thought. *It's not exactly the face they're thinking
about.*

Melanie collapsed into her chair. She had an instant message
from Julie as soon as she signed on.

> WrigleyJules: Maybe we can get her fitted with an electronic monitor. I'm
> worried she's not even going to make it to the studio.
> Thortonology: I'm worried she *is* going to make it to the studio.
> WrigleyJules: I wasn't this nervous before you started being nervous.
> Thortonology: You weren't with her for two hours.
> WrigleyJules: I'm refusing to believe this can't work. This will work.
> Thortonology: You sound like a Nader voter.
> WrigleyJules: Ack! Ack! It's on . . .

She considered going to watch on the big TV in the war room,
but she saw in a glance that the entire fucking campaign staff was
there. *It's my most successful earned media strategy ever,* Melanie
realized, *and I'm not even going to get a raise out of it.*

Melanie had a small television on her desk. She changed it from
the soothing political white noise of CNN to America Now. The
daytime anchor was Margaret Finn, a frosted brunette with
tweezed eyebrows and the face of a starved cow. She tended to zero
in on slice-of-life stories about kittens and lost children who had
been found. She also did not like "filth," and those tweezed eyebrows editorialized whenever America Now booked the usual culture war suspects, from NARAL to PFLAG to the ACLU.
Melanie's nerves ratcheted up a notch.

She opened gently enough. "Now, here to talk to us about the hottest scandal in Washington right now is Heather Mason, known now to all of D.C. as 'Capitolette.' "

And there she was, on the split screen for all the world to see. *Oh, good, her nipples as well,* thought Melanie. America Now tarted up female guests—Julie always complained about it—and with Heather, they had gone for a full-on streetwalker look. Her fair skin was pancaked into a facsimile of a glow, her eyelids were gilded, her lips wet, and her hair rose above her head in a perfect approximation of Pamela Anderson. Melanie thought Heather looked pleased with herself. Indeed, she kept glancing over to her lower right, which is probably where the monitor in the studio was. *I should have told her to have them turn that off,* Melanie thought. *Next time. If there is a next time.*

Julie sent Melanie an instant message exactly then: "Tell her to have monitor off next time."

Yeah, yeah, yeah. Let's just see how she does, Melanie thought, suddenly impatient.

Finn interrupted Heather's brief giggle fit: "So you are the writer behind the 'Web log' Capitolette, where you chronicled your . . . well, romantic adventures."

Melanie tensed. Heather smiled, glanced at herself in the monitor—which made her look kind of shifty—and drawled: "I don't know if they were that romantic. They were adventures."

Heather was mostly looking at the camera now.

Julie's instant message instant commentary continued: "Good answer, I think."

Finn's eyebrows were in her hairline. "Yes, well, your claim to have dated a lot of Washington figures—I know everyone has been kept very busy trying to guess who they all are. But how do we know you really dated them?"

Fuckfuckfuck, Melanie thought. *Why didn't we prep her on this?* The question had come up often enough during the early interviews and in e-mail to Capitolette.

Heather shifted eyes again: "Would you like photos?"

Melanie's mouth dropped open. Her IM program boinged alarmingly as Julie spat out panicky notes: "WTF? WTF? Where is she going with this? We can't promise photos?"

Finn's expression at this surprising response was hard to read. Offended? Eager? She found the idea of photos obscene, thought Melanie, and she'd like to have several copies. "You have photos of you with your . . . 'partners'?"

Julie had already come out on the other side of panic: "Maybe we could fake some. . . . Kidding . . . Mostly . . ."

Melanie glanced at the message and wondered when she and Julie would get to a line even they couldn't even think of crossing.

Meanwhile, Heather was responding to Finn's inquiry. "Partners? Well, I guess it was a kind of business relationship." She giggled again.

Finn kept pursuing: "You can prove you had relationships with all these Washington figures? A television journalist? A campaign manager? You have pictures of yourself with them?"

Heather smiled. "I didn't say I had them. I just thought you might get off on looking at some."

Finn raised her eyebrows so high they threatened to pull her lips into her nose. Heather giggled. *We're going to have to work on that,* Melanie thought. Then again . . . There was a crazy innocence to the way Heather was handling this. A rawness that was like a big "fuck you" to Washington's media elite. Then Melanie remembered the clear acquisitiveness that crept into Heather's eyes as Julie and she had explained that her role as Capitolette would require her to go on television. Heather's rawness wasn't a fuck you. It was a fuck me.

I'm not sure what I'm watching, thought Melanie, *but it is good television.*

Nostrils flaring, Finn spat out a final question: "Do your parents know about your sex life? Do they know the kinds of things you've been up to here in Washington?"

Heather giggled again. "They do now."

Julie messaged her final pronouncement: "She's going to be a star. It's time for her to make her social debut. Let's bring her to the Brompton party this weekend."

13

Friday, August 20

To: emilybrompton@kensingtonco.com

From: Julie.Wrigley@clevelandparkgroup.com

Subject: party crasher?

Sent: Aug 18

Hey, Emily—I'm RSVPing very late for your shindig Friday, and I'd like to bring Mel Thorton. I know I'm pushing the boundaries of your good graces but I hope Southern hospitality will win out over your (or my) manners. And maybe I can make it up to you with a tip: Have you thought about maybe inviting Washington most newly famous face, Capitolette? I saw her on America Now yesterday and she was *amazing*—totally fresh and very cute, in a bloggery way. In any case, it would certainly give everyone something to talk about. And you wouldn't want the Holden-Riches to get to her first, eh? The bookers at AN must have her contact info. Anyway, looking forward . . .

Cheers,

Julie

"Guys like me because I'm thin but stacked," Heather was saying. "That, and I don't have any hang-ups about sex."

Julie smiled. "You don't have any *limits* when it comes to sex, I think you mean," she said, smoothing her palms over her blue-and-white Marc Jacobs halter dress.

Heather giggled. "Whatever."

Heather wore a strapless black dress that made her considerable assets obvious. It tended to slip down in such a way that her assets became more than simply obvious—they were drink holders. When nipples threatened, Heather would lean over a bit and kind of shimmy the whole dress into place. She did it unselfconsciously and in the middle of sentences, like some people would pick their nose or a cheerleader would twirl her hair. *Except, of course,* thought Melanie, *she isn't getting ready to go on, she's already onstage.*

They were drinking Cosmopolitans—"pre-partying!" as Heather put it—in Julie's kitchen, prepping their newly minted mini-celebrity for a party at the home of Republican power couple Hugh and Emily Brompton. Julie paced the hardwood floor, her heels clicking out an impatient tattoo as Heather steadfastly refused to take seriously their warnings that this was going to be an Important Party. "How important can it be if no one famous is going to be there?" she cooed.

"Jesus, it's Washington, Heather," Julie said. "The bar is pretty low. *You're* famous now."

Heather liked the sound of that.

Melanie watched from a perch on the other side of the kitchen island. She'd shimmied into a Banana Republic sheath that approximated something Gucci had done last year. It almost fit. She added a pair of black stilettos she'd bought to replace the Charles David graham cracker heels. The pitcher of Cosmos was close at hand. Normally, she wasn't much for sweet, girly drinks ("Nothing with more than three ingredients" was her rule of thumb), but

Heather had insisted and Julie agreed: "Her idea of cool is *Sex and the City;* I have no trouble playing along as long as I don't have to be the slutty one. Or the one with the baby. Please not the one with the baby."

We're both the one with the baby, Melanie thought, watching Heather puff her cheeks and pout as Julie ran through a list of some of the people she might meet.

"There's the head of NBC's political unit. He seems mousy but he's razor sharp. Comes on like your high-school civics teacher but he's probably got photos of the principal doing unspeakable things with a thirteen-year-old in a safe-deposit box somewhere."

Heather perked up at the mention of "NBC." Or maybe at the mention of "unspeakable things." It was hard to tell. "And what do you want me to do with him?" she asked.

Julie sighed. Getting Heather to understand that she did not need to *elaborate* on the Capitolette scandal had been a persistent problem. "It's not what we want you to *do* with him, it's just . . . these are the people who will be there. According to what 'you' have written on 'your' website, you already know them. In some cases— we've implied at least—intimately. So it would be bad if you drew a blank meeting them now."

Heather nodded slowly. Then she smiled. "I can always distract them with my charms."

"For your charms to be any more distracting, my dear, you'd have to be wearing that dress as a skirt."

Melanie almost choked on her drink. *I suppose I should jump in,* she thought. *The student council president in Julie just can't quite get her head around taking the trailer park princess to prom.*

Julie's vague antagonism with Heather seemed hardwired to Melanie. There was an element of magnanimity in her efforts to give Heather a crash course in the Washington hierarchy, but something of a sneer as well, maybe left over from Julie's prep school days. It probably *was* as simple as the hidebound high-school social cliquery that governed so much maneuvering in D.C. *In which case, I suppose even I should be snubbing Heather, too,* Melanie thought. But even in high school proper, Melanie hadn't been able to muster disdain for the girls who put out easily and often. She was editing the paper, performing in chorus, planning the Spanish Club's trip to Cancún, and generally too busy padding her college application to participate in the high-stakes roulette of high-school popularity contests. Just popular enough to escape active derision, Melanie had thought of herself as more of an anthropologist than a tribe member. Her high-school journals, indeed, read more like field notes than diaries at times. Sure, there were random pages filled with variations on "Mrs. Colin Paige, Ms. Melanie Paige, Mrs. Melanie Thorton-Paige," but there were also observations on the mating habits and dining rituals of sixteen-year-olds:

I am beginning to wonder if the girls who hang out outside Troy Parker's locker recognize each other by the scent of their Juicy Fruit gum. Or maybe that's how Troy recognizes them. They also have similar costumes—the denim skirts, the tiny tees, and those ridiculous microscopic backpacks. I've been thinking about those backpacks a lot: Are they like what sociologists say about high heels? Do they signal a kind of learned helplessness? Instead of "I have knowingly hobbled myself so that you can catch me," it's "I am purposefully carrying something that makes me look like a four-year-old tagging along with Mommy to the store."

Now, Melanie could barely read her high-school prose; her eyes squinted too much with embarrassment. But she was quite certain that, in the back of her closet, Heather had just such a tiny backpack. *Of course,* Melanie thought, *I'm the one with twenty pairs of three-inch heels.* Who's learned helplessness now?

THE BROMPTONS LIVED in Georgetown, in a house that used to be an embassy. It was large and grand but sort of generic, a stage set for the fabulous life that was lived in it. Its anonymous wealth made it exactly the kind of house you'd see in thick-paged glossy lifestyle magazines, its rooms empty and sterile except for the opening spread in which Emily and Hugh stood, their three children posed purposefully beside them.

Now the rooms were full and sterile—crowded with diplomats and pols who smiled and nodded at one another while reporters fidgeted in line for the bar. Gaggles of young, single, and presumably Republican women had flocked to the corners—Emily ran some kind of underground railroad for them, Melanie suspected. She was always introducing them as "my odalisques," a Faulknerian fillip of slightly creepy grandiosity that was in keeping with her Mississippi roots. These understudies dotted the city throughout summer but there was usually at least one recent graduate from an approved-of small college bunking in one of the house's thousand or so bedrooms while she interned at the RNC or the Fed or maybe even Emily's own lobbying group. Melanie nursed some envy for the system—to be among Emily's charges meant an automatic introduction into Republican power circles, a full social calendar, and more likely than not a summer's worth of blind dates. In addition to getting her girls jobs and introductions, Emily also seemed intent on getting them married off, pairing the lobbying intern with the *Weekly Standard* writer, the Senate aide with the pollster. It was like a grand conservative eugenics experiment. And there was more than one going on: on the other side of northwest Washington, Ann-Marie and Justin Holden-Rich ran a slightly more subdued Kalorama breeding ground. Julie preferred the Holden-Rich parties because Democrats seemed more welcome there. "They're probably just using us as decoys or target practice, though."

"IF ONLY THERE WERE a Democrat equivalent to these political speed dates," Melanie had once complained to Julie.

"There is," Julie said. "Saturday night at Stetson's."

Emily booked her parties the way chat shows booked guests: She loved introducing a token not-so-wild card from across the aisle like James Carville, or snagging the latest celebrity to trip through Congress on an awareness-raising mission for the fight against teen pregnancy or junk food or unneutered pets. Capitolette's presence would give Emily a vicarious sheen of unpredictability and feed Washington's favorite kind of scandal: the insulated ones. Capitolette's apparent bipartisanship, Heather's genuine lack of political attachments—at least the ideological kind—made it hard to politicize her. Emily would not have to worry about debate breaking out over what Heather meant or who she'd damage the most. Of course, that was only because no one was aware of who she had saved.

JULIE AND MELANIE had arranged to get there before Heather did, though the possible advance work they could do was limited.

Indeed, Julie had almost decided no advance work was so valuable that it was worth risking leaving Heather alone in her apartment for thirty minutes. "I wonder if I can write off replacing whatever it is she breaks," Julie had mumbled as they climbed into her Jetta.

"Don't worry," Melanie said. "The only thing she's in danger of breaking is the seal on your peppermint schnapps."

At the party, Emily greeted them at the door with a perfumed hug and double air kisses. Her tight, trim figure was wrapped in a green silk cheongsam and her sunshine-colored hair was piled in an elegant tumble on her head. *It would take me an hour to even get my hair to stay in place like that and then it would still look as though it was some forest creature's nest.* "Welcome across the aisle." Her drawl was honey-coated. "Hugh's over by the bar. I'm sure he'll be happy to see you, Melanie. . . ." Emily dropped a slow, unnerving wink.

Julie gave Melanie a puzzled look. Melanie shook her head curtly and shrugged, then answered Emily. "If so, he'll be the only one who's not the most excited to meet Capitolette, no?"

Emily clasped her hands. "Oh, I *know!*" She then leaned forward and inclined her head, as if about to impart a secret. When Julie and Melanie didn't bow down with the same conspiratorial gesture, Emily grabbed their shoulders and pulled them in. "You know, some of my invitees are—ahem—more interested than others in meeting her." She grinned. "And then there are those who I think might already"—she issued a ladylike fake cough—"know her." Emily straightened back up. "It's going to be *so. Fun.*" She turned to greet the next arrival.

Julie and Melanie stood back up themselves.

"What did we get ourselves into?" Melanie hissed to Julie.

"Hush," Julie said. "It's all going exactly according to plan."

"You have a plan?"

"I know the next step."

"Getting another drink."

"We are, as usual, on the same page."

THEY CROSSED the packed entrance hall to the bar set up in the living room. The party was definitely more crowded than usual. In Washington, Emily's parties held the same position in most people's datebooks as going to church or the doctor might in other parts of the country: You didn't go because you wanted to go, you went because you were worried about what might happen if you didn't go. The town's social agenda was no longer set by the old-money families who populated the indexes of Katharine Graham's and Sally Quinn's autobiographies anymore. Two decades of newcomers who promised to reject "Washington-style" politics made for a dinner party culture that was more entrepreneurial than hereditary. Newt Gingrich had failed as majority leader, but he did make Emily possible. In fact, Melanie was pretty sure she saw Newt there.

Emily was a former aide to the Senate majority leader and currently a low-key lobbyist and kingmaker. She devoted what were probably billable hours to party planning. Melanie imagined spreadsheets for every guest, tallying party invitations received versus those declined, possibly weighted according to who or what the party was for and, of course, who the invitee was. There were the presentable journalists (television, mostly), the connected consultants, the must-have Republicans, the must-have Democrats, the in-a-pinch Republicans, and the permissible Democrats.

With a guest list that strove so hard to be bold, it was hard to pin down why the parties themselves were so dull. Perhaps it *was* all those bold-faced names that were the problem. Everyone there was either the kind of person who got written about or one of the ones doing the writing—a situation designed to bring out nothing but the best behavior. Best boring behavior. But, then again, none of these people had gotten to where they were by being interesting. "Interesting" rarely translated into power. "Interesting," in fact, often gave people ammunition to get you out of power. And if "interesting" got your foot in the door, you unlearned "interesting" on your way up.

Which is what made Capitolette such a breath of fresh air in this careful room.

LUCKILY, there was always lots to drink. Hugh's law firm had a connection to the Distilled Spirits Council of the United States—hands down the most popular lobby in Washington—and the bar was top-shelf and well stocked and probably free if not entirely tax deductible. Hugh watched over the proceedings from the side, dressed in a seersucker suit and holding a large bourbon. He was posing, and Melanie realized that the glossy mag the Bromptons were aiming for had to be *Southern Living*. And, indeed, he was happy to see Melanie. "Hello, darlin'," he said, leaning over for a one-handed half-hug. "What are you ladies drinking?"

"White wine," she replied. He looked to Julie.

"Same here, Hugh. How are you these days?"

Hugh passed their orders to the bartenders.

"I'm good, Julie, I'm good. Excited about meeting this new girl in town, I have to admit." He smiled. "She seems a little more . . . adventurous than most of Emily's charges."

Julie's eyebrow raised: "You think she's Emily's latest charge?"

Hugh chuckled. "A boy can dream, can't he?"

"Ah." Melanie was growing slightly nervous about being stuck in conversation with Hugh when they should be gathering intel. "Ah, Hugh, it's been lovely. I need to pull Julie away, though. . . ."

"Oh, yes." Julie started to pivot already. "Thanks for the drinks, Hugh."

"A pleasure, ladies." Hugh took Melanie's hand again. She thought he might kiss it.

"Uhm, bye." She pulled away and joined Julie in an empty corner. "That was weird. Why have I not noticed the plantation-owner fetish of his before?"

"It's a summer thing, when he breaks out the seersucker."

Julie looked at her drink: "These aren't wineglasses, they're fishbowls." Hugh had confided in Melanie once that the secret to barline management was to make every drink a double: "They don't have to come back as fast."

"Appropriate enough," replied Melanie. "At least it's not Chilean. That's how you can tell when they really don't care."

"That's when you switch to bourbon." Julie replied, eyeing the goblet. "Oh well." She took a sip. "Drinkable."

Melanie was already proving her right.

Julie's fingers fidgeted around the edge of the glass. "Fuck. It is really crowded."

"Nothing brings out bipartisanship like a sex scandal," Melanie observed, wondering if she was already too far down the road to drunk to stop. The air in the room was heavy—the Bromptons would need an industrial-strength air conditioner to keep pace with the sheer number of people in their house, let alone the tang of sweaty excitement that had become more than just figurative. Capitolette had, indeed, brought together both the left and right sides of the aisle. *And if you believed her blog, she had also passed fluids between them,* Melanie thought, wondering if part of the tension in the room stemmed from people trying to figure out if Capitolette's sex life had lowered the degrees of sexual separation between them.

JULIE HAD SET DOWN her wine and was thumbing away at her Berry.

"You sending Heather tips?" Melanie said. "You might mention that Chris Matthews is here, and that she should not try to steal the Nilla wafers from his pocket. Also, I see Chris Wallace and that third-string White House chick from ABC. She does not have Nilla wafers in her pocket, because they would double her weight."

Julie frowned into her Berry.

"You get all that?" Melanie resisted—just barely—the urge to peer over Julie's shoulder. "And tell her to avoid Ann-Marie and Justin unless she wants to be a pawn in their crosstown social Cold War."

"Right, she's our pawn. I'm just sending names for now. Names she'll recognize, I hope. Maybe she'll even stay halfway sober."

"Oh, it's too late for that. Much, much too late."

There was a kind of clatter in the hall. Julie looked up.

HEATHER WAS STANDING under the arch that led from the entryway to the living room, at the top of a short jump of steps. *Got to give her credit for knowing how to work the stage,* thought Melanie. Her arms were akimbo and she held her shoes, dangling by their ankle straps, in one hand. Her dress had slipped down perilously. She smiled broadly, either not caring that everyone in the room was looking at her or—more likely—very pleased indeed that everyone in the room was looking at her.

Just behind Heather's right shoulder, Emily stood with her arms crossed, evaluating. *She doesn't have a spreadsheet for this*, Melanie thought.

"Hope you don't mind that I took my shoes off," Heather said, addressing the crowd. "They were kind of tripping me up and I didn't want anything to keep me from getting to the bar!"

Melanie's mind raced. It wasn't that funny. It wasn't unfunny, either, but it was also coming from . . . nobody. If Golden had said it, everyone would laugh. If Emily had said it! If it had been said during an Oscar telecast . . . Melanie was just realizing that she was holding her breath when the giggles erupted—naturally, from near the bar. And from right next to her! Julie was either laughing or choking on her wine. She grabbed Melanie's free hand and hissed. *"Laugh!"* Melanie began with a hesitant "heh," but by then the entire room was going and there had been a Red Sea–like parting between Heather and the bar.

As the laughter died down, Melanie whispered to Julie, "What happened?"

Julie was watching Heather wiggle across the room. She shrugged. "People want her to succeed. She's like the spoiler candidate—for both parties. Everyone thinks she can only hurt the other side."

"She could hurt *us*."

Julie gave Melanie a sideways glance. "Not as much as she's already helped us."

A squeal of laughter pierced the room. Heather had gotten her drink and was giggling at the epicenter of a scrum of men, all suited and staring at her. One of them—Jason Hoover, a nervy correspondent from America Now with a buzz cut and too-broad shoulders—had maneuvered his hand onto Heather's bare back, and it had started to migrate south.

"Should we get her out of there?" Melanie asked. "I only recognize Hoover. We should get her over to Matthews or— Jesus, is Lead here? She totally needs to talk to Lead."

Julie was watching Heather appraisingly. As was every other woman there, Melanie noticed. The party's political divides were helping Heather, as each side secretly wished for her to blow up (as it were) in the other's face, but Melanie realized there was definitely a Capitolette gender gap.

"Training wheels, my friend," Julie declared. "Training wheels. Hoover's a perfect start."

Emily sidled up beside them: "You think she'd aim higher." Emily half-smiled and gestured toward the Capitolette fan club.

"Just above the upper thighs, really," Julie murmured.

"Excuse me?" Emily inclined her head.

Julie cleared her throat and started again: "Oh, I think any guest at your party is starting quite high enough."

Emily smiled. A real one, Melanie noted. Flattery traded very high in Washington, even when it was fake. Emily floated onto the next knot of guests.

"You want to go steal some of her cigarettes and go to the patio?" Julie glanced around, double-checking that the well-oiled party machine was clicking along. "There's no one to smoke with since Campbell Brown left. And"—Julie's eyes turned back to Heather—"we can watch the show from there just as well."

Melanie's eyes scanned the room as she made her own estimate of what direction the party was moving in. Toward Heather, it seemed. In the meantime, Hoover's hand had settled—with some finality—on Heather's ass. "Do you think she's safe with Hoover?"

"Sure," Julie replied, "she's doing just fine for now. We'll sic her on someone more deserving later."

THE AIR ON THE PATIO was still and warm. It seemed like the smoke from the cigarettes hardly moved when they exhaled.

"I can't believe this is really happening," Melanie said, waving her hand in front of her face to help the smoke along.

"It does have a dreamlike quality," Julie mused. "But then again, most campaigns do."

"You mean nightmares, then."

Julie laughed. She stood with an arm crossed in front of her, her hand supporting the other elbow as she smoked. It was a pose out of a movie, Melanie was sure. She just couldn't remember which one.

"The other thing I can't believe," Melanie continued, "is that you've never done anything like this before."

"You're kidding, right?"

Melanie shook her head.

Julie's head shook, too, ruefully. "No, I haven't. Almost wish I had. It's turned out to be so . . . easy."

Instinctively, Melanie looked for wood to knock on. Julie saw the gesture before Melanie could contain it. "My sweet child of the corn. Do you throw salt over your shoulder, too?"

"Only when I can aim it for someone's eye," Melanie said. "Which brings us back to dirty tricks . . ."

"Well, to be honest." Julie straightened up and squared her

shoulders. *Honest?* Melanie thought. *Julie confesses!* To what, she didn't know, but it would be a first. Julie went on: "To be honest," she repeated, "I haven't done *that* much campaign work."

Melanie continued her disappointment. "Ah. So it wasn't that you weren't willing, it's that you didn't have the opportunity."

"It's true." Julie gave her a closed-lip smile. "Day-to-day Hill work doesn't lend itself to stunts. It's a deeper game, as they say."

Melanie nodded and disguised her slight bit of discomfort with another drag. She knew next to nothing about life on the Hill. It had taken her parents weeks to understand that she didn't work underneath that big white dome on all the postcards she sent home. But campaign culture was almost totally distinct from the everyday machinery of government, and about the only time Melanie was in the same zip code as Congress was to accompany Skoloff to a television hit.

Julie interrupted her thoughts. "Did you hear about Altamont, by the way?"

"Nope."

Julie dropped her cigarette and ground it out with a very pointy toe. "She got a fucking book deal out of that stunt with the recovered memory. She's made it about the environment and gamma rays or some shit, so the Clearheads are staying far away, and I don't see it impacting us"—Melanie cringed at the verb—"but she is also . . . wait for it . . ."

"Starting a blog."

"Hey, I thought you said you didn't know!"

"Who doesn't have a blog?"

Julie smirked. "She probably won't write it herself, either."

With that, they turned to look back through the patio doors. Heather was gone.

. . .

THE EFFECT OF HER departure on the party was as if the center had been ripped out of a painting or a fire had disappeared from a hearth; where there had been a focal point, there was now a vacuum surrounded by nothing but frame. Heather must have left suddenly, too—people were only just now starting to drift into the space left in the middle of the room; somehow the impression of her remained there, a dent in the air like the body-shaped hollow in an empty bed.

Melanie and Julie walked forward, trying not to rush, or at least trying not to appear to rush. Melanie scanned the living room for the male swarm so sure to follow Heather everywhere while Julie checked her BlackBerry: "Nothing," she said.

They marched into the smaller dining room, dominated by a table groaning with cheese plates, mini-quiches, and orchards of fruit. Nothing.

Melanie noticed that the other guests displayed a distinct lack of interest in their search. In the hour since they had arrived, the party had turned some corner—or maybe it had gone over a cliff. The keen and constant eye-swiveling had been replaced by slightly glassier looks; the stagey half-turned-out postures of people partly engaged in conversation had been replaced by more intimate knots of two and three. Melanie already knew that she, Julie, and Heather had arrived late, but now she surmised they had arrived after the third round.

They were plunging ahead into the kitchen when Melanie stopped, putting a hand on Julie's arm to keep her back, too.

They dropped into a huddle.

"Okay, let's slow down. If we're going to find her, we'll have to be more methodical," Melanie said.

Julie took a deep breath. "Right." She glanced around the room, less searching than buying time for a thought: "If I were a slightly sloshed harlot, where would I be?"

Julie and Melanie met each other's widened eyes, both knowing the answer to that question.

Melanie spoke first: "How many bedrooms do you think this place has?"

THEY EDGED OUT of the dining room toward a sweeping staircase that rose out of the front hall. Guests dotted this less populated orbit of the party but climbing up those steps would leave them exposed. *Even Heather's not that shameless a party guest,* Melanie realized. "Is there a back way?" she asked Julie.

"A servants' entrance? There has to be, there are enough servants."

They reversed course, threading their way through other guests. Melanie noticed that for once, Julie was barely bothering to acknowledge people, much less say hello. She wondered if that in and of itself was too conspicuous.

Melanie heard someone say, "Oh, he's *definitely* one of the ones who's sleeping with her. You can tell from the blog," but she couldn't quite make out whose voice it was.

As they approached the kitchen, Julie stopped in front of a doorway and put her back to it. "Pretend you're talking to me."

"I am talking to you."

"Yes, well, pretend you're talking to me while I pretend I'm not seeing if this door is unlocked."

They were in a smaller hallway that continued off the main entrance and had entrances to the dining room and kitchen. The door Julie was trying faced the kitchen entrance. People walked through, probably looking for the bathroom, but it was a little too narrow for conversation.

Julie's hands fiddled with the knob behind her back and the door cracked. She smiled. The hall was mostly empty. They both ducked inside.

A narrow staircase rose at a sharp angle. Melanie's stilletos—a very pointed toe, a very high heel—were precarious on the shallow steps. "People were supposed to carry dishes up and down these things?"

Julie's back bobbed as she jogged up the steps. "Bring it up with OSHA." She was nearly to the top. Melanie hurried to catch up. As Julie reached the head of the stairs, she said over her shoulder, "You go left. I'll go right."

She turned. Melanie headed to the left. The hall was dimly lit but fairly wide. Two women wearing matching simple cotton dresses and aprons were leaning up against the wall, speaking Spanish—Melanie recognized them as the ones who had stood ready to take coats in case anyone at the party had somehow stepped into the August heat wearing one.

They stopped as Melanie approached and looked at her with slight confusion in their eyes. The slightly shorter and older one spoke first: "Coat?"

"No, uhm, no coat." She was unsure of how to proceed. She felt self-conscious about talking to the Bromptons' help. "Girl?" she asked, then immediately berated herself for it. *At least I didn't shout and make hand gestures,* she thought. Before she could stumble into her high-school Spanish, she noticed that the women's expressions had shifted slightly: Was that confusion in their eyes or amusement?

She pressed on: *"Chica?"* Then the younger of the two women started nodding, barely suppressing a giggle. *"Está allá,"* she said, pointing to a closed door a little farther down the hall. *"Con los otros."*

Melanie spun around and headed toward the room, barely processing what the woman had said. *Others?*

SHE TRIED TO OPEN the door but something was blocking it. Someone, actually: "Hey! Watch it!" a man's voice said on the other side. Through the crack in the door she saw the room was dark; a suited arm rose and flicked a switch.

There was a pause. Then quickly "Hey!" in a different male voice. And then "Hey" in yet a different male voice. The arm reversed its movements, and the body it was attached to pushed the door shut. Melanie heard a scrambling on the other side, the sound of another door opening and slamming, and a distinctive giggle. Just as she opened the door to the bedroom again, there was a blur of movement at the other end of the hall. They saw the backs of three men as they peeled around a corner and out of sight.

Julie jogged toward Melanie from her end of the hall: "What the fuck was that?"

"Leftovers?" Melanie suggested.

"Did you see who they were?"

"I saw a seersucker suit. . . ."

"Let's hope that just means they're all the rage," Julie replied, still looking in the direction the suits had fled. "I'm sure they were all just looking for the bathroom."

. . .

THEY WENT IN.

Heather perched cross-legged on a big four-poster bed made with white and peach linens. Her clothes were on, thank God, and she smiled at them sweetly: "Hey."

"Having a little after party of your own?" Julie ventured. "I think you need to work on the guest list a little more thoroughly. Usually, you can count on some no-shows, but in your case . . ."

Heather laughed outright at that. "It was just a little mix-up," she said.

"Ah," Melanie said. "What part of 'yes' didn't they understand?"

Heather shook her head. "That's not it. I just said I was going upstairs to lie down for a bit." She smiled. "I mean, I guess I expected *some* company . . ."

". . . But not a bridge game," Julie finished.

"Bridge?" Heather's eyebrows knitted.

"Never mind." Julie crossed her arms, looking so authoritative that Melanie wondered if Heather was going to get grounded.

Julie shook her head. It wasn't really a shake but more of a single whiplash swipe, a sharp gesture that Melanie didn't see that often. It cut off debate when there was debate and signaled some kind of unpleasant change of conversational direction. *Her kids are going to be so fucked,* Melanie thought.

Melanie ventured a thought before Julie's anger threatened to upset Heather and ruin everything. "I have to say, Heather, I'm impressed," she began. *When in doubt about what to say, stick as close to the truth as possible.* Hal Prentiss had taught her that. She continued: "Reporters leaving a room where there's free food and drink usually means there's a bombing or a missing child in Idaho or at least a hurricane."

Julie harrumphed. "Oh, there's a natural disaster happening."

Heather flicked her eyes at Julie. The glint in them could be anger or amusement. "I don't see what the problem is." She looked back to Melanie. "After all, no one got caught."

Well, thought Melanie, *that is basically the same as being innocent in Washington.*

Julie interrupted: "Who, exactly, didn't get caught?"

Heather opened her mouth to reply but Melanie cleared her throat conspicuously and raised her eyebrows at Julie.

Julie sighed. "Or maybe it's best not to know." Her shoulders relaxed and she uncrossed her arms. With a deep breath, she smiled. Melanie wondered if Julie had made an executive decision to smile. "On the bright side," Julie said, "I doubt if anyone downstairs is talking about the Clearheads."

"You know, you've never explained who these 'Clearheads' are," Heather said, jumping lightly down off the bed. "Aren't they touring with Coldplay?"

"Not quite," Melanie, answered. "But they might be handing out leaflets in the parking lot."

Heather looked at Melanie doubtfully, then wrinkled her nose with a grin. "I'll see you both downstairs?"

"It's probably best if we don't all leave together," Julie decided, opening the door for Heather. "You go ahead. You'll go home, right?"

"Sure," Heather replied, then winked.

"Heather." Julie's voice made the room temperature go down a notch.

"Oh, please," Heather replied, rolling her eyes. "I'll never break curfew again, Mom." She sashayed away.

Julie closed the door again.

"You trust her to just leave?" Melanie asked.

"Sometimes you have to give a child responsibility in order for them to take responsibility."

"You've been watching Dr. Phil again, haven't you?"

"I just taped that one mental health care coverage hearing on C-SPAN and suddenly my TiVo thinks I care."

"Yes, I know better."

Julie smiled, a genuine smile this time, and Melanie could feel herself relax a little bit, too. She continued: "You know, they say any landing you can walk away from . . ."

"Oh, let's not assume we're able to walk just yet. We still need to inspect for damage. I hope to Christ whatever horny bastards who were up here knew enough to zip their flies and their lips before crashing into the crowd downstairs."

"I think we'll be fine. Everyone seemed pretty lit when we were down there earlier," Melanie said.

"Listen to you: 'lit.' I'm totally stealing that."

"I'm trying to bring it back. Also, I think 'tight' should come back into circulation. The fifties were a good era for drug and alcohol slang."

"Weed should be called 'grass.' "

"I've always liked 'tea.' "

"We could write a memo."

"We're delaying, aren't we?" Melanie asked.

"I think so."

They were quiet for a moment, then Melanie opened the door and Julie followed her downstairs.

THE PARTY WAS as they had left it, though perhaps a little less crowded. Female cable correspondents, reed-thin in their boldly colored suits, swayed slightly in their small groups, like underwater grass. They, in turn, had been set upon by burly pundits, more red-faced than usual but talking just as loud as ever. *Blowfish*, Melanie thought.

There was no sign of commotion, no disturbance in the Force. Melanie turned to Julie and shrugged. Julie seemed more skeptical: "It's not like us to be lucky," she said.

"I know," replied Melanie. "But do we really want to investigate further?"

"I suppose you're right. I could have sworn I saw . . ."

Melanie looked at her inquiringly. "I could finish that sentence myself but I don't think I should. Whatever group-grope was about to happen, didn't, after all. And, to be honest? I actually buy her excuse. She got careless with her innuendo and three guys thought it was an invitation. It may not happen to all of us, but Heather isn't all of us."

"You're right." Julie looked around one more time. "You're right."

Emily approached them from the side, a little glassy-eyed herself. "And where have you two been?" she asked. "Doing something Democratic with each other?"

"Au contraire, we were casing the joint, just like good GOP girls would," Julie answered. "Your collection of inaugural shot glasses should fetch a pretty penny on eBay."

Emily laughed.

"Especially if Hillman wins," Melanie added.

Emily laughed louder. "Oh, stop. You're killing me." She wiped her eyes.

Julie was disdainful but amused. "Drrr-unk," she whispered to Melanie. Melanie knew that Emily was kidding, playing out the partisan divide as burlesque. But as she thought about the scene upstairs and the heart-racing panic it induced that had only just now started to subside, anger tugged at her. All they were doing, all they were risking . . . it had to be about more than just showing each other up at cocktail parties. There was something at stake besides ego and earning potential. *Of course there was, of course there was,* she reminded herself. *The fate of the free world, right?*

"Thanks for the party," Melanie told Emily, with polite and cheerful insincerity that made her wince even as she said it. As Julie said her good-byes—always more intricate than her own—Melanie tapped Julie on the shoulder and gestured that she'd meet her outside.

She walked toward the door, automatically glancing into her purse for the reassurance that she had her tools—her phone, her Berry, her wallet. In the alcove in the living room, the waiters were finally dismantling the bar, empty bottles turned upside down in cases, glasses racked. Without its heavy white tablecloth, the bare card table they had served from looked out of place and lonely.

It was warm and damp out. Melanie waited for Julie as Emily's guests dribbled out. Men steadied their dates, wives drew up beside their husbands watchfully. *Wives,* Melanie thought with a pang. *People have wives.* The idea that she might someday be a wife wasn't quite real to her, and the more she saw of Washington's social structure, the less certain she was she wanted to be one.

You could be a husband and still be "the wife"—it just meant you didn't swim in the same water and breathe the same close air. Invisible, ignored, condescended to, and worked around. Washington was not a place that's kind to people who can't be cutthroat. A lot of wives—and male wives—just opted out, skipped the everyday cocktails and most of the events. Why be ignored when you could be doing something else? *That was,* Melanie thought guiltily, *Kathy's approach.*

For a long time, she had even assumed Rick was single. He didn't talk about his wife, and she was never around. *Of course, he just acted single.*

JULIE SHOWED UP at her arm. "It's always an obstacle course to get out of there," she said, searching her purse for the valet ticket. "Emily won't take yes—or no—for an answer."

"About what?"

"About anything," Julie said, giving the valet ticket to a uniformed man.

"God, this is complicated."

The Jetta came around and Julie put a packet of folded ones into the valet's hand.

Sunday, August 22

THE LUXURY OF mid-afternoon assignations in mostly anonymous hotel rooms, takeout from restaurants that normally didn't do takeout (Rick would call and somehow cajole a carefully wrapped goat cheese and leek tart or porterhouse for two out of the manager)— one could get used to that life, and sometimes Melanie worried that she had. She'd had expense accounts before, and she knew the lines that separated sources from colleagues from clients from recruits only became clear when the Federal Election Commission was looking, but it still amazed her how much fun could be had on someone else's dime.

To be fair, the campaign didn't spend that way. Melanie was perpetually on someone else's tab—if not Rick's, then Julie's, if not Julie's, then Prentiss's, if not Prentiss's, then the guy from Bloomberg or someone from the *Washington Post* or even Emily and Hugh if they were around (and, mysteriously, they usually were).

There was always confusion at the end of the night—a round of plastic would get thrown on the table and start a round of minor and mostly good-natured squabbles over who had paid last time, but the people who paid were the people who could: consultants, television folk, newsmagazine types. Newspaper reporters and campaign staff were charity cases. It was Washington's one true socialist system.

Heather had upended that. She was a charity case, too, Melanie supposed. She and Julie certainly couldn't afford to bankroll her by themselves. But she somehow drew out the charity from the uncharitable—people who couldn't afford to buy her drinks bought her dinner and people who couldn't afford to buy her dinner wanted to pay for hotel rooms, dresses, teeth whitening, or college tuition.

That last one would be a nice touch, Melanie thought: the kind of magnanimous gesture that could not possibly be taken up. It was a classic Washington move, and Melanie suspected that it was the real reason why everyone seemed to know newspaper and magazine publication schedules and television taping times by heart: invitations could be timed for maximum chance of their not being accepted. Because while it was easy to pay for someone else's meal, sometimes the company wasn't quite worth it.

And maybe this was why people seemed to like Heather so much. Most relationships in Washington were transactional, but

Heather's transactions weren't under the table. *Well*, Melanie thought, *only literally*.

When Melanie and Julie had invented Capitolette, they had decided to make her frankness a running joke. Had they realized that people like that really did exist? Heather was conniving in her own way, but she was also without guile.

Heather called Melanie at one in the morning while Melanie was watching a TiVo'd version of the morning's episode of Rick's show. She paused the show and slumped back against the couch. "Heather?"

"Yeah, yes. I mean, of course. I mean, sure."

"What are you up to?"

"Ohhhh . . . nothing."

"Just shooting the shit, huh?"

"Well, no."

Melanie could feel someone else in the cab. Melanie could hear wind in the receiver. She assumed Heather was in a cab. She asked, "Headed home?"

Slight pause. "Well, no." Was there a smile in Heather's tone?

Melanie closed her eyes. It wasn't that she didn't trust Heather. Heather's lack of shame made her more honest than most people in Washington—she had no reputation to protect, just one to live up to. But within the narrow scope of what Julie and Melanie needed her for, she had discovered a kind of latitude—or depth, depending on how you looked at it—that the two hadn't been able to predict.

"What are you doing? Or what are you thinking of doing?" Melanie asked, trying to keep the exhaustion out of her voice.

"You said before that you didn't want me to actually fuck any of these people."

Melanie still had a hard time believing that Heather found that many people in D.C. she *wanted* to fuck. Maybe it was just her way of killing time. She was going to have to take up knitting: "That is correct."

"How long is that going to last?"

"Well, at least through the night."

Heather sighed. "Yeah, I know. But one of the guys from that party you dragged me to—I thought he was probably harmless . . . I gave him my number. . . ."

"Your raging libido, while definitely impressive, needs to be harnessed for good and not evil."

"You both keep saying stuff like that," Heather pouted. Melanie felt like she was denying her the family car. Heather continued: "But, Jesus. It's just fucking."

Could someone really have lived through Monica and still think that there was such a thing as "just fucking" in Washington? Maybe people "just fuck" in New York or Los Angeles or Kalamazoo, but in Washington people enter into strategic relationships or they sign nondisclosure agreements or at the very least they pretend to forget it ever happened. Melanie remembered a months-ago drunken fumble in the bed of an eager lobbyist. A Republican, no less. She shuddered. They were at the same parties all the time; both of them just smiled and said hi and shook hands. Sometimes a bad memory was as important as a good one.

"I'm sure with you, there's no such thing as 'just fucking.'" Melanie offered ice cream to soothe the loss of the family car.

Heather giggled. "Wouldn't you like to know . . ."

Melanie now suspected that Heather was an actual, clinically diagnosable nymphomaniac. She would be impressed at her determination if she weren't so tired and not quite convinced that Heather wouldn't sneak the family car out for a joyride as soon she got off the phone.

"Do me a favor, Heather?" Melanie aimed for a tone that was less parental. "Just go to bed."

A giggle. *Who knew a dirty mind could be so active?*

Melanie pushed on: "Your own bed. Really. I know it's tough. You're used to having more fun than this."

"Oh, I'm having fun. I'm just used to getting a little more out of it."

Melanie's mind flashed to Capitolette's e-mail inbox, still full to bursting with offers both legitimate and shady, though none particularly lucrative. Not yet. She thought Heather would probably get a lot out of this, indeed. *And if she can keep her pants on, we could all get nationalized health care.*

But Heather's mind, while concerned with physical well-being, was not at all focused on a Hillman-Langley victory: "Is there such a thing as 'blue balls' for girls?"

"Perhaps. But there are home remedies. Do-it-yourself projects." The gutter was a hard place for a mind to get out of, especially when talking to Heather. Melanie remembered, with a twinge of shame, that the banter she was pretending not to enjoy at the moment was, in fact, what she and Julie did best. And it was how and why they had created Capitolette.

She heard laughter on the other end of the line, and a murmured instruction to the driver to head to a different address on Capitol Hill. Melanie's jaw relaxed. She hadn't realized she'd been clenching it. She wondered if Heather would tell her whose house she had been headed to when the conversation started. She wondered if she really wanted to know.

"So is DIY gonna do it for tonight?"

Heather was quiet for a bit. Melanie could hear the wind in the receiver again, then the crush and squeak of breaks. "Hello?"

"I'm still here," Heather said. "I was just thinking."

Wonders never cease, Melanie thought, then immediately felt bad. "About?" she asked.

"It would really fuck you—I mean, you know, screw you," Heather laughed. "I mean, it would cause a real problem if I didn't listen, wouldn't it?"

Melanie batted back the instinct to just say "yes." Admitting weakness was the first step to defeat. Or would Heather be swayed by a sympathetic appeal? Could she win an expectations game? Campaign clichés tumbled through her brain before she could even think whether Heather represented the opposition party or a renegade wing. Was she Golden or Zell Miller? A sigh built up inside her but she held that back, too.

"Good night, Heather."

"Good morning, you mean."

"Let's hope."

14

Monday, August 23

To: PRESS.RELEASE@lists.whitehouse.gov

From: PRESS.RELEASE@lists.whitehouse.gov

Sent: Mon Aug 23 18:20:15

Subject: POOL REPORT #3, 8/23

Pool report 3

Aug 23

President Golden—who your pooler has observed clearing approximately a jillion acres of brush on his ranch in Arizona—today participated in ceremonial tree-planting at a middle school in Boynton Beach, Florida. He was accompanied by Ag Secretary Jerry Miller and Rachel Squall, the principal of Christa McAuliffe Middle School—your pooler has learned that the school is a polling place come election day, that Florida is apparently an important swing state. Your pooler believes in coincidences.

At the tarmac departing Boynton, the presidential dogs were on hand. One seemed to have the president's attention as he was asked questions by the pool. Here is a transcript of that exchange:

Q: "What do you think of the initial reaction to your Social Security plan?"

POTUS: "C'mon, Sally."

Q: "How much should gas be, since you are calling for it to be affordable and you want it to come down?"

POTUS: "C'mon, Sal."

Q: "Are you concerned about the protests that are planned for during the Republication Convention?"

POTUS: "Don't be a bitch, girl."

Your pooler assumes the president was addressing his pet. After straggling and sniffing suspicious wet spots on the pavement, "Sal" eventually heeded and trundled up the steps to AF1.

Kendra Herman, Cox Newspapers

MELANIE CAME IN at five, which felt so early she couldn't quite believe herself. But the Golden convention loomed large and close, a pretty, bunting-festooned façade that covered a massive artillery store. And work had to be done before he rode the Clearheads to a convention bounce very different from her own.

She had spent the last few days in a blur of videotape and blogs, trying to promulgate negative stories about the Clearheads and keeping her eye on Golden's increasingly amusing ad-libbing. Actual campaign work was punctuated by missives from Julie about Heather's progress through the Washington media food chain. After the Brompton party and her turn on America Now, the real shows had come calling—crumb-picking early afternoon financial shows, late-night shouting head fests, morning shock jocks. Julie did a good job of weeding out the setups, and Heather followed the script just enough that Melanie was able to sleep.

She could almost pretend it was all normal.

At seven, the real staff started to come in. Someone had brought Cinnabons. Someone always did. The sickly sweet smell would forever make Melanie think of two things: airports and meetings.

She grabbed one and balanced it on her stack of newspapers and notebooks.

"These poll numbers are crap," Skoloff announced, taking her seat at the head of the table. "I haven't had whiplash like this since Ted Kennedy in eighty."

Melanie glanced up from the USA Today she had folded to fit in her notebook, like a teenager sneaking Playboy into The Sun Also Rises. The meetings were increasingly useless and, well, simply increasing. Melanie sat shoulder to shoulder with one of the interchangeable interns (they were all named Ashley or Brandon or Joshua). She looked at the notes he was writing with a "Hillman-Langley" pen into his "Hillman-Langley" pad of paper: "Polls crap → whiplash. (Kennedy?)"

The best and the brightest, thought Melanie. Though, to be fair, she had once been clueless and intimidated, too. Sometimes she still was. But at least I don't wear my campaign swag to the campaign. Very gauche. Like wearing the band's T-shirt to the concert. Everyone already knows you're a fan.

The room was crowded with junior staff, their young faces drawn into serious, thoughtful expressions that seemed a little too rehearsed to Melanie, like the facial equivalent of playing dress-up. They wore expressions they had stolen from actors on The West Wing. Skoloff continued: "We're seesawing and taking one step forward and two steps back because Golden has gone so completely negative. It turns people off but it also makes them pay attention."

Melanie had already heard all of this on the senior senior staff meeting conference call.

The more restrictions Skoloff put on the war room, the more likely it became that there were people sitting on the floor at other meetings. What comfort people got from these meetings, Melanie would never figure out. Perhaps it was just the way that strangers huddled at the scene of car accidents or dogs piled on top of one another for warmth. The stress made the war room's faint Pandora's box (or was that Bluebeard's dungeon?) aroma even more tempting—the less you knew about what was going on in there, the more you believed it must contain the kind of brilliant strategies that would save the campaign. In reality, the war room hatched the same kinds of strategies as any other meeting. They just cost more.

Melanie remembered a meeting from the week before, when in the middle of a discussion about Hillman's health care platform, she had noticed someone sitting quietly in the corner, a *Wall Street Journal* held in front of his face. It was a clumsy, Inspector Clouseau–style attempt at espionage and, of course, it was one of her interns. *So much for dirty tricks,* Melanie thought.

Skoloff continued to lecture on how the polls did not actually say what they appeared to be saying. "If you'll look at the delta in the 'trust with the future of our country,' you'll see the actual change is very small. . . ." Skoloff took a drag off her cigarette; Melanie noticed the Marc Jacobs–purse-carrying intern (Charlotte? Charlize? She wished the interns would wear name tags) look as though she were about to cough in a very directed, you-realize-this-is-a-nonsmoking-workplace way. Marc Jacobs Girl thought better of it and swallowed the cough, turning light green in the process. Skoloff appeared not to notice. "The delta is very fucking small indeed."

Melanie glanced to her seatmate's notes: "delta = fucking

small." She suppressed an urge to roll her eyes and turned back to her paper, confident that the steno pool's notes would catch her up if Skoloff called on her.

She scanned the front page of *USA Today*. Its crayon-colored Dick-and-Jane approach to stories was easy to mock, but it was the Official Newspaper of Flyover Country, a good snapshot of what the rest of the country is thinking or at least a snapshot of what people who care about what the rest of the country is thinking think the rest of the country is thinking.

The lead story focused on the sorry job prospects for recently graduated college students—"for many, this first summer of their adult lives was spent learning adult disappointments." Predictably, the article veered into the job-growth plans the two campaigns had put out, or, rather, the sound bites describing those policies (Hillman: "Let the government give a helping hand to the future" versus Golden: "Young people graduate from college and join the 'bootstrap society'"). "Bootstrap society," Melanie hated to admit, was brilliant. It made cutting student loan programs sound like a favor.

Skoloff, meanwhile, was holding forth on the campaign's next move. They needed to both make a point about the opposition and "capture the public's imagination." *Well, at least they were learning something from the Clearheads,* Melanie thought.

Someone in the back of the room asked if that meant they'd finally make use of having the Hobbit actor's endorsement.

Skoloff's cigarette dangled out of her mouth as she gestured impatiently: "They have these tinfoil hats they wear, right? So we need something. Remember how the giant chicken followed H. W. Bush around when he wouldn't debate Clinton?"

The troops' expressions of earnest concentration faded for a moment into blankness. Skoloff took out her cigarette and ground it into the floor. "Christ," she half-muttered, "of course you don't. You were watching *Sesame Street* at the time."

Chuck—Melanie hadn't noticed he was there—raised his hand in the back of the room and drawled, "Actually, Karen, it was *Care Bears.*"

A few careful titters ruffled the edges of the crowd. He smacked his gum and grinned. Melanie caught his eye and he winked at her. He continued: "What about if we get someone to follow Golden around dressed as a giant cock?"

Skoloff looked at him quizzically: "Like a rooster?"

"Like a big dick," Chuck said calmly, "because he is one."

Half the room burst into laughter, the other half tried to decide if they were offended. Skoloff smirked. The giggles faded quickly. Skoloff's voice oozed with mock pleasantness: "That's a terrific idea, Chuck, but I don't think the campaign can spare you."

Chuck continued to grin, but he tipped his head a little in recognition of Skoloff's slap.

Skoloff drew herself up and said appreciatively, "Still, way to think outside the box."

Chuck stage-whispered: "As it were."

Titters again, but the exchange had done something to loosen the sludgy thickness of everyone's desire to *help,* where concern about having the right idea to save everything made any legitimately new idea impossible to formulate.

MELANIE PUT THE PAPER under the table and cleared her throat to cover up the rustling of its pages. She hoped the cough did not sound accusatory.

Bringing the paper back up into her lap, Melanie glanced over the op-eds. *Oh, my,* she thought. *Oh fucking my.*

THE MODERN RULES OF SKANKETTE
by Marilyn Talcum

Once upon a time, there was decorum in the nation's Capitol. Women wore gloves, men wore hats, and the way you got ahead was to work hard and play by the rules. Today, there are new rules: If long ago men showed their favor to young ladies by opening the door for them, now they open their flies. And young women? The ability to take dictation is not as prized as the ability to give a blow job.

Which nation could she possibly be talking about? Melanie thought. *Must look into consulting gigs there.* But her automatic sarcasm couldn't stop the tickle of excitement that ran down her spine. She read on:

It probably started with Monica, the intern who taught a generation that public service could be performed on one's back. But these rules have a new paragon and her name is "Capitolette." Actually, her real name is Heather Mason. "Capitolette" sounds more glamorous, so it's no wonder she adopted it. Considering the shame she's brought to her family name, if I were one of her parents, I'd suggest she start using it permanently.

Usually, the weather in Washington during August is hot, not the news. This year, however, Capitolette has come to town. A self-professed "slut," the strumpet made a trumpet of an Internet "Web log," turning that massive government-supported "information superhighway" into a dirty diary, detailing her alleged liaisons with staffers for an unnamed presidential campaign (I wonder which one, don't you?), journalists (somehow not a surprise), and other denizens of the District (in case she left anyone out). Somehow I don't think Al Gore had this in mind when he invented the Internet.

And, of course, Washington loves her. She's been feted by a Georgetown hostess, embraced by cable television, and is adored by the *Washington Post,* which ran an unquestioning interview with her—lobbing softballs and cooing compliments in a way that stands in stark contrast with how the official newspaper of the liberal establishment treats the president of the United States.

How is Capitolette different from your average, run-of-the-mill skank, the kind of girl who'd meet the entire football team in the parking lot or flash fishnets at the prom? For one thing, those girls were just whispered about, their exploits were the subject of speculation. We don't have to wonder what Capitolette has done: She's told us. It's the difference between having a reputation and having a résumé.

Capitolette's résumé hasn't gotten her a job. . . . Not yet. Right now, her prospects are somewhat limited. Washington may be populated by liberals, but Jim Golden still runs the country, and I believe his example of candor and courage and decency will keep Capitolette out of the bookstores and off the magazine covers. But for Capitolette, a Hillman administration would be a full employment plan.

Melanie fumbled her Berry out of her bag, dropped it. The LED light blinked urgently and she had seventy new messages. She looked around. No one seemed to notice her clumsiness; the room's palette of young faces projected tense concentration onto the white board. In the time that Melanie had been poring over the Talcum column, they had added four possibilities to the list of "anti-mascots" who might tail Golden:

- chicken
- hawk
- chicken hawk
- pirate

Pirate?

"I don't think we can get Goofy," Skoloff was saying. "Copyright issues. But . . ." and here you could hear the strain in her voice as she swallowed whatever barb she might have usually flicked at an inept idea. "But," she continued, "I'll write it down anyway." There was a certain slope in Skoloff's shoulders that said more than the current poll numbers did, and it made Melanie's own sense of possibility seem all the more bright.

She had to get out of this room.

Stuffing her paper and notebook into her bag, she resisted the urge to check the Berry right now. She shuffled back her chair, smiling apologetically to her seatmates. Walking out the door, she noticed Skoloff's face pinch into a quick glare at her. And for once she didn't care.

"WHAT'S *USA TODAY*'S circ again?" Melanie asked.

"What?" Julie's voice crackled over the line.

"Circ for *USAT*," Melanie said, looking around the office's ladies' room and trying to deduce the area of least cell phone interference.

"Ah, you saw the Talcum piece," Julie said as Melanie pressed herself into the corner nearest a small, high window. "It's either two or three million, but of course it's not just the legion of horny business travelers we've broken out to—"

"It's flyover country—my people."

"You sound like you're at the bottom of a well."

"I'm in the ladies' room."

"The reception is shitty."

"At least I don't have to worry about Skoloff barging in."

"Yes, I heard she pees standing up."

"Right now she's pissing all over the interns."

"What else is new?"

"Actually, I should give her credit. She's trying to be nice to them."

"Things look that bad, huh?"

"Depends on your point of view," Melanie countered. "If you look at it through the candy-colored lenses of the nation's hometown paper . . ."

"Christ. I know. Have you checked the Capitolette inbox yet?"

"No, I came straight here from the meeting. You think Heather's checked it?"

"Unclear. I don't think so. I don't think she's up yet." Julie let out a low whistle. "It's very full."

"I bet. What are the headlines?"

Melanie listened to the series of soft clicks from Julie's keyboard.

"Hm," Julie said.

"Hm?"

"Well, there's a predictably sizable portion of 'you ought to be ashamed of yourself you jezebel harlot whore whatever.' There are also several publishers. A few agents. And, uhm . . . it may not be real, but there's at least one e-mail from someone at Larry Flynt publications."

"What do they want?"

"Pictures, of course."

"For personal use? Or business?"

"Is there a distinction?" asked Julie.

"Ha," Melanie exhaled. "What are we going to tell Heather?"

They were both quiet. Melanie could hear Julie's office waking up around her: the crisp click of heels on the wood floor, a whirr of computers starting up. Julie's voice dropped into the pause: "I can't stay on the phone much longer."

"Yeah, I have to get things done today, too."

"We could discuss over lunch."

"I have a lunch."

"Ah." Julie made it sound accusatory. Obviously she knew that "lunch" meant "Rick."

"Besides, I don't think we have that long. She's going to get up soon."

"We could delete the money stuff," Julie offered, her voice a little quieter than before. To Melanie, she sounded like the devil on her shoulder. *And is there an angel?* she wondered.

"No . . ." Melanie took a deep breath. "No, we should let her read it. She's been itching to get more out of this and it's about time she did."

"Think she'll give us ten percent?"

"I'm not sure if we're in a position to ask."

BY THE TIME she got back to the main office, the meeting had begun to break up. She glanced in at the white board and saw that a handful more mascot suggestions had been thrown out in her absence:

- octopus
- snake
- weasel
- really mean pirate

She tried to hurry past the door but Skoloff called her over.

Skoloff straightened the papers in front of her as though she might slap one of them for getting out of line. Melanie took deep breaths and tried not to think about the to-do list that was multiplying behind her eyes—the tasks both on the books and off the books, from feeding reporters a puff piece about the Hillman family to figuring out just how much of Heather the public was going to get to know. *Oh, and fuck: Rick.* An inward smirk: *Fuck Rick, indeed.* That was at one. Heather would be up by eleven or so—would that give her time to pitch the story about Hillman's daughter doing outreach in Watts?

Skoloff's sigh interrupted Melanie's thoughts: "I don't know where they grow them. They're eager to be here, sure, but they think they're auditioning for *West Wing,* not working on a real campaign." She blew out a thin stream of smoke, aiming halfheartedly at the cracked window ten feet away. *How thoughtful.* She continued: "Do you think They have the same problem on the other side?"

For all the strategizing and obsessing and planning done in this very room, it was strange to hear Skoloff refer to the other campaign so directly and even personally. Melanie thought of some of the younger, less familiar faces she had seen at the Brompton party. How were they different from the faces she saw every day here? She wanted to believe that maybe their clothes were more expensive, their haircuts more precise, their politics impenetrably conservative. And of course they played dirty. This thought reminded her: Could she get any more play out of the flat-earther president of Clearheads?

These thoughts spun quickly through her head. She was beginning to feel dizzy, actually. Maybe it was just the cigarette smoke. Or the coffee. Or the lack of sleep. She realized the pause in conversation was in danger of growing uncomfortably long.

"They probably don't have as many *West Wing* fans, it's true," she said. "And, you know, the skills you learn campaigning on behalf of the rainforest or debt relief or sweatshop workers maybe don't translate as smoothly to what we do. The conservatives have always been better than us at making activism like an election, and at making elections like activism."

"Elections like activism, activism like an election," Skoloff reflected. "Hm." She ashed her cigarette. "That's a nice bit, wish it meant something."

Skoloff's mosquito-bite insults didn't bother Melanie as much as they used to. That was one benefit of not being quite so invested in the job. In this aspect of the job. Everything she did was still working for the campaign, she reminded herself, it just wasn't all working for Skoloff. Still, she flinched a little.

Skoloff continued: "Anyway, with all these munchkins in need of leadership as much as an education in campaigning, maybe it's best not to dump a meeting just because it's not as important as, oh, I don't know . . . What was it, exactly, that was so important this morning?"

Melanie met her eyes squarely: *"The Post* is fishing for information about unrest in the campaign. I thought you might want me to bat that down."

Skoloff squinted. Melanie kept her eyes soft, her expression neutral. It wasn't exactly a lie: A thumb-sucker about disorganization/disquiet/lack of direction in the campaign was traditional about now, and Lord knows it would be true enough.

"You know," Skoloff said, "those stories would be less appealing if we had something to give them on Golden."

"Truuuue," Melanie said. Should she tell her about her Goldenisms idea? She decided to test the waters a little. "I've been thinking about his Goldenisms."

"Those aren't stories, they're punch lines," Skoloff sighed. "Besides, everyone thinks they're 'cute.' " Skoloff practically snarled.

"They're cute enough," Melanie continued, "but I've been watching them, looking for a pattern or something . . ."

"And?"

"Well, they do seem to increase when he's traveling. And when he's in a friendly atmosphere. It's like he doesn't worry as much so he just lets his mouth go."

"This helps us . . . how?"

Melanie sighed herself. She hadn't thought it out at all. Her mind was elsewhere. "I . . ."

Skoloff ashed her cigarette again though it didn't need it. It was like a gavel banging: "You can go," she said, and turned back to the white board. Melanie heard her mutter under her breath: "Where the fuck would we get a pirate uniform?"

Back at her desk, Melanie tried to concentrate on the pitch letter she was writing:

*Citizens for Clear Heads president and co-founder Craig
Donnelly:*

*Smearing a presidential candidate is just his first act. Don-
nelly's ultimate goal is the invention and marketing of an "anti-
psychic" shield device to schools and government agencies.*

*The holder of patent number 6,079,081, Donnelly says his
device would, as he has written, "protect those who need it the
most from the harmful mental pollution that permeates the
lower atmosphere, thanks to years of sexed-up prime-time television, filthy rap music, and the disappearance of Christian
morals from our classrooms."*

Melanie didn't know how much play the patent story would get.
The Clearheads campaign succeeded in part because its leadership
was so singularly unhinged. Their antics made good copy and their
allegations gave Hillman's better-established critics an easy, jokey
delivery system for more subtle smears.

Voters knew, or at least they thought they knew, that candidates
didn't think for themselves anymore. If, in Hillman's case, it was
mad scientists and not the education lobby pulling the puppet
strings, what difference did it make?

Melanie clicked over to the Capitolette inbox as if she were
checking scores. In part, she supposed, she was. There was another
wave of mail around ten, when all the various Washington news tip
sheets went out. Predictably, the backseat pundits were scrambling
all over one another to produce an opinion that didn't already
belong to someone else.

America Now's *Morning Juice* called the column "just what the Golden campaign needs to set the stage for a convention that will apparently focus on the 'growing moral divide' between real Americans and 'elites.'" *Hotline* tossed it into a wrap-up of "bloggers in the news," noting that "Capitolette's rising media profile, along with the Citizens for Clear Heads' successful strategy of releasing new ads and scoops directly to bloggers, suggests that small operations can bypass the mainstream media if their message is compelling enough." *Or if their tits are nice enough,* thought Melanie. *The Point* was priapically smug: "You know you've arrived when you get your first hit piece. You'll know where you've arrived when you roll over and see who's next to you," but Taylor couldn't resist trying to go big-picture as well:

> We hate to point it out, but the Gang of 500 can't keep pretending Capitolette is an apolitical or at least bipartisan (heh) event? She's good for someone's campaign, and Talcum's apPointing her as a figure in the culture wars hurts, but, arguably, there's only room for one freak show at a time. Have the Clearheads run their course?

Swamp Thing just excerpted the diatribe and put a new headline on it: 'She's so getting a book deal out of this.'

AN INSTANT MESSAGE from Julie opened.

WrigleyJules: I assume you saw the various hits from the morning reads.

Thortonology: yup

WrigleyJules: talked to her yet?

Thortonology: not yet. You?

WrigleyJules: no but I'm thinking we should be proactive

Thortonology: always

WrigleyJules: if she's going to flip this into a profitable enterprise, we can at least guide the process.

Thortonology: listen to you. You working up a white paper?

WrigleyJules: seriously: of all the things she's been offered, what works out best for us?

Melanie flipped back to the inbox. Publishing houses, book agents, movie agents, a line of clothing geared to the "trashy girl in all of us" . . .

Thortonology: I think we're forgetting something.

WrigleyJules: what?

Thortonology: She's not really capitolette.

WrigleyJules: what do you mean?

Thortonology: we MADE HER UP.

WrigleyJules: your point?

Thortonology: if she writes a book or sells her life story or, hell, if she goes on oprah, at some point it will occur to people to try and find at least one of the 50 or so anonymous leches she supposedly fucked.

WrigleyJules: You have far too much faith in American journalism. You work with those people, remember?

Thortonology: I just think it might strike some people as odd if they can turn up absolutely no one who has actually had sex with capitolette. Surely someone will notice

WrigleyJules: not if she doesn't have a shirt on

Thortonology: well I guess that narrows down the options as far as what deals you'd like her to make.

WrigleyJules: unless nightline is going topless, yeah

Thortonology: she got an offer from nightline?

WrigleyJules: they're a little desperate these days

Thortonology: aren't we all.

Melanie's BlackBerry buzzed before she could wrap up the conversation with Julie. It was Rick. The missive was to the point: "M St. Ritz. Order lunch when you get there."

Sort of brusque, even for a BlackBerry message, Melanie thought. She started making excuses for him: *Busy day, someone looking over his shoulder, feels so comfortable with me that there's no need to gussy up instructions.* . . . Then another message tumbled into the queue: "Looking forward to it, gorgeous."

She smiled, then a part of her wondered what he wanted.

BEFORE SHE COULD get back to Julie, a reporter called from *Newsweek*. He spent the absolute minimum on chitchat ("Hi," really) before rescuing Melanie from the lie she had just told Skoloff: "What's this I hear about Prentiss not showing up at meetings anymore?"

Somehow, she wasn't grateful.

She spent half an hour batting back his feelers and then lost herself in a blur of returning other messages and slogging through clips on Golden. She was closing up her desktop to leave and meet Rick when her cell phone rang.

"Hiya, it's Heather."

"Hey." Melanie slung her purse over her shoulder and continued the conversation as she walked out of the office.

"So who is this Talcum lady, anyway? People keep mentioning her in all these e-mails I got this morning."

"She's a thuggish prude. But we should probably write her a thank-you letter."

"Why?"

Melanie sighed. She wasn't ready to have this conversation. "Can I explain in a minute?"

Melanie snapped the phone shut. She pulled out her Black-Berry and tapped out a message as she threaded her way across the room.

To: Julie.Wrigley@clevelandparkgroup.com

From: ThortonM@hillman.com

Subj: the eagle has landed

She called. Did we come to a decision? Don't particularly want to steer her toward porn what about—

"Ooof!" Melanie was bounced backward a step by a sudden collision with Prentiss.

Prentiss's center of gravity was such that the impact did not rock him at all. Instead, he chuckled. "You okay, there, Mel?"

Actually, she had half-sat/half-fallen onto a desk corner, the point jabbed into the back of her thigh. The bruise was probably darkening as they spoke. So much for swimsuit season, she thought.

"I'm fine," she said, smiling tightly.

"You looking at new numbers or something?" He grinned. "Must be important. . . ." He stepped forward and cocked his head to look at the Berry.

A flash of panic made Melanie blink. She instinctively dropped her hand and pressed its screen against her leg. She tried to recover: "Sorry, Hal. Not sure how I could have missed you."

Prentiss rocked back on his heels and crossed his arms. "Not numbers, eh? What could possibly be more important? Love letter, perhaps?"

Melanie's eyes stayed level and her voice light: "Why spoil the surprise, handsome?"

His eyes twinkled. "I'm free after seven."

"I'll put it on my schedule." She made to move past him and as she did, he gave her a firm pat on the rear.

Anger rose in her throat, but then she thought about where she was headed. *Maybe he can smell it on me.* She wondered if this was how Heather got started. *Oh, shit: Heather.*

She pulled her cell out and dialed, turning out of the office to go down the stairs—the elevator blocked cell reception and the office was only slightly less public than Times Square.

Her shoes clicked down the steps and the phone rang on the other end of the line.

"Hello?"

"Hi, Heather, it's Melanie." She stopped on a landing and leaned back against the cool cinder block.

"So I was, like, actually *reading* the e-mails and you're so fucking right! This is so exciting! Where does this Talcum woman live? I definitely want to thank her—or at least get her to pose with me in *Penthouse.*"

"That would be a scoop indeed." Melanie remembered her unfinished Berry message to Julie. They hadn't settled the *Penthouse* question at all.

"I just can't believe this one bitch's column did this. I was on TV like a week ago! And look at these book deals. But then I'd have to write it, too, right? The *Penthouse* thing would be easy. I mean, you know, I *know* how to take off my clothes and look sexy . . ."

As Heather cataloged the possibilities, Melanie felt a pressure on her chest like someone had tightened a belt around it. *I should be excited, right? This will be great for the campaign, right? Fate of the free world . . .* She put her phone in the crook of her neck and resumed the message to Julie:

. . . Don't particularly want to steer her toward porn. What about Maxim or something? She's on the phone now . . . I'm just worried about, uhm, overexposure . . .

By the time Melanie's attention turned fully back to Heather, Heather was back to musing about a book: "I guess I would be using the blog, and there's already a lot written in that. You guys wouldn't mind, would you?"

"No," said Melanie. "I mean, no, wait, the blog . . . well . . ." Her mind raced as that belt tightened around her chest more. The blog had way too much in it that was, if not true, then at least gestured at truth. It couldn't be fact-checked, but it could get people in trouble. But how could they keep her from using it? Then it was obvious: "Heather, the blog is fiction."

"You're saying I can't use it?"

"I'm saying you can't say it's true. If, however, you wanted to market it as a novel . . ."

"Like a romance?"

Melanie smiled to herself. "You could call it that."

"Huh. But how much would you get paid for a novel?"

"I don't know. Maybe not as much as for a tell-all. But think about it, Heather: What, exactly, do you have to tell?"

"A lot, actually . . . I mean, unless you don't want me to put this part in the book."

"Touché."

"I'll think about it. I'm calling the *Penthouse* people, though."

"You really think that's a good idea?"

"Why not? I'm proud of my body. And they must like it, too."

"I just . . . this whole thing makes me nervous, Heather. If you really ride this out, people are going to start asking questions about where you came from and how come none of the men in the blog will come forward? And if anyone connects you to the campaign . . ."

"Guess you should have thought of that."

"What?"

"I'm not trying to be mean. It's just, it seems like you knew you were taking a risk. And hey, why not just bail on the campaign? You could write my book!"

Melanie sighed. "I can't bail on the campaign. It's important."

"What's important? The campaign? Seems like you care more about winning than you care about the campaign."

All the air left her chest for an instant. Maybe Capitolette's frankness wasn't an invention after all. But she'd thought about this before. Or, rather, Julie had. She used the line she'd heard from her: "That's only because the campaign doesn't matter if you don't win."

"Oooh-kay. Whatever. I am going to make some calls."

"Promise you'll at least let us know what you decide."

"Sure. Why not."

She's granting us favors, Melanie realized. They clicked off and Melanie straightened up from her slant against the wall. Air filled her lungs again and as she left the building to flag a cab, she repeated to herself, *Fate of the free world, fate of the free world, fate of the free world . . .*

The air felt thick as she stood outside waiting for a cab. When she had checked the *Post*'s Web page earlier, its real-time image of the city's skyline looked as though someone had smeared oil on the camera lens. "Code orange" air quality, indeed.

SHE WAS EARLY. She was always early when Rick got the hotel room the night before—it was a way of making up for the extravagance of having to let it stay empty all that time. But it was easier to get a late checkout than an early check-in and, for now, few of the finer hotels rented by the hour, even to a Washington power broker.

The M Street Ritz was boring and lush at the same time, like an overgrown condo complex with complicated bathroom fixtures. The first time she and Rick had met there, she had called building maintenance because there was no hot water. They came immediately; and as soon as the handsome and compact Guatemalan (Jorge, the name tag said) started his investigation of the problem, Melanie realized she had been turning the knob the wrong way.

She shooed him away as fast as she could over his polite protests, stuffing a five-dollar bill in his hand for his trouble and grateful that Rick had already left to do *Inside Politics* or *Capitol Report* or *Inside the Capitol Political Report* or whatever campaign porn he had been detailed to that day.

Today, she would gladly do without hot water.

The cool shower worked to rinse off the sweat and dust but it did nothing for the bad taste that the conversation with Heather had left in her mouth. Wrapped in a plush robe, she ordered room service—salads, it was too hot for anything else—and thought about calling Julie. Radio silence was unlike her. Julie clearly had a definite opinion about what direction the Capitolette brand-extension plan should take and it seemed to Melanie that she should be pushing it on her. Julie didn't give things up.

Rick would be there any minute, but Melanie tried Julie's office line anyway. It rang through to an assistant. "Would you like to leave a message?"

"No, no that's okay."

She walked to the window and looked at the pedestrians baking in the street.

Melanie had gained enough wisdom—*especially lately,* she thought—to write a how-to book on having an affair. She had learned the tricks of a covert carnal operator, and part of her was as proud of this newfound skill as she was of memorizing the names and faces of each senator before she came to town. She knew which hotels in Washington would guarantee a noon check-in, what restaurants had separate entrances to the garage, and how many pairs of underwear she could fit into the side pocket in her purse intended for a cell phone.

It was not as easy as it looked and required a sometimes draining amount of organizational skill and forward thinking. Having an affair was like having a second job, Melanie thought, but the benefits made it worthwhile.

Or did they? She thought about her acid stomach and tight chest. Then a soft knock at the door made her smile. She was exhausted, but she had Rick.

HIS POST-TAPING high made him buzzy and kinetic. He was talking fast through his grin: "Did you catch it? Was on with some guy from the *Washington Times*—I guess that's their idea of balance. Turned out okay, though. He was saying the poll numbers are showing Golden losing it because of the economy, but Jesus those numbers are old . . . and anyway, the dog and pony show in New York is going to avoid the economy issue like it was a gay hooker. They're pitching the whole show around *values* and *integrity*, which I guess they can win with, especially if Hillman is still sinking under the weight of tinfoil hats. . . ." He paced as he talked, undoing his tie and throwing his jacket over a chair.

Melanie sat on the bed and raised an eyebrow at him. Rick smiled.

"Sorry, babe. I mean, you're working wonders with what you have over there. And this values thing is really tired. I almost don't even want to file on it."

"I find that hard to believe," Melanie said. She stuck her leg out, corralling his pacing with her calf. "But maybe you want to talk about something else for a while? Or maybe talk about something else without talking . . ."

He unbuttoned his shirt. "Maybe we could use body language?" he suggested.

Melanie pulled him toward her by his belt: "Now you're talking."

He pushed her robe apart and kissed her neck. It was still damp and cool from her shower, and so his lips and breath felt hot, a post-card from the weather outside. On his cheek she could smell baby powder and rubbing alcohol layered over the loamy mineral-oil scent of makeup not quite removed. She closed her eyes as he pushed her back, aware of her wet hair on the back of her own neck, aware of the goose bumps rising on her arms and breasts in response to either the air conditioner or the relief and thrill of Rick's attention. His hands ran down her sides, lips traced her collarbone. She could smell his shampoo now—its spiciness (pepper and orange and cinnamon) expensively subtle. *Frédéric Fekkai for Men,* she remembered, and a small laugh escaped her. *Never trust a man whose hair products are more expensive than yours.*

"Ticklish girl," he said, looking up at her from her belly. His hair hung in front of his eyes boyishly.

"Yeah," she said. "But I know you're ticklish, too."

She put her hands inside his shirt and started to brush at his ribs. He wriggled and made a protesting yelp; then he grabbed her hands and pushed them over her head in a pose of mock surrender. Or not so mock. "Not right now, okay?" he said, a little sternly.

Melanie blinked. "Sure, honey," she said. She tried to strike a tone both comforting and firm.

He smiled apologetically: "Guess I'm a little sensitive today."

"Well," said Melanie, "that's not necessarily a bad thing."

"No, no, it's not." He shook his head, clearing it. They looked at each other and Melanie tried to find the glint of mischief she was used to. *We're all under pressure,* she thought. *Of course we are.*

He leaned down to kiss her, his tongue slipped around the edges of her teeth and one smooth hand reached down to open her legs. Her worry melted.

SHE FROWNED at Rick's back. It was pale and slightly pockmarked and shook with a soft snore. But Melanie's head buzzed; her mind flitted from a worry to a task to a memory and occasionally to a new thought. Lying beside Rick, she tried to still herself. This is an oasis, she thought. The curtains drawn against the hot bright day, the air-conditioning set to "stun," the room's purposefully bland décor: They were in a space capsule, a desert island, a Martian colony, Minnesota. She glanced at the bedside clock: She probably had another half hour, which meant showering in ten minutes or so. And with those ten minutes . . . She made her breaths deep and regular, looked at Rick's freckled and dented back, and began to softly trace the paths between the marks with a whisper-light touch. Walking down Eighteenth Street on her way to the Metro, Melanie had seen tourists and congregants walking in the labyrinth outside St. Thomas Parish. Eyes downcast and moving with deliberate slowness, they looked as though they had all simultaneously lost their contact lenses. But now she understood.

And this dot, to this scar, to this freckle, to this mole . . . Rick stirred and Melanie pulled her hand away.

"Mmmm, no," he mumbled. "Don't stop. That's nice."

Melanie smiled and went back to the task. After the interruption, though, it was not quite as meditative. She started wondering if her touch was too light or too hard and if she was getting the left more than the right. She shook her head against these thoughts and her focus shifted to the campaign. *Sigh. Might as well take advantage* . . .

"Hey, Rick . . . You were saying about the values message? I think I interrupted you. . . ."

"Hm? Ah, yes." His voice was still somewhat sleepy. But his back straightened under her fingers. She felt and heard him take a deep breath. "Values. That's Golden's theme for the convention, as you know. But it's boring. I'm supposed to do a big pseudo-sociological walk-up to the election and we can't just keep pretending to worship at the altar of David Brooks with these color-by-numbers— literally—thumb-suckers on Red/Blue. I have an idea, though."

"You have more than one, I'm sure."

Rick turned over so that he faced Melanie.

"I have many ideas about what to do to you, beautiful," he said, and here he put a hand on her naked hip and drummed his fingers.

"We'll get to those later." He pulled his hand back and propped himself up on his elbow. And gestured with a sweeping arm: "Values. What if we're at a turning point when it comes to values? Golden's pushing Mom, flag, apple pie, pickup trucks, and mortgages—there's a whole generation of young people who live a life based on absentee parents and McDonald's vegetarianism, credit card debt and one-night hookups. They're entering the professional class now, and their mores and norms will define the new middle class. Playing by the rules used to mean keeping your nose clean and playing fair. *What if the rules have changed?*"

He glanced back at her and wriggled his eyebrows. Melanie half-expected him to say "ta-da."

"That sounds familiar," she said, sitting up and facing him, her arms crossed over her chest. Her heart seemed to beat sideways. Rick was in mid-rant, though, and he hardly seemed to notice she'd changed position. His eyes were set on the middle distance. She realized she was holding her breath.

"Well, yes. That Talcum woman's column this morning. But hear me out: She's onto something, she just didn't blow it out big enough. This is about more than Capitolette. this is about how the old appeals don't land on the same ears anymore. Politics used to be about avoiding scandal. Now scandal is an entry point. It's a publicity stunt."

Melanie could barely hear Rick over the sound of blood rushing in her ears.

"The Clearheads fit into this, too, actually. People know they're full of shit—for the most part—but it's engaging and it's fun to watch, and saying a candidate can't think for himself confirms some cartoon version of the beliefs we already have."

Melanie looked around for a glass of water. Rick continued:

"And Capitolette is especially interesting. She's like the entrepreneurial Paula Jones—no, she's like Colette—no . . . wait, I'm getting it. She's like Mary Kate and Ashley meets Fawn Hall."

She half-stumbled out of the bed to the cabinet and found the remaining half of a glass of the water that came with lunch.

"You okay?" Rick said, breaking off from his riff.

Melanie picked a robe up off the floor. "I'm fine. Just, just . . . suddenly really tired." She turned around and smiled at him. "All this exercise in the middle of the day."

"Right." He continued: "So it's a whole trend piece, really—kids using MoveOn to make the moves and MeetUp to hook up, politics and sex. It's not mudslinging, but it's dirty."

Melanie could hear him writing the piece in his head, or at least writing the memo. The memo would sell the story, promising a cover that would pass from gimmicky trope to pop wisdom—the next "Red and Blue America," the next "soccer moms," the next "Generation X" . . .

And there it was. " 'Generation Sex'?" Rick wondered aloud. "No, been done. 'Generation Sexy'? 'HookUp-dot-org' . . . better, better . . ."

He wasn't even talking to her anymore. Melanie started toward the bathroom for her shower.

"Hey, hey, where are you going?"

"I've gotta get back to work," she said, not looking at him. In the bathroom, she turned on the water in the stall but suddenly felt claustrophobic. She closed her eyes and thought of the empty dome of sky she used to take for granted back home. A shiver crackled through her and she turned her face upward into the water. *This is gonna totally fuck with my hair,* she thought absently.

As she showered, she tried to get her head around the panicky feeling that seemed to shadow her. *Heather straining at the bit, Julie's radio silence, Rick pushing the very story I can't let him know about . . .*

The last clouds of lather rinsed down the drain and Melanie wondered: *Can I let him know about it?* Maybe it was that easy. She could control the story if Rick wrote it, maybe. She would at least know what direction he was taking it. She knew him. She could figure out what might keep him from digging too far. Whatever bogus trend piece he was dreaming up wouldn't be that bad. *In fact, it could be great.*

She emerged from the bathroom to Rick going through his e-mail on his BlackBerry. "I know I can get her e-mail address from Lead, but I'm having trouble getting a phone number." He looked up at Melanie, towel-drying her hair. "And I would hate to owe Lead something."

Melanie almost said something then. The opening was right there: *What about owing me?* She held back, though. Some vestige of guilt or uncertainty or concern made her tongue thick. "Mmmm," she said.

Rick raised an eyebrow at her. "*You* wouldn't happen to have it, would you?"

"Mmm," Melanie said, grabbing her underwear off the floor. She bent over to put them on and Rick gave her a light spank.

"You know something, don't you?" He was flirting, his attention fully on Melanie. She turned around and gave her shoulders a slight shimmy for him, a Betty Boop flourish she hoped would keep him from remembering the question. She shrugged into her bra and slipped her dress over her head: *Tip #34,* she thought, *wear clothes without buttons.*

"I gotta run," she said, finding her sandals. "We can talk more about this later." She headed toward the door.

"Actually, we can't." Rick's voice called her back. It sounded sharper than it had just a minute ago; there was a teacher-keeping-you-from-recess tone Melanie recognized as the same tone he would use to quiet her down so her voice wouldn't be picked up while he was on the phone.

"Oh?" said Melanie, turning around.

"I meant to tell you earlier—we're headed back to the beach early this week. Last chance to relax before Golden's convention in New York and all that."

"*Think* is letting you go?"

"I'll file from there. I've done the reporting, I just have to polish and keep the editors from fucking it up."

"Oh." It was the last week of August and they hadn't seen as much of each other as Melanie had wanted—and of course, as much as she had wanted just hadn't seemed possible. Now she wouldn't be able to see him for the rest of the month.

Rick was now putting on his robe. His hair was spiky and the robe too small. *The robes are always too small.* Yet he had put on his mask, the Business Rick mask, which made him seem both more ridiculous and more distant—a CEO in a suit and ballet slippers, laughable but imperious.

"Sorry I didn't mention it."

"You don't seem sorry," Melanie said, torn between wanting to have the fight that was unfolding—a spat is a kind of connection—and wanting to run away.

"I guess I just hoped you'd realize that I do have a real job, and a real life," Rick said, snapping the robe belt tight. He approached her. "You know, none of this is free."

Melanie supposed he meant the things he paid for: the hotel, the ridiculous room service lunch, the clothes he bought, the bottle of single malt he gave her to keep on hand. Or maybe he meant the lies he told his wife, the ones that had to be painted over with a different kind of currency—a surprise early return, flowers, dinner at home.

Of course, the relationship had cost her, too.

He was standing in front of her, face self-consciously placid. "I really am sorry, Mel."

She wanted to believe him. "You don't have to be sorry. I get it."

"Of course you do." He half-smiled. "That's why we get along, Melanie my dear." He put his hands on her shoulders and gave them a quick squeeze. "I'm just tired. These convention issues should be easy—they're almost fill-in-the-blanks—but they're huge and the real challenge is to find a theme for the thing that doesn't just echo the fucking press release."

It occurred to Melanie that she had written several such fucking press releases.

A huff of amusement escaped Rick and his smile broadened: "Though some press releases are better than others."

She smiled back.

"That's my girl," he said, giving her a peck on the forehead. "Now, my turn." He stepped beside her to get to the shower. He paused at the bathroom door and turned, shaking his head as though marveling at some slight or error that happened long ago. "You know," he said, "that's probably why I was so into that stupid Capitolette pitch—and no, no, I know, I was straining—it would be a nice last easy piece before the campaigns are full speed again."

"Oh, she's an easy piece, all right." Melanie was getting seasick from the conversation's changes in speed. *I shouldn't have had that glass of wine with lunch,* she thought. *Or maybe this is just life returning to normal speed.*

"I guess that's the point. Anyway," he continued, "if you can dig up some contact info, I'd appreciate it."

Melanie considered. "I'll see what I can do." She hoisted her purse onto her shoulder and walked to the door.

"What? No kiss good-bye?" Rick called, leaning against the bathroom doorjamb.

"Next time," Melanie said.

IN THE CAB back to the campaign, Melanie's cell phone rang. Finally, Julie.

Melanie flipped open the phone: "Where have you been?"

"Whoa, Mom, did I break curfew or something?"

"Sorry . . . It's just . . ." Melanie calculated the time she had actually not heard from Julie . . . a couple of hours, maybe. She felt her face flush and was glad Julie wasn't there to see it. "Well, you sort of left me hanging."

"Ah, right. Yes. Our girl's earning potential. You talk to her?"

"As a matter of fact, I did."

"And?"

Melanie got a small guilty pleasure out of parceling out the information at her own speed.

"She seems pretty set on a book, possibly the centerfold."

"Hmm. We should find her an agent."

"So you think this is a good idea? Really?"

"I think it's where we are. And I think it could be fine. More than fine."

"Remind me how this is helping the campaign."

"Ah."

"What, ah?" Melanie's jaw was tight. She was almost to the office. She felt weighted down by just the idea of going back.

"Well, I was wondering why you were resisting this. Is it because Heather's no longer an asset to the campaign specifically? She's outlived her usefulness to you?"

"No, no, of course not!" *Right,* Melanie asked herself, *of course not?* She continued: "I'm resisting because I just don't see how this will end well. She becomes some kind of media figure and people will ask questions. People will find out who she is, and, well, maybe they'll find out how she became what she is now."

"I don't think so."

"How can you be so confident?"

"People don't really want to know. Also, remember: We've created a more sordid past for her than she actually has. Why would people want to uncover something that makes their media darling more boring?"

There were too many layers here. Melanie followed Julie's logic but it didn't seem to take her where Julie wanted to go. What Melanie was really thinking couldn't be said out loud. That if Pandora got out of her box, Melanie was the one who stood to lose the most. She was the one who'd had the affair. She was the one who had to keep her spinning and strategizing wrapped in a wholesome package or risk the fate of the free world. And Julie, after all, was just doing what she could feasibly be getting paid to do anyway. "I just . . ." Melanie started. "I just can't . . ."

"Just what? Mel, if we can't control her anyway, we have to stay on her side."

The cab pulled up in front of headquarters.

"I'm here," she told Julie. "I should go."

A sigh on the other end. "Fine. Call me later. I can explain it over a drink if you want."

"I'm sure it will all make sense then."

"Or it won't matter."

"Bye, Jules."

She paid the cabbie and got out. Her knees almost buckled in the heat. *It is so fucking hot.* Maybe she shouldn't begrudge Rick his extra time at the shore. She'd take it if she could.

MELANIE GOT HOME from work at seven, just seven. There were hours of daylight left. The apartment was streaked in light and stuffy. It smelled like dust and orange juice—she had left a glass on the counter, now slicked with orangey film and spackled with bits of pulp.

She dropped her bags and crossed the short distance to the kitchenette purposefully. In the sink were assorted pieces of cutlery, dirty from her halfhearted grazing among the leftover take-out boxes. She grabbed a dish towel and started to work. It would feel good to focus on something that had nothing to do with the campaign, Rick, the Clearheads, or Capitolette for a change.

JULIE CALLED as she was finishing, instantly reminding her of what she had just barely been able to forget. Melanie felt bad, and she knew it was ultimately more her fault than Julie's, but lately just hearing her friend's voice could heighten her anxiety level.

"What's that noise?"

"The faucet."

"Are you in the bathroom again?"

"No—it's a little more unnatural than that. I'm cleaning."

"Really? What's that like?"

"Well, it involves soap, and hot water. And when you're done there's a pleasant sense of accomplishment." Melanie hung the dish towel through the handle of the refrigerator. She did feel like she had done something. *Behold, I have made order!*

"Oh, I know that sense. Which reminds me—you want to get that drink?"

Melanie looked around. Dust motes floated over a place that wasn't so much dirty as unused. "Would you be terribly upset if I didn't feel like it?"

"Not so much upset as surprised."

"I just think I might try to get some sleep."

"Riiiight."

"No, really, sleep."

"What about our protégée? Where's she sleeping tonight?"

"Shit." Melanie knew she should call Heather. But the situation still made her nervous. "Do you really think she'll make a move without us?"

"Move? How do you mean that, exactly? I don't think she's going to run into Larry Flynt's office and strip all of her clothes off in the next twenty-four hours, but she might in the next thirty-six. She seems . . . eager."

"You talked to her?" Melanie was a little surprised by this. Julie and Heather's wary relationship had never warmed above "tolerant."

"Yeah. I just thought I'd get, ahem, the lay of the land."

"What did she say to you?"

"The exact same things she told you, I think. She's itching to finally make some scratch. She wants to scratch an itch. Whatever. She's not going to stay in the starting gate for long."

"Yeah."

A pause. Melanie wondered what Julie had told Heather, if she had weighed in on the options. It would be impossible for Julie to not weigh in, really.

"Soooo . . . that drink?"

"What did you tell her?"

"Heather?"

"Yes, Heather."

"I didn't tell her to do anything, except wait. She's gonna call tomorrow to check in. Really, though, Mel: It's much better for us if she thinks we're on her side. We can have a say in how this plays out."

What was "this," though? Melanie saw her Berry flash in the shadowed fold of her bag. She went to go pick it up while Julie finished: "Is the feminist thing hanging you up about the centerfold?"

"No . . . no. I guess it just seems, well, sleazy," Melanie said, distractedly.

She scrolled through the messages as Julie talked. There were more Google alerts for Heather than for Clearheads . . . a rapidly diminishing number of alerts for the Clearheads, actually. "Sleazy is part of the brand," Julie decreed.

"But doesn't it bother you that if she gets linked up with the Dems, that sleaze will rub off? It worries me."

"We're insulated."

"What do you mean?"

"I mean don't worry about it."

"You keep saying that."

"I keep meaning it."

Melanie knew Julie had something to say that she didn't quite feel comfortable enough to tell her on the phone, but Melanie didn't have the energy to fish for it. She wandered over to the window. It wasn't even dusk yet. "Well, I'll see if I believe you tomorrow. What are you up to tonight?"

"Not sure yet. Want me to ping you if we do anything fun?"

"Sure."

They both hung up and Melanie glanced down at the windowsill. She ran a finger through the dust.

SO MELANIE KEPT CLEANING. She made five roundtrip treks to the basement laundry room. She winced and half-retched through the entire contents of the refrigerator—a process that was not unlike going through old photo albums or boxed-up toys in the garage: Every take-out container brought back memories. *Oh, yeah, that time we went to Ten Pehn and almost ran into Mary Matalin* . . .

She almost even called her parents. Instead, she wrote a letter. A real letter, on paper, with a stamp. It was chatty and inquisitive about how things were in Iowa. She included two short clips where she had somehow gotten quoted by name.

She folded her clothes in front of C-SPAN's rebroadcast of *Washington Journal* and forced herself not to tune out completely when the guy from *Washington Monthly* started talking about actuarial tables and Social Security reform.

When she finally slipped between her freshly washed sheets, it wasn't that much earlier than her usual, more drunken bedtime. But she wasn't drunk. She had made tea. It was too hot for tea, but it was what normal people drank at bedtime.

15

Tuesday, August 24

SHE WOKE UP EARLY, slightly embarrassed by the clarity of her head. The back issues of *The Economist* she had brought to bed with her were on the floor and the light was still on. *Is it still passing out if you're sober?* she wondered, heading for the shower.

Even the shampoo smelled better than usual, and Melanie

found herself humming along to the *Morning Edition* theme music. She made coffee at home—wincing a bit when she stopped to think about how much her usual morning lattes added up to. The mail was still unopened, but she told herself she'd deal with it later.

At seven, the streets were only dotted with pedestrians and last night's cool hadn't quite burned away. Melanie started to hail a cab, but then thought about all those lattes and headed to the Metro instead.

Riding down the escalator at Dupont Circle, Melanie realized how long it had been since she'd been in public. Public as in with real people. People who weren't working on a campaign or writing about one, people who went to work at nine and got out at six, women in suits and running shoes, men with their names on their shirts. She passed sleepy interns and somewhat shell-shocked tourists, and Melanie remembered her first awkward forays into the subway, like that time she had accidentally wound up in Virginia.

Rush hour was only just starting, but the cars were already crowded. Melanie grabbed a seat next to a man in a suit with powdered sugar on his lapel. *Probably powdered sugar,* she thought.

Mixed in with the Metro's omnipresent faint whiff of diesel, Melanie could smell soap and shampoo and aftershave. A hopeful scent.

This inspired her: She pulled a pad of paper from her bag and started a list.

- Catch up with J re: H (steer her to novel, worry about nude thing)
- Send R email and phone for H

- Are we really renting pirate costume? (If so, who to where? How to pay? Cash collection?)

There, it all made sense now. She wondered if she were kidding herself by placing the Rick task in the middle. She wondered if she were kidding herself that she would do it at all.

No, she would. Order. Control. If Julie was right about Heather—give up some control in order to stay in good—then the logic applied to Rick as well. Besides, there was a thrill in being able to give him something he wanted but couldn't get on his own. He'd owe her. She smiled.

She added more things to the list:

- List of bloggers at convention, who would be receptive to posting pix of pirate?
- Teeth cleaning?

Doable, she thought, *doable.*

Then the other things she had to do snuck in through cracks like ants. Pay rent, for one. And look at that mail. When *was* the last time she had actually opened a piece of mail? What kind of bills sat on the kitchen counter, slowly turning red? She really should have called her parents. And fuck, Skoloff still was sitting on the spontaneous reel from two weeks ago.

She added these to the list as the movement of the Metro car made her handwriting quiver.

THE DAY THAT had started with such promise opened and wilted like a cut flower left in the sun. By eleven, Melanie's to-do list had spread across the page, and the margins were filled with phone numbers and jagged box-shaped doodles. Arrows pointed from a task to a list of subtasks and tasks that needed to be checked off before the current task was undertaken.

Even getting her teeth cleaned necessitated a strategic plan drafted by the Army Corps of Engineers—between the insurance company forms and finding a free hour to do it and getting the records from her old dentist . . . *So much for structural integrity,* she thought.

Giving Rick Heather's contact info had been the easiest thing to cross off all day, especially since she had just refused to scribble out what escalating avalanche of consequences she might have to cross off once he had the information. She would give him the phone number. She would be done.

Thortonology: Yt?

StosselR52: Yup

Thortonology: Still need that contact info for c'ette?

StosselR52: as a matter of fact, I do . . .

Thortonology: I have it . . .

StosselR52: Hold. Are you callable?

Thortonology: Y

Call? Really he'll call?

And he did. There was an odd sense of playacting to taking a call from Rick while at work. She could hear the stiffness in her voice: "Well, hello."

"Yes, hello, Ms. Thorton. I understand you have a tip for me."

"Yes, well, yes I do."

"Excellent."

"Ah . . . yes, the person you want to get in touch with . . . I'll e-mail you the number itself."

"Oh," he said. "Well, that's fine, too." Did he sound disappointed?

"Look, Rick . . ."

"Probably better to e-mail it, I suppose."

"Sure. Just, look . . ." What was she going to say? She felt she had to give a warning or make a show of knowing something but the knot in the pit of her stomach was making it difficult to think.

"Hmm? Look at . . . Looking at some new ads right now. You seen these for Golden? They don't actually have apple pie in them, but . . ."

"Funny. Anyway, look: I just wanted to let you know that this Capitolette girl . . . She's a handful. She's also fairly unpolished. She's pretty much exactly the person she appears to be." Melanie wasn't sure who she was protecting.

"Well, that is refreshing, isn't it?"

"Yeah, I guess that's the point."

Melanie put Heather's number into an e-mail and punched "send."

"Sent."

"I'll look for it."

"Right."

She felt like there was a thing she should be saying. Some line of the script that she had forgotten.

"And, Melanie?"

"Yes?"

"Thanks," he said. *Ah, yes. My line.*

"Uhm . . . you're welcome."

Somehow hearing it wasn't nearly as satisfying as she thought it would be.

. . .

JULIE WAS THRILLED with Melanie's change of heart about expanding Capitolette's media profile, though she was still pushing the centerfold idea. "It would put the final nail in the Clearheads' coffin. Or final strap in their straitjacket: NUDE GIRL IN WASHINGTON is the only sexier story than CANDIDATE IS MINDLESS AUTOMATON."

AT THE CAMPAIGN, there had been another pirate meeting. The honchos dickered:

"Now, if it's a pirate, is it *Golden* as a pirate," Prentiss asked, "or is it a *Golden supporter?*"

"We could put a Golden mask on the person in the pirate costume. . . ."

"He could carry around a bag labeled 'Social Security Funds'!"

When the hat was passed—actually, it was a not-very-clean Tupperware server from someone's long-discarded lunch—Melanie put in ten dollars toward the rental and struck out. "There's no time to find a 527," Skoloff snapped as Melanie hustled out the door, grateful that her angry attention was focused elsewhere.

At her desk, she sunk into the task of returning calls. There were people to be dealt with who were sniffing for process stories, hunting down rumors that new campaign strategists were coming in at the top—Carville? Begala?

"The campaign has a wide-ranging group of advisers, some informal. We're listening to all kinds of ideas," she told them. Off the record, she tried to game it a little: "Things always get hairy right before the other guy's convention. We're looking at new ways to go about this but since we don't know how they're gonna come out of New York, there's no way we can say for sure what they're going to be. We have lots of tricks up our sleeve."

Our billowing, puffy pirate sleeve, she thought.

Hank Lensky called about the Donnelly story, sort of: "Well, you seem to have proved that he's insane, you know, I mean, it's not news but who can say you haven't added to the weight of everyone's assumptions? That's gotta be the kind of thing you're best at, Melanie. How'd you dig this up anyway? Whew, I can't imagine the time you spent."

He was just eating around the edges of the Donnelly thing, like a guest too polite to say the meat loaf was dry. "Thanks, Hank, I do what I can."

"I just look at you working there, what, coming out of nowhere and you're doing some of the best work there, really. . . ."

Melanie's eyes narrowed and she bit the inside of her cheek. Flattery from a reporter was pretty much never a good sign.

"Don't know where you find the time to get out."

"Well, you know. It's August. It's usually kind of slow. I just take advantage."

"Didn't I see you at Emily's party last weekend?"

Melanie dreaded where this was going. "Hank, you talked to me for half an hour."

"I did?" She could almost hear the dials clicking inside his head on the other end of the line.

"No, I think you just said hi." It had seemed like half an hour at the time, Melanie realized.

"Well, I was just wondering because, you know, that Capitolette was there, too. And you were talking to her and of course I thought at the time how wonderful to see two of the most beautiful and successful women in Washington chatting with each other."

"She's a whore, Hank. I'm just . . . for hire."

"Ha. Yeah. Heh. Anyway . . ."

The campaign continued to grind loudly behind her—fax machines screeched, electric staplers thumped, and occasionally someone had an idea—but Melanie tuned it out. She could hold this conversation squarely in her sights only if she didn't look down. She didn't want to know how high up off the ground she was, without Julie acting as her net.

"You know her? I mean, you were talking and I guess of course you know her. But I'd love to talk to her for real, you know? She's out and about around town, I hear, but she's only given that one print interview. And you just seemed to know her."

Melanie cocked her head and parsed the conversation. There was no way to tell if he was hunting for an angle or for dirt or for a connection or maybe he just wanted to get laid. She hoped the latter.

And actually, Melanie was pretty sure she *hadn't* talked to Heather at the party. She scanned her memory banks and avoided the trap: "I don't think I did talk to her at that party, Hank. You sure it was me? I know her by reputation only. And it is, as you know, quite a reputation."

"Ah. Okay. Uhm . . ." Hank's patter sputtered out. He lost his momentum and pulled the starting cord out again: "Ah . . . Well, anyway, back to this Donnelly thing. Interesting stuff, real interesting stuff . . . You have anything more? I mean, just, it would be great to get this stuff into the magazine . . . a real coup for you, too. They don't appreciate you there, do they?"

She had to give him points for persistence. Lensky got most of his stories by wearing people down. She started multitasking, only half-listening to him make feints at the "campaign in disaster mode" meme while deleting all the campaign spam from her inbox ("MoveOn.org Announces 'What Does Freedom Taste Like' Contest/Feed the People, Not the Rich Recipes for a Democratic Majority"; "GOP Launches 'Blogit and Poddle,' the Cartoon Duo Who Fight Lies and Innuendo on the Internet"; "Jibbery.net Brings You the Funniest Flash Animation of the Campaign Year").

Maybe he sensed her distraction. He wound it down: "Anyway, thanks. You going to Russia House tonight? That blogger girl sent around an e-mail. A whole shift of folks is back from Arizona for some R and R before the convention and they're thirsty. Or at least that's the excuse she gave."

Melanie considered his invitation. She could definitely use a drink. The blogger girl aspect meant that it was unlikely her drink would be free, however.

"Thanks for the heads-up, Hank. I'll try to make it."

"I'll buy you a round."

"Of course you will."

Wednesday, August 25

THE AIR-CONDITIONING in the cab was broken. Of course. Melanie had woken up with a vague, fuzzy hangover from drinks at Russia House, and in the still, humid air of the cab, it soured and threatened to turn mean. Waiting in traffic on Pennsylvania Avenue, Melanie wondered whether her apartment would still feel clean if she felt this dirty.

Her hair was only semi-clean and just marginally tamed by a butterfly clip and a pair of oversized sunglasses perched on her head. Her flip-flops gave anyone who cared to look a full view of a ravished pedicure. She wore a faded shirt from Carol Moseley Braun's campaign in 1992 (bought by mail when she was in high school and long before Moseley Braun's financial scandals made her first term as the first female African-American senator her only term). Skoloff and Prentiss had flown out to Hillman's ranch in Montana that morning and so today could count as a day off. *I don't want to spend it hungover.*

A workout would help. She would sweat it out. She had a day pass for the spa at the Georgetown Four Seasons that had come with the room from an early summer tryst with Rick. Management had graciously extended its expiration date when Melanie batted her eyelashes—and after she had paid for a night and a day's worth of room service in cash.

The doorman looked surprised when she stepped out of the cab, though he had the class to ask if she needed help with her bags. She slung the ratty backpack over her shoulder and said no.

The lobby wasn't the quickest way to the spa—there was another entrance—but Melanie relished the crisp hit of air-conditioning. She had perhaps overestimated her capacity for shamelessness, however. She avoided the eyes of the well-preserved patrons in the smoothly beige lobby and concentrated on looking forward. The lobby was airy enough and the furniture was probably expensive, but the Four Seasons was the only luxury hotel in America to have borrowed its architecture plans from a San Diego singles' condominium built sometime in the mid seventies.

Propelling herself to the stairs she passed the restaurant. She was about to make her escape when she heard a familiar voice: "Please. This isn't about what could hurt us. It's about . . . how we can help each other."

Julie. Melanie froze.

"Darlin', if you can figure out a way to make this about mutual back scratching and not a catfight, your name should be much higher on the letterhead than it is now."

She now placed the other voice without much trouble: Hugh Brompton, Emily's husband. She walked a few steps backward. The restaurant was open walled-in glass; it wasn't hard to spot Julie and Hugh, sitting at the periphery. Melanie ducked behind a brick pillar without thinking about it.

"Don't worry, it's climbing," Julie responded, confidently.

The maître d' approached and gave her a polite but wary smile. "Can I help you with something, miss?"

Is it the flip-flops, Melanie wondered, *or that I have a huge black woman's head on my shirt?* She took a deep breath and aimed for charming: "Oh, hi. I, ah, yes. My boss left his sunglasses here, ah, yesterday. They're . . . black. Kind of round? I, ah, would have called ahead but I'm on my way out of town."

His smile became more certain. *Of course it's okay to be dressed like this if I work for someone else.*

"Right," he said. "Wait here for a minute and I'll check in lost and found." He started to turn to leave.

Whether or not she actually intended to eavesdrop, she had succeeded in buying time to do it.

Melanie felt exposed and obvious; she pressed up against the wall, willing herself invisible. *A sweatshirt would help. . . .*

She tuned back in: "Unless you have digital pictures of the three of us playing naked Pictionary—and I know you'd like to have them—I don't think your allegation would get very far."

"Capitolette herself doesn't have much more than her say-so, honey." Most of the time Hugh was semi-pleasantly unctuous, toeing over the line only with his focus on your tits. Now he just sounded oily.

It was his seersucker-clad back she and Julie had thought they had seen coming out of the room with Heather back at Emily's party. He continued: "As far as what I have, well, the three of you have more phrases in common than a Joe Biden speech. Then there's the timing. All very advantageous. Seems to me that the Hillman campaign was hit with two pieces of bad news at the beginning of the month. The Clearheads, sure, and also an item about a communications aide and a prominent journalist."

"Hm."

"And I seem to recall that it was you who put the idea into my lovely wife's head that it would be 'amusing' to invite Miss Mason to our home."

Melanie's heart chilled. Julie had been so certain that no one would put two and two—or two and one—together. And now Hugh had done it? *Fuck. Fuckfuckfuck* . . .

"And then there's the question of what you and Miss Thorton were doing upstairs when Capitolette retreated from our soiree of the week."

Ah. It was him.

Julie's voice dropped and Melanie could barely make it out over the clatter of cutlery. "Hugh, friend, if you know *we* were up there, then I know *you* were up there. And I don't think you can plausibly argue you were looking for the loo."

It was all very intriguing, though Melanie wondered why Julie hadn't mentioned it. There was no reason not to. *Maybe I should just say hi. Why not? Am I that embarrassed about poor Ms. Moseley Braun? No, of course not. I'm embarrassed in general.*

Hugh was talking again: "Maybe I saw you head upstairs."

"Maybe your wife saw you head upstairs."

Julie didn't sound like she needed rescuing, that much was true. Hugh pressed on: "You could try to throw a wrench into my marriage, dear Julie, but all that causes is a fight. If someone connects you to Heather, that throws a wrench into the campaign."

"Let's just say, for the sake of argument, that I've done some . . . freelance consulting for Ms. Capitolette. She asked me who I thought she might want to get to know, that kind of thing."

"I'd say that if you're getting a cut out of these introductions, you should trade that VW of yours for a Cadillac."

"And if I'm not?"

"Then why don't you introduce me?"

"Interesting."

The maître d' would be back soon—perhaps even with a pair of sunglasses. Melanie would have no excuse to be standing here. *I could Berry her, tell her I'm in the neighborhood, if she invites me by, well, then . . . Then what? What will that tell me? Why am I not going in there?*

"What do you mean, 'interesting'?"

"I would think you'd think larger than that. You can risk ruining your marriage in exchange for maybe hurting Hillman—or you can not risk much and get more than just a lousy fuck."

"Are her fucks so lousy?"

Julie started to answer: "I wouldn't know, but what I do know—"

"I'm sorry, miss." Melanie jumped. "I couldn't find any sunglasses that fit that description." The maître d' had returned.

Melanie tried to follow the conversation but the maître d' was already gesturing toward the door. "Something else? Maybe you'd like to leave a name and number. . . ."

"Ah, uh, no. No."

He looked at her narrowly, and suddenly Melanie felt like it was all written all over her—the affair, Capitolette, the stupid lie she told her dad in eleventh grade about sleeping over at Nancy's when she was really at Josh's. . . .

"Thanks," she muttered, pushing him out of the way and stumbling toward the exit.

MELANIE THOUGHT ABOUT going to work out somewhere else. She thought about calling Julie. She thought about calling Rick. There were so few people to call. She could call Lensky or Taylor or even that blogger girl but, Jesus, those conversations would have less emotional depth than a *New York Times* editorial.

At least this cab was air-conditioned. The driver had asked where she wanted to go and her first thought was "home." Home not as in her inescapably dingy apartment, but home. Home with a four-poster bed and milk in the refrigerator, home where they would go to the Country Buffet for dinner and no one assumed you had a cell phone. Instead, she had him take her back to the campaign.

She could try to stay busy or at the very least not dwell. There wasn't much to do at the campaign at the moment but there was even less to do at the apartment. She could make calls, do research, come up with another to-do list, and enjoy the frigid air-conditioning.

Chuck saw Melanie come in and grinned. "Hey, Moseley Braun!" he called from across the room. "Did you work on that? You had to have been twelve. Awful young to be getting kickbacks."

She gave him a tight smile. *I should have changed first,* she thought. But the key to the rinky-dink gym in the basement was in her desk.

At her desk, she rummaged through the drawers. *Fuck, it was around here somewhere.* She realized she might not have any shampoo in her bag. *Had sort of been counting on the Four Seasons to provide that. Had sort of been counting on the Four Seasons to provide a lot.*

"If you're looking for the gun, it's taped under the center desk drawer." Chuck appeared beside her. "But it's a little hot for murderous rampage. Besides, Karen's not even here."

She slumped in her chair, then gave a minor sigh. "Right. It's a good thing I don't have any bullets, then."

"Yes, well, the entire campaign is shooting blanks." He smiled at her. "Now, really, what's up? It is retro Wednesday and I didn't get the memo? Or is it the last day before laundry?"

Melanie tried to smile back. "Actually, believe it or not, I have clean laundry."

"Mom came to visit, eh?"

"No, I used this odd machine in the basement of my building."

"You have an Old Navy in the basement of your building?"

Melanie's smile was finally real. She shook her head. "The truth is that I was hoping to get a workout in. I just can't find my passkey."

"I think I've got one somewhere, if it isn't rusted beyond recognition." He strolled off toward his nook.

Melanie glanced at her Berry. Many, many messages. The LED light blinked placidly. She hesitated, then slowly thumbed in her password. The list of new messages included two from Julie and one from Heather.

"Here you go, milady." Chuck returned, grinning and presenting her with the key laid across his arm like a very, very tiny Excalibur. "As fresh and new as the day it was minted in the smithies of ye olde building manager."

"Ah . . ." She was going to have to put the Berry away. She did, sliding it into its holster and vowing to get the fucking workout over with first. "Thanks, Chuck."

"No problem. By the way, you know it's fine if you just bail on the afternoon. I'm not gonna tell and there just isn't that much to do that can't be done remotely."

"Easy for you to say—you've been phoning it in from the beginning." Melanie winked at him, shouldered her bags, and turned to head downstairs.

"That really hurt!" he called after her.

SHE DIDN'T HAVE any music of her own to listen to while sweating out the remainder of her hangover in the airless little gym below. The ancient boom box sitting on a folding chair in the corner picked up mostly static, but Melanie found whispery reception for one of the local NPR stations. The host's rasp was barely audible over the squeak of the treadmill. Melanie found it comforting, though—somewhere in D.C. thousands of people were listening to a discussion of the future of the National Botanical Garden under a second Golden administration.

She paced along, facing the mirrored wall. Instead of looking at herself, she stared at the flecks of dust and shadows of water spots that dotted the glass. Her own reflection blurred.

To: ThortonM@hillman.com
From: Julie.Wrigley@clevelandparkgroup.com
Subject: where are you?

Hey, is this payback for the other day or are you just still too hungover to answer the phone? I just wanted to let you know I've been sniffing around about publishers and agents and I think there's a few we can bring to Heather's attention as, you know, real options.

And, of course, if you want to grab a drink tonight. . . .

Melanie did not want to grab a drink tonight. Did not even particularly want to respond. Her hair was still damp from her shower downstairs; the mini-gym's mini–blow dryers did about as much good as a stiff breeze.

The office was almost completely empty. She could go home, though she wasn't sure what she'd do once she got there. She pecked out a reply to Julie just to get it over with.

To: Julie.Wrigley@clevelandparkgroup.com
From: ThortonM@hillman.com
Subject: Ghost town

I'm here, though I probably won't be for long. Hangover sweated out, now feeling like I need to hydrate and watch old debate tapes. Maybe will play the Bob-Dole-refers-to-self-in-third-person drinking game—with water.

As for Heather: Let's deal with it tomorrow.

Melanie packed up her stuff and headed home, dimly aware of the dozens of unopened e-mails and message icon blinking on her phone.

At the apartment, she considered cleaning again. Or maybe she really would watch those debate tapes. They were from Golden's unsuccessful gubernatorial run and she was on the lookout for what seemed to make him nervous or if there was a pattern to his flubbed lines. She had a theory about Goldenisms that would make them seem far less cute. Sure, she'd watch all five hours and write a memo and then she'd probably be asked to find a Tinkerbell costume to go with the pirate suit.

Her phone rang as she rummaged in the freezer for limeade. It was Heather.

"Hi, Heather. Made any decisions yet?"

"No. Not yet." She giggled. Melanie did not trust Heather's giggle. "I was out with this guy who says he's your friend last night. It was fun, it was really *interesting.*"

Friend, Melanie thought. *Friend?* Her mind didn't race. It seemed to crawl: *friend. . . . Friend who Heather knows . . .* Her breath became shallow. *No. No, it couldn't be.*

"Friend," Melanie croaked.

"The TV guy?" Heather chirped. "He's kinda old but really nice and I think he's totally loaded."

Melanie felt her arms go numb. The air went out of her lungs. She felt as though she'd been thrown against a wall. When she found her voice, it seemed to be coming from far away: "When you say *interesting,* do you mean that you discussed the works of Proust? Or that he laid out his theories on the likelihood of success of parliamentary governments in former colonies?"

"Uhm . . ."

"Or do you mean you fucked him?"

"Welll-ll," Heather said. Suddenly, Heather's schoolgirl casual-
ness infuriated Melanie. "Welll-ll," Heather repeated. A laugh. It
raked against her exposed emotions like sandpaper.

"You did." The world lost all color. Melanie had to sit down. No,
she had to stand up. No, she had to move around. No, she had to
throw the fucking phone out the window. She had to throw up.

"It's not like it's a big deal," Heather complained. "It was just one
night!"

Melanie's head was still molasses-slow. "One night."

"We were kind of drunk. Look," Heather said, her voice taking
on the tone of an older sister. "I don't think anyone saw us after we
left the restaurant." A pause. A soft laugh. "I don't think *either* of us
planned it. . . . And, you know, he's married. I don't think he'll tell
anyone."

"No," Melanie agreed. "I don't think he will." Her throat was
thick and the words scraped through her vocal cords.

She could observe two scenes: In one, she was chastising Capitolette for stepping over the boundaries she and Julie had set. In
the other, she was falling apart.

Melanie willed hot tears to dry. But would her lungs ever fill
again? Outrage snuck into her voice: "Is there *anyone* you won't
fuck?"

"What do you mean?"

"I mean, Jesus, Heather . . . it's not healthy. To let yourself be
used like that."

"Used?"

Melanie finally sat down. *Used, yes.* She could try to convince
Heather that fucking Rick was a bad career move but mostly she

wanted Heather to believe it was just a bad idea. *You have no idea how bad.*

The tears threatened again. "I mean, what will you get out of this? He got laid. You? What did you get?"

"He thinks I could have a show. I *am* going to get a book deal."

"He said all that to you?" Melanie felt shivers now, and she remembered the last time she spoke to Rick. He had thanked her. Anger seeped into her chest. "Did he paint this gorgeous future before or after you had sex with him?"

"It was before, but he said it again after."

Melanie couldn't keep a resentful snort from punctuating the thought. "I'm sure he did. Was that before or after he fell asleep?"

"They don't fall asleep with me."

"Come on, they always do."

Melanie waited for Heather's response and watched the high summer clouds drift by in the sliver of visible sky. *Still daylight,* she thought. *How can so many bad things happen when there's still so much daylight left?*

Finally: "I had no idea you'd be so upset," Heather said.

Yeah, well, neither did I. But she tried to retreat to girlfriend mode. "I'm not upset, Heather. I'm disappointed."

"Gee, Mom. I wouldn't want to disappoint you." Melanie could almost hear Heather's eyes roll.

"Heather. I'm not your mom, I just . . . hate to see this happen to you." *And that much is true.*

"Well, thanks for the advice, then."

"Yeah. Heather . . . ?" Melanie wanted to ask if they had made plans to see each other again. She found she didn't want to know. "Good luck, Heather. That's all."

"With what?"

"With everything."

She sat on the couch with the dead phone in her hand. Thoughts flickered across her mind, chased by images from the early summer. Rick smiling at her from the tarmac at a stop in Dayton, Rick buying her a drink in South Carolina at a bar decorated like a Wisconsin hunting lodge, Rick working on a story in his bathrobe with a pencil behind each ear.

He was supposed to have been out of town last night, too. Her jaw clenched and somehow that small detail lit the kindling anger into a blaze. Regret fueled it, too. And helpless frustration at her own stupidity. *Of course he fucked her. Of course he did.*

SHE COULD ADMIT it to herself now: She hadn't so much fallen for Rick as felt like she *earned* him. Being with him was the payoff for the late nights and the cold coffee and the driving around Illinois in a duct-taped-together Hyundai asking people to vote for someone they'd never heard of. His attention meant she belonged here, that no one was going to come out from behind a corner and tell her it had all been a horrible mistake and she should take the first available flight home.

But it had been a horrible mistake, all right.

Her knuckles were white in their grip on the phone and as her breathing grew more regular she stared at the phone as though it had simply appeared there. *I could call him,* she thought.

Wait. Really? Just call? Just like that? No strategy session, no breakdown of possible outcomes, no consulting on how to frame.

As she went to dial, her finger froze over the dial pad and she pulled back. *Julie. Maybe call Julie.* Julie had pushed Capitolette as useful trash. Julie had never trusted Rick, either. Melanie had always thought she had the better read on those two. That's what you do in Washington, you evaluate people and you figure out what button to push and dial to turn and Julie had done it better. She closed her eyes. *But that is not how grown-ups behave.*

And suddenly the anger was right there again, a hot, heavy thing in her chest that made her eyes water.

She dialed. With each tone and click she imagined the connection being made—an electric pulse flashing through the ether, a string that would pull taut when he picked up. When the phone on the other end rang her mouth went dry. She felt like she was talking through a mouthful of cotton. "Huh," she said, coughed, and started again: "Hey."

"Well, ah, hi there."

"Can you talk?"

"Uhm . . . Sure. Sure I can. Let me close the door here."

"You're at work?"

"Of course I am."

"I thought you were headed to the shore."

"Ah," he said. "Ah," like he had figured something out or had been shown an interesting word problem. His coolness made Melanie's back shiver with rage.

He continued: "Well, you know. It was going to be tricky to get out in the first place. Better to keep some chits in reserve for a time I really need to cash them in."

"Right." She closed her eyes but she couldn't stop the image of Heather and Rick together coming to her mind. A naked thigh, a hand, a hank of dark hair. *Stop. Stop. Stopstopstop.* She opened her eyes and with her free hand clenched her fist so that her nails dug into her palm.

"So I heard you went out with Heather last night."

"Oh, yeah, I did. Was about to tell you that. I figured you had other plans and I guess she's headed up to New York in the next couple of days." The words stung like kicked-up gravel. "And you know," he said, "you were right."

Cute, she thought. *A pat on the head to distract me.*

"She's . . ." He gave a low whistle. "She's kind of wild."

Melanie had always thought rage flowed freely. That anger was like lava and would just ooze out when given a chance. But no; it was more alive than that. She held the thing inside her chest tightly; she felt like she was trying to hold down a thrashing, feral thing but she held it. Her voice was level and cold: "I bet she was. I hope you used protection."

He paused. *He shouldn't have paused.* In the pause she could hear him making the calculations and running the cost-benefit analysis.

"What do you mean?" he asked.

"If you're stalling for time, you're going to have to do better than that."

"Why would I need to stall for time?"

"That's better. That's much better. But, oh, fuck, Rick. I thought you were smarter than that."

Now he just didn't say anything. It was another trick that Melanie recognized: Let the other person fill in the blanks. Don't say anything until you know how much is known. She gritted her teeth. Did he really believe she was so easily spun? "You have no idea where her cunt has been," she spat. "I know you don't keep up with the website like I do."

"What do you mean?" he asked again.

"God, you are a real fucking disappointment. 'What do you

mean?' I'm not insulted you fucked her anymore. I'm insulted you're not trying harder."

"What do you mean, I fucked her?" His voice was quiet but oddly pleasant, as if the charge he was denying was the violation of an obscure custom—as if he had put his elbows on the table or served from the left and cleared from the right.

"She told me, Rick."

"Obviously, she's lying." The finality was impressive. And for a second, Melanie felt a chill of doubt. Not because she believed him, but because she feared her anger was meaningless to him. That she could rage and wail and he would just sit there; he was a stone statue and she was a weak wind.

She gathered herself up again. There was comfort in knowing she was right. "She wouldn't lie to me about this. She has many faults and maybe a different moral compass than most people, but she also has no shame whatsoever. It makes her honest, Rick. More honest than you." *Or me.*

"She must be trying to impress you or maybe her stories are little tall tales." *Ah, there.* She heard the reach in his voice. *Finally.* "What do you really know about her, anyway?"

"You don't understand. I know her better than she knows herself, at least in some ways. There was no Capitolette before three weeks ago."

"You mean the website."

"No, no I don't." It had all been so painful, but now Melanie could feel a cold glee: "You have no fucking clue. While you were busy making up excuses for your magazine to run cover stories on the Clearheads, I was trying to save my career and your marriage. Julie and I created Capitolette. She's ours, and she's about as real as

Batman. Heather—whatever else she might be—is a good actress." Delivering this news gave the pleasure of driving a knife home, that feeling of cutting through something that had been solid.

She could not resist twisting it: "Maybe you know about the acting part, darling? How convinced were you that you made her come?"

He was breathing hard enough now that she could hear it.

"Now, slow down a minute. This is crazy."

"You're stalling for time again." Melanie had an urge to drum her nails on a table like a hard-edged moll in a gangster movie.

He exhaled. "I don't know," he said. "I . . ." He exhaled again. Melanie knew he was running his hands through his hair and pursing his lips like he had tasted something sour. Melanie supposed he had. "Do you want to talk about this in person?"

Melanie wasn't sure if she had the stomach for this in person. She shook her head and then said, "No. But, tell you what: You can report this. You're the journalist. Call Heather. Or better yet, I'll conference her in." She wasn't sure where this gall was coming from. It just seemed to rise up in her, the kinetic energy of that wild anger inside her expressing itself as daring.

She walked to the phone's base, knees weak in a way that made her glad he wasn't here. Dial tone. Digits.

"Wait, wait, wait," he said. "Wait a second here . . ."

Melanie ignored him. Heather's voice mail picked up: "You've reached Capitolette. I can't come to the phone but I'll come when I can." Melanie's stomach lurched at the sound of Heather's giggle.

She recovered. "Oh, isn't that cute? You're lucky—she's not home."

The machine beeped.

Melanie plunged on, past caring, past trying to figure out the roil of emotions that propelled her. "Do you want to leave a message or should I? Here, let me: 'Heather, this is Melanie. I'm just here talking to Rick Stossel, chief political correspondent of *Think* magazine and host of *Capitol Insider*. Perhaps you've heard of it. We've been discussing your date last night and I was going to update the blog, but some facts conflict. I told him I'd go to my deep throat.'"

The line went dead. Rick had gone off to regroup.

AND NOW WHAT?

The buzzy high of her anger dissipated. She was alone in a hot apartment with a melting can of limeade concentrate in the sink. Her shoulders were tight. Her jaw hurt. She felt like she had been in a fistfight.

Melanie didn't want to think about what she had done. She wanted not to think at all. She approached her memory of the conversation carefully, afraid if she moved too fast the emotions would rush back to her all over again.

She forced herself to make the limeade. She picked up the wilting cardboard can and sloshed out the slushy mix. The Brita pitcher smelled like the refrigerator, so she used water from the tap. A simple, concrete task. She did this and she inventoried what had happened, wincing at every recalled exchange. But what had she done, really? *Aside from losing Rick, what else have I lost?*

The phone rang with "Champagne Supernova." *Julie.* Melanie thought about letting the call go but knew she couldn't. Somehow she had been pushed onto the other side of the hill and while the slope was slight it was impossible not to keep running. Why not run harder?

"Hey, Jules."

"Oh, sweetie . . . Heather told me what happened. She really doesn't understand what she's done. She thinks you're mad about the book. Or because it's a bad move, you know, brand wise."

Melanie laughed once, harshly. "That I wouldn't know."

"You want to talk about it?"

"Not really." She took a deep breath. "I sort of got it all off my chest with Rick about five minutes ago."

"You didn't," Julie said, though her voice was too flat to make it a real challenge. Julie knew she had.

"I did, I really, truly did."

"How much did you tell him?" Julie asked.

"I told him everything."

There was a silence and now Melanie wondered how she had ever talked to anyone without knowing that silence was really a recalibration, and that every pause was someone gaming out all the possible next moves. *More people in this town should play chess,* she thought. She poured herself some limeade.

Julie spoke: "Everything like, she's not real or everything everything."

"Everything everything."

"What do you think is going to happen now?"

"I don't know, Julie. I'm not sure if I care."

"Of course you care."

"Yeah, maybe. I care enough to at least have thought about the consequences."

"Before or after you told all?"

Melanie gritted her teeth. "After. But it'll be fine." She swirled her ice in the glass. "Trust me."

Melanie took a sip of her drink. She had really only just come up with this, but saying it out loud might make it seem more real. "He may be a shitty boyfriend, but Rick isn't stupid. He can't write about the setup because if he does, I can out him. Mutually assured destruction, remember? It worked for superpowers, and it will work for supersluts."

"Which one of you is playing the Soviet Union here? It didn't work so well for them."

"I'm the Republic of Freedonia."

"What is that supposed to mean?"

Melanie sighed. "It means . . . it means I was watching Marx Brothers movies when I should have been building bombs."

"You're not making any sense."

"You're the second person who has told me that today." Melanie smiled at this. References beyond her grasp would usually send Julie scurrying to Google, but there was no time for that now. Julie would just have to not understand something for once. Melanie rolled the ice-filled glass across her forehead. The gesture reminded her of her father and she set the glass down. "Look," she continued, "I think it's going to be fine. I do. But why do you care? You're the one who insisted that the Capitolette background story would never matter."

"I didn't think that anyone would go digging for how the blog started or who started it; I didn't think they'd try to connect it back to us." Julie's voice was soft and sharp: "I never imagined that some-one would hand over that part of the story to a reporter on a silver platter."

Melanie's face contorted in a quick grimace.

Julie went on: "Because, you know, just because Rick doesn't write about it doesn't mean that others won't. Especially if Rick decides that he can safely leak the story to someone else, for instance."

She sounds like she's in a meeting, Melanie realized. *I feel like I should be taking notes on a white board.* "Thanks for reminding me."

"But I think I've fixed that."

"Oh?"

"Before I tell you, remember that the most damaging part of Heather's backstory getting out was connecting it back to Hillman."

"Riiiiight . . ."

"But what if Capitolette wasn't connected to just Hillman? What if she had connections to the other campaign?"

"Are you switching sides or something?" Melanie didn't know if her question was a joke or not.

"No. No, I'm not. But I'm bringing someone else on board."

Someone you had lunch with at the Four Seasons. It made sense. It was Julie's own Cold War–style insurance. Melanie fought the urge to tell her she knew the plan already.

Julie plowed through Melanie's silence: "Hugh."

"I see. Is there a reason he's joining up? And are you going to get a commission of some sort? Will I see you around town wearing big hats and bling?"

"He's not joining up to fuck her."

"Of course not. I'm sure he's joining up to help provide food to needy orphans."

"He's going to help with the book deal."

"Book deal."

"She needs an agent, right? And he can steer her to that conservative imprint his sister works at."

"So he doesn't want to have sex with her, he just wants to make money off of her."

"You say that like it's a bad thing."

"I don't know, maybe it is . . ." Melanie's head hurt.

"Don't you understand? If Hugh's on the team, and if she does this book for a wingnut publisher, the Hillman angle disappears. There's no Democrat conspiracy—it's the biggest blow for bipartisanship since the Senate compromised on Clinton's impeachment. Hillman's protected, *you're* protected. . ."

Melanie was sick of being protected. "And you join up with Hugh just like that. Why do you care about Hillman? Her book will sell no matter who wins."

"I know."

"Then why did we do this? I thought we were trying to win. What's the point?"

"The point, Melanie, is to keep playing. Think about it—she's a brand now. She's not just some scandalwhore; she represents some weird generational mascot. A book, a magazine spread, I'm thinking we could probably get a clothing line out of it. She could consult! We've got clients here who would fly across the country just to hear what she has to say about Internet marketing . . ."

Melanie hung up without saying good-bye.

MELANIE BARELY REMEMBERED where her car was. *In an alley off of Swann Street, yes.* She left her phone and her BlackBerry rattling on the table and took her keys. The sky had become gray and steely, and a wind kicked up the hot air, but Melanie could smell rain.

Like everyone in the campaign, she'd let her car mostly atrophy over the summer as she tossed taxi receipts into file folders and clamored into town cars. Neglected for weeks, her Olds had started to collect flyers and dust and mulberry stains.

She hadn't squeaked across the pleather since the night she and Julie had created Capitolette, but the gas gauge showed half a tank. She got in the car and drove to the George Washington Parkway.

Traffic was stop-and-go until she crossed the Key Bridge, leaving the forced quaintness of Georgetown for a brief glance at the brutal anonymity of Rosslyn's concrete towers. Then she turned off the bridge onto the parkway. The curves melted under the wheels as the old car got its momentum. A cool damp breeze rushed into the open windows.

In Iowa, she used to drive like this after exams. Just find a country road that split a cornfield or two and let it unspool in front of you. Her car then—Lawnmower One, she guessed—hadn't even had a tape deck. She had listened to AM oldies stations; Peggy Lee crackling out of the speakers as the sky went dark.

She had splurged on a satellite radio with her "victory bonus" after her triumph in Illinois. It was worth more than the car, but it had made the drive bearable. Now it was tuned to the alternapop station and the smooth orchestral melancholy of the Pernice Brothers fluttered in and out of the roar of the wind. *Thank God it's not Elliot Smith or Kurt Cobain,* she thought, before realizing that she was turning around near where Vince Foster committed suicide. She laughed. *No, nothing that drastic,* she thought as the parkway wound back to the airport.

The signs for National Airport rose up in front of her. Freedom. Normally she'd be racking through all the permutations and spin she'd dish out to Rick, Skoloff, the press, her friends, and her parents, but now she didn't even bother. She had fucked up so badly she could only get away with the truth. Novel, that: the truth. She let off the accelerator.

The bills. The teeth cleaning. Something real to eat. The pooch of her belly over her jeans. When was the last time she had talked to someone who didn't have some kind of official ID around his neck at some point in the day? Who was the last person she had had dinner with who couldn't plausibly charge the meal to a boss? What was the current best-selling book? What song was annoying parents? Had Madonna done anything interesting recently?

And Rick's neatly folded socks at the edge of the dresser and the glasses cases: one for the sunglasses, one for the reading glasses. His way of sucking air in between his two top teeth. How sometimes his breath smelled like peanuts. All those times she had waited for him to finish a call, silently creating white noise and trying not to hear.

She started making lists: She would work out more. She would learn to make sushi. She would fill in the gaps of her music knowledge—*what's the difference between an alto and a tenor sax? What's the deal with Glenn Gould?* She realized she'd been making secret tallies of all the things she wanted to do that she had put aside for the campaign, the affair, and the endless cocktail hours.

I am going to read all the great books! She laughed to herself.

She pulled into the departures lane and slowed to a stop, wondering how long she could idle before being shooed away. *If only there was a way to take the damn radio out, I could leave now. But go where?*

She remembered her dad's comprehensive pre-vacation checklists, his somehow comforting insistence on getting "an early start." And then her mind zeroed in on what she supposed she had been circling around as surely as he had been looping the parkway: *Dad. How am I going to explain this to Dad?* Suddenly, she was there in his office. He was in one of those odd white short-sleeved buttondown shirts, smiling at the wrong time as she explained it to him.

"There was no merit to the claims the Citizens for Clear Heads political action group made," he would say, taking her hands in his. "I don't know why you were so concerned. Also, Hillman was the better man, you know that."

And then, "As long as you're happy, honey."

She pulled up to Northwest's terminal. She could abandon the car. The satellite radio could come out. She could buy a ticket for San Miguel (she had a picture on her fridge from *Travel & Leisure* she'd ripped out at the doctor's office months ago). She'd buy a swimsuit in the lobby of the hotel and the cell phone and Berry wouldn't work there.

This is the kind of thing they did in the movie of the week, she thought. *And I'll meet a handsome Latin lover who likes kids and bad TV and detective novels, and we'll discover treasure!*

She laughed and pulled out of the departures lane, looking at the Northwest sign in her rearview mirror. She would leave soon enough.

16

Thursday, August 26

To: ThortonM@hillman.com

From: OwenThortonENG@aol.com

Subject: How are you?

Date: Aug. 26

    I saw the new ad from Mr. Hillman today and thought of you. Your mom and I are concerned we haven't heard much but of course we understand that you're busy.

    I am ordering a new book *Bioterrorism: Mathematical Modeling Applications in Homeland Security* and another book: *Spatial Deterministic Epidemics.* I read the reviews in the recent *Notices of the American Mathematical Society* and cannot wait to study them.

    Please write when you can. We love you

THE TEARS CAME the next day. Huge, racking sobs that embarrassed her and made her cry some more. There was a deep well of self-pity to draw from, regrets about Rick, about Heather, and about Julie, too, she supposed. The tears made her face hot and red; when she went to go splash water on her cheeks she laughed at the clown that looked back at her in the mirror.

Around midnight, she was too exhausted to cry anymore. She lay on her bed, the air-conditioning whooshing over her. Rain finally started to fall. She thought of her movie-of-the-week fantasy again. *What would Valerie Bertinelli do?* "Dear Mrs. Stossel . . ." She shook her head. *Overly dramatic. Wrong. Is it a movie of the week on Lifetime or Sundance? Can we get away with a moody mandolin soundtrack as I slink out of town to become an itinerant preacher? Or what about the Sci-Fi Channel: I will be eaten by a giant bug.*

Her eyes flicked to her laptop and she wanted to smash it. She stared back up at the ceiling and wondered what she would do.

WHAT SHE DID was call in sick for two days. There were pings from Chuck, from Julie, and others, but with the chieftains still in Montana, no one at the campaign really seemed that concerned. She changed her voicemail message to ask people to e-mail her and she forwarded press inquiries to others.

She watched action movies and drank Diet Coke and made peace with her laptop. Tidying her electronic desktop was therapeutic and mindless work. She had spent four months dumping every new document she had typed into her My Documents folder. There were thousands—from press releases on the candidate's position on bovine hormones to the list of enemies she'd made after her first week. She untangled it all, placing each item in its proper folder.

The only folder that didn't need tidying was labeled simply "Social Security." She'd chosen that name because clearly no one snooping in her open laptop would care to look into a folder on that subject. That's where she'd put the whirlwind of Capitolette material—the posts, the e-mails, her own mid-scandal musings, even saved Web pages from Frederick's of Hollywood. She'd been so terrified of being found out when it had all started that she'd dutifully kept it all in one file she could quickly toss if she ever needed to.

Sunday, August 29

AND THEN RICK WROTE.

To: ThortonM@hillman.com

From: Rick.Stossel@thinkmag.com

Subject: Heads up

I just wanted to thank you for helping to set up my interview with Heather. We're looking at a cover package for next week. It will focus mainly on Heather as a new archetype for political women, contrasting it to the values shtick at the Republican convention I would have called you but since we're really not doing anything on how she started blogging or where she came from, I didn't think it was necessary. Chuck Reed covered for the campaign.

A punch pulled, Melanie thought.

Monday, August 30

MONDAY WAS SKOLOFF'S first day back at the office from Hillman's ranch. Melanie went in, too, and Skoloff called her in right away.

In the corner of the war room, Melanie could see a mermaid costume hanging next to the pirate outfit. Skoloff coughed: "We're thinking something about the 'siren call of campaign donors.' "

"Creative," Melanie said. She stood in front of Skoloff, shifting slightly on her feet.

Skoloff cleared her throat again: "We looked at the spontaneous reel on the ranch, by the way. John was very impressed. He said he had no idea that listening could actually look like listening. We're running him through listening rehearsals now." She gestured for Melanie to sit down.

Melanie nodded, then shook her head. "No, no," she said. "I think I better stand." In every movie she'd seen, people stood when they handed over their resignation letters. And then she did.

Skoloff took the pages from her, an eyebrow raised. She took the letter in quickly, inhaling sharply when she flipped to the second page.

While Skoloff read, Melanie looked at her shoes—appropriately humble, she hoped—and went over a checklist in her head. She had paid the rent. She had hired a cleaning service. She had stopped the mail. She had preprinted the boarding pass. She had worn shoes she could take off easily at the security check. She had written down where she had parked her car.

Melanie realized that Skoloff hadn't said anything. She looked up. Skoloff was leaning back in her chair, smoking lazily. "I really think you should sit down," she said.

Melanie sat down, which made it hard for her to continue to stare at her shoes. She cleared her own throat. "I . . . I am sorry."

Skoloff chuckled. "I guess you are. Of course, if I didn't have to fire you, I'd give you a raise. I always knew you were better at this than you let on."

Melanie tried to smile but her stomach flipped. She swallowed and parried: "Well, that will come in handy when I'm working on the state senate primary race in North Dakota."

"Or when you've got your own show on Fox. I can see you across from Dick Morris. You didn't by any chance have a prostitute suck your toes, did you?"

"Just a reporter."

Skoloff stabbed out the cigarette and lit another. "Fuck me," she said, taking a vicious drag. "Fuck. We can keep this quiet for a week, I guess. Shit, Melanie. Your conscience really should have kicked in before this started. I can fire you, but that isn't going to keep your stink away from the campaign."

"I think there's a way, actually." Her voice was weaker than she intended.

"You really are a child," Skoloff said, cutting her off. "You've actually *created* a fake sex scandal for a Democrat. Jesus Christ, Hillman's dick is the one lifeless part of him we've been thankful for. And she's already on the magazines. She's recognizable. Fuck . . ."

"I have a plane to catch," Melanie said. She had timed this carefully.

"Wait." Skoloff leaned forward on the table. "You know, you don't have to go. I don't have to accept your resignation. And this . . . this part of the Capitolette story . . . it doesn't have to get out."

"I think it does," Melanie said, getting up from the table.

"You frosty bitch." Skoloff shook her head in awe. "You . . . I . . ." She drew herself up. "You'll be right at home in North Dakota!"

Melanie walked out of Skoloff's office, put a folder on Chuck's desk marked "Goldenisms," with a note: "I've found the dots—maybe you can connect them?" Then she walked out the door.

To: plead@washpost.com

From: ThortonM@hillman.com

Subject: CAMPAIGN AIDE REPRIMANDED, RELEASED; OFFICIAL STATEMENT

Paul—Thought you deserved to get the first nibble on the exciting climax of the Capitolette saga. I know I've put you through a lot—consider this a thank-you note. I'm not available for calls but you can reach Karen Skoloff on her cell.

Begin forwarded message:

CONTACT: Karen Skoloff (SkoloffK@hillman.com)

RELEASE

After a lengthy internal investigation, communications staffer Melanie Thorton has been released from the Hillman-Langley campaign after acknowledging off-duty participation in an Internet prank. . . .

The ambiguity was artful, Melanie thought. People always trusted the math more when they did it themselves.

AT THE AIRPORT, Heather's face looked out at Melanie from a tiny box. She recognized the picture. It was from Emily's party. The convention dominated but, sure enough, Rick had figured out a way to roll her up into a tart, airy bubble of non-news: "The New Permissiveness: What Chance Do Values Stand?" Melanie rolled her eyes.

She dragged her new wheelie bag past the racks and farther into the store. She hadn't read a newspaper or a newsmagazine in days and she wasn't going to start now. She was trying to decide between bad airport fiction thrillers when her cell went off. Julie.

"Hey."

"So you're really leaving, eh?"

"I don't see how I can't. Oh, and another thing: I want to." Melanie put down the Clive Cussler and picked up the Lawrence Block, wondered if they were actually different authors. "My room faces the ocean. There are two pools. I am going to order lots of drinks that come with umbrellas in them from handsome waiters in tight white shorts. I am going to start doing that about nine A.M. By the time the network anchor says good night I'll be seeing him in stereo and those white shorts will be on the floor." Her plans were actually a little less debauched than that. A lot less debauched than that: Her plane landed in Davenport at seven P.M. She hoped to be done explaining her trip home by at least the next morning. And who knows what after that. Detasseling corn, maybe.

"That sounds great. Wish I could come."

"So come. The airport is empty, I'm sure there's room on the flight." It was a decidedly Washington invitation.

"No room in my schedule."

"Ah, right. There's a presidential campaign or something going on, right? Remind me who's running?"

"Two rich white men. That's really all you need to know."

"Actually, I think I could stand an update." Melanie closed her eyes and leaned against a wall of romance novels.

"Well . . . apparently someone got fired from the Hillman campaign today." Melanie opened her eyes. The clerk was staring at her. She resisted the urge to stick her tongue out at him. "Hillman, he's the slightly more stiff white man."

"You said 'stiff.' "

"Yes, well, apparently sex is involved." Julie seemed genuinely curious. "I wonder if people know how much."

"They might find out."

"Melanie. Who are you trying to hurt here—Rick or yourself? Hillman? Me?"

"I'm not trying to hurt anyone. I'm trying to make up for something. And you're going to get out of this just fine. I know you. Maybe Hugh Brompton will help."

"Hmm."

"You always had better taste in men," Melanie said. She stood up and turned around to face the racks again. The gilded covers of the romance novels reflected slivers of Melanie back at herself in their gold script. Her jeans seemed looser, though that might be wishful thinking, and her running shoes were dirty and creased. *That happens when you actually use them,* she thought, smiling.

A staticky announcement for a flight to Miami burst through Melanie's thoughts. "Hey, they're calling my flight. Gotta go."

"Oh, uh, hold on a sec." Julie's side of the phone went silent. *I can't even brush someone off anymore,* Melanie thought. Julie came back: "What was that? You have to go?"

"Actually . . . well, yeah, I gotta run."

"So."

"Yeah, so. I'll send you a postcard."

"Do that, pal." Julie clicked off.

Melanie stared at the silent phone, and then looked up, wondering if throwing it in the nearest trash can would bring airport security running.

She bought a Stephen King novel and headed toward her gate.

Once in the departure lounge, she settled down and started typing. She was early, very early, for the flight. Dad would be proud. By the time the flight was called, she'd tapped out three pages.

Glancing over the passages, she exhaled apprehensively, then saved the file inside her Social Security folder.

She looked at her fellow passengers. Future voters, she thought, and wondered if she should do some focus-grouping right now. *If you discovered that a junior aide lied in order to save her own career, would that make you very likely, somewhat likely, somewhat less likely, or very less likely to vote for that candidate?*

Going home was definitely the Hallmark channel ending, though she supposed it would help if she had learned something from the experience. If there was a moral. She wasn't an innocent corrupted, she had just become more corrupt than she'd been when she started. *I screwed up, I cheated, I cut corners—and I didn't have to. I chose to believe all these shortcuts were in the service of the greater good, but I didn't have to take them.*

There was a whole floor of people at the campaign headquarters she hadn't done more than say "hi" to in all the time she had spent there. People who made charts and wrote white papers. She was one of the hacks and, she admitted to herself, she didn't think she'd ever want to write white papers. She smiled. She liked the gray area. Maybe too much. Live your life there and it can start to seem like black is just another shade of gray.

Now I'm making up Grateful Dead lyrics.

Her BlackBerry winked. There was a message from Chuck: "I don't know what happened," he wrote, "but I definitely want to hear more. Glanced at your file—where did you find the time? Are you okay? Call me, please?"

Melanie smiled. Maybe she would, that is if he didn't want to lynch her after news leaked. The Goldenisms file could tip the balance in her favor. Maybe. Chuck had been with Hillman since he was a Senate intern. Whether Melanie had been a renegade in an otherwise upright campaign or whether boredom and lack of a story line would force editors to make her a symbol of the campaign's poor management and rot would spin out soon. "How can we trust him to fight terrorists if he can't hire good people," she could hear any number of pundits saying.

She would try to reverse that story line. On board, the stewardesses were reciting that familiar refrain about approved electronic devices. Melanie drew out her laptop again. She had one last thing to do. With the plane doors still open, her wireless modem would be able to make a connection, and she had something she needed to put out there. She opened the file from the departure lounge and pasted it into a website form. She hit "publish."

"Your entry is live," the screen said. She went to the blog's home page—www.makeamonster.net—and read:

> The champagne was cold and expensive. The room was crowded and hot. And you couldn't swing a Democratic convention credential without braining a network reporter, a campaign staffer, or a hit-or-miss celebrity . . .

Epilogue

MELANIE THORTON: Most of political Washington turns her barely veiled account of August into a favorite parlor game, but some treat it as a résumé. Three weeks into her Iowa exile, she is still sending all 202 prefixes and potential job offers to voicemail. By November, applicants are sending her the résumés.

JULIE WRIGLEY: After her part in the Capitolette scandal is exposed, Julie prepares a resignation letter, but is then greeted in the office of the founding partner by champagne and balloons. In addition to her raise and promotion, she now handles the Cleveland Park Group's tobacco lobby account.

CHUCK REED: Melanie's Goldenism file provides the basis for a pitch to the *New York Times*. In October, the *Times* runs an article highlighting a pattern in Jim Golden's ever more frequent and disturbing malapropisms, demonstrating that he is a persistent and dismissive lech. Many agree that the Goldenisms themselves are less damaging than a sound bite from a psychologist at the University of Colorado: "You don't have to be professional to interpret these statements. Jim Golden is a small-minded sadist."

KAREN SKOLOFF takes credit for everything.

RICK STOSSEL, facing an ultimatum from his wife, gives up life on the road as a reporter to head a think tank devoted to issues facing parents of gifted children. A noted speaker, he demands that payment for any engagement outside the Beltway must include first-class travel . . . for two.

HEATHER MASON poses for *Maxim* and keeps her top on. Her book, *Washington: A View from the Bottom,* comes out, to great titillation, from Regnery Publishing after a lucrative deal negotiated by · Hugh Brompton.

JOHN HILLMAN, despite misleading early exit polls, becomes the next president of the United States.

ABOUT THE AUTHOR

Ana Marie Cox is best known as the voice of the hugely popular political blog *Wonkette* (www.wonkette.com), and has written for *Elle, Wired, Mother Jones, Slate, Salon, New York,* and the *New York Times Book Review,* among other publications. Originally from Lincoln, Nebraska, she lives in Washington, D.C., with her husband, two cats, and dog.